# SINISTER

# EXTREMITY

## A LOVE STORY

### HUGH NEILL

**Sinister Extremity**

Copyright © 2025 by Hugh Neill

All rights reserved.

ISBN: 978-1-968319-00-7 (Trade Paperback)

No part of this publication may be reproduced, distributed, or transmitted in any form or by any means, including photocopying, recording, or other electronic or mechanical methods, without the prior written permission of the publisher, except as permitted by U.S. copyright law.

For permission requests, contact castellatedpress@gmail.com.

*This is a work of fiction. The story, all names, characters, and incidents portrayed in this production are fictitious. No identification with actual persons (living or deceased), places, buildings, and products is intended or should be inferred.*

No artificial intelligence was used in the composition or editing of this novel, nor the design of this book.

Book design by Castellated Press

First edition 2025

*To G, for putting me back together.*

# Content Warning

This story contains repeated amputations, explicit sex, a level of gore beyond all plausibility, general disgusting filth, and modern American labor standards.

**SINISTER** *adjective*

SIN·IS·TER

    1. Suggestive of evil or malevolence.

    2. Designating the left side of the body.


**EXTREMITY** *noun*

EX·TREM·I·TY

    1. The utmost degree (as of emotion or pain.)

    2. A limb of the body, especially a human hand or foot.

# Part One

## The Invisible Hand

1

Every day, Griffin Batt went to work at his job where he cut off his left hand in a single swift strike. Griffin Batt hated his job where he cut off his left hand in a single swift strike.

Here is what Griffin Batt would do every day when he went to work at his job where he cut off his left hand in a single swift strike.

He would wake up in the morning to his fat orange cat, Mr. President, sitting on his chest and screaming in his face to demand food. Griffin would eventually rise and stumble over to Mr. President's bowl, which he would fill with a couple of scoops from a twenty-two pound bag of kibble, comprised of fish flavors on alternative proteins. Mr. President would then dive in with the frantic desperation of a creature that had been starving in the desert, though the bag of kibble was visible at all times, with an open top that Griffin had not bothered to clip shut, which Mr. President, despite it all, would not eat directly from unless circumstances were truly dire, as Mr. President appreciated the ritual of the process. Griffin had left the bag out and open due to not wanting to pay for a refillable container and not having anything that could truly be called a closet or kitchen storage space. What might have served as a closet to store clothing or personal objects had been retrofitted to serve as the utility closet that contained his electric water heater and no drain.

Mr. President would eat in the soft morning light, which was diffused by a sheet of frosted plastic that Griffin had adhered to the windows of his ground-level apartment so that passerby would not be able to see into his home as if it were a dollhouse occupied by a lanky 28-year-old man. There was one stripe of uncovered window he'd cut out at eye level for looking outside when necessary, and a similar small low viewport for Mr. President to see all the exciting action of the concrete courtyard.

Once Mr. President was crunching away at his breakfast rather than screaming, Griffin would turn on his electric kettle and examine his left wrist to see how yesterday's work was looking, and therefore how today's work was going to go. Depending on how well he'd done the day before, as well as the quality of his sleep and levels of protein intake, he would be looking at anything ranging from a thick band of scar tissue solidly holding the hand to his arm with all the grace of an apprentice welder's first work, to a surprisingly seamless connection with only the remaining sutures as evidence of his grim task.

Once the kettle clicked, Griffin would use the boiling water both for a mug of instant coffee with soymilk and a bowl of instant oats. The coffee was more for its laxative effect than its stimulant effect, as it was important to have a bowel movement before leaving his apartment. As you can imagine, it would be much harder to go to the bathroom in the middle of his workday and wipe properly with one hand that was still a bloody stump.

Griffin Batt's workplace did not have bidets.

After breakfast, he would brush his teeth while staring at himself in the mirror, regarding the look of idle despair in his blue-grey eyes. Now, depending on how much money Griffin had blown on getting drunk enough to briefly forget how awful his life was on any given week, he might pack a lunch to save money. He would usually go for a basic peanut butter and jelly sandwich, due to how easy it was to eat one-handed, which he would put inside a plastic bag inside a paper bag inside his messenger bag. If he was being thrifty, either out of the successful deployment of self-control or absolute necessity, he would load his rice cooker and set its timer for right around when he usually got back from work, so that there would be the beginnings of a meal waiting for him in the form of some nice steaming hot rice upon his return.

Every day he was in horrible pain and deeply miserable. Nothing he did made any difference and he felt abandoned by God. His life was hell, and nothing was good.

Once the rice cooker was set, he would strip off the boxer briefs and t-shirt he slept in, step over the huge protruding lump in the floor that kept his bathroom door from fully opening, and scrub himself thoroughly in the shower. He usually showered twice per day— once in the morning and once in the evening, since his work could get a bit messy and when at work he was more eager to be done and get home than to be fully cleaned and stay later.

But in the mornings, after he made sure he didn't smell bad and wouldn't shit himself at work, he put on business casual clothing that he had never ironed, but that he always hung to dry on a rolling rack near the radiator because he was unwilling to pay for the extortionate scam that was laundromat dryers. He had six white oxford shirts on rotation that he would wash and bleach once a week because old blood stains had never been in fashion, as far as he knew.

Griffin would then turn on his TV and put on a playlist of bird videos for cats to watch so that Mr. President could be entertained while he was away, despite being unable to look out the window or go anywhere. Mr. President was the cat version of the chained man in Plato's allegory of the cave, seeing shadows on the wall that were a pale imitation of reality. Fortunately, without any frame of reference to what he was missing, Mr. President appeared to be perfectly content with his lot in life. Once he was situated on his little pillow in front of the TV, Griffin would give him a skritch on the chin and a kiss for the road, then head out the door.

Stepping out of his front door, he would see directly in front of him the stairwell, going up to the second floor apartment landing and down to the basement. The basement was unfinished, full of spiders, and prone to flooding. To the left was the front door to the whole building, which he would exit through on his way to catch the bus.

Every time Griffin got on the bus, the driver gave him a look as if he'd just said a racial slur the moment the door opened, though this had never been the case, whether when the door opened or at any other time. Griffin would tap his phone on the paypad, say thank you, get a slightly different look like he'd just spat in the driver's face, and go sit down. He was usually seated next to various weary-looking men who smelled strongly of pepperoni or other fragrant lunch meat products and appeared to have been up all night.

As the bus made its way towards his workplace, he would skim through his video feed to look for people doing jobs that were actually clearly good for the world. He enjoyed seeing woodworking, power washing, and animal husbandry— his favorites were the farriers who dealt with cow hooves. There were few things more satisfying to Griffin than watching a man carve into an infected hoof that was so internally pressurized with pus that it would shoot out in a bloody stream, instantly relieving the animal of a great deal of pain. He appreciated the effort these men went to to ensure the health and comfort of these cows before they were sent off to a swift and violent death, and fantasized about anybody making an effort to reduce his suffering in a similar way before he died. He also fantasized about similarly being able to do work that seemed to help anyone or anything in clear and concrete ways.

Griffin Batt held a master's degree in economics.

Here is what would happen when Griffin Batt arrived at his job where he cut off his left hand in a single swift strike.

The bus let Griffin off at a stop near the edge of the parking lot in front of the large, drab building. The complex technically housed several companies under one roof, though they were all similarly under the same corporate umbrella, and each subsidiary company had its own entrance. He would cross the parking lot, enter the building through the front, swipe his ID keycard for entry, and make his way through windowless, labyrinthine corridors towards a small room with a metal chair and table. He would pass the supply station, where he would tell the attendant Hey Dave and the attendant would reply Hey Griffin and as Dave went to fetch the day's hardware and regenerative cooling gel, he would think for a moment that Dave could be pretty cute if he actually bothered to take care of himself a little better. Dave would then wheel out a cart bearing a container that looked similar to a deep fryer, but full of a pale pink liquid, so innately cold that coils of condensing vapor poured off of it like dry ice. He would take this cart and roll it to his station.

Common, lanky Griffin Batt came from the hallway, bearing a tub of regenerative cooling gel upon which sutures and a cleaver lay crossed. On a lower level of the cart there sat an insulated cooler of ice and gallon-sized sealing plastic bags. He entered a small wedge-shaped room with a metal chair and table, atop which sat a large end-grain cutting board. At the narrower end of the room was an interrogation-room-style two-way mirror that gave him the impression that somebody or something was behind it and watching and enjoying the sight of him in pain, but he was yet to confirm this one way or the other.

Griffin would spend the first hour of every day sharpening his large carbon steel Serbian cleaver, hoping to get it to a point where it would slam through the skin and flesh and fat and bone and sinew of his left wrist like it wasn't even there. The name of the game was a single swift strike, not several slow slices, and he was a professional. As he sharpened his instrument, he mentally steeled himself for the performance of his contractual obligation.

The first time he ever did this, emotionally preparing to emancipate lefty from the homeland had been a long and harrowing process, but over time it became almost automatic. He had set up a pavlovian connection in his mind at this point, wherein the sharpening was a meditative, or perhaps dissociative, process. Through classical conditioning he had trained himself to associate the inimitable shine of the perfect razor edge of a carbon steel cleaver with absolute mental, emotional and physical preparedness for the task at hand.

You might think it takes intentional grit, courage and resolve to cut off your left hand in a single swift strike, but this is not the case. It might've been like that the first time, but Griffin had been at it so long that it was hard to remember. In truth, the mental state required to do this every day on a professional level was a resigned, dissociative numbness. When he felt like his body was not his own, when he felt like he was watching someone else wield the cleaver, then he knew he had achieved the optimal state of readiness to disconnect his left hand from the rest of his body.

From that point forward, the process was fairly simple. He would apply a tourniquet to his left arm to restrict blood flow, place his hand upon the chopping block, hit a button that indicated he was about to amputate so that personnel could be on standby if anything went wrong, and pick up the cleaver. He felt the sturdy weight of the blade in his right hand and knew that if not for the bone, it would go through him like meringue just by resting its weight on the wrist. Unfortunately, Griffin Batt was a bone-in man, so it did require a bit more precision and force. He would hold the cleaver precisely at its intended point of contact, draw it back to a good high starting position, then slowly return it in reverse, repeating this process a few times to get a feel for the ideal groove of the swing like a golfer resetting his stance before every shot.

No matter how practiced you are at something, it's not an excuse to get cocky and sloppy with your work.

Then he would swing down hard and cut off his left hand. An indescribable pain incapacitated his mind and body for a few seconds as his brain scrambled to figure out how to process the complete cessation of all nerve input from what was formerly the location of his hand. This passed in a few minutes.

If he had done it right, and usually he had, there wasn't much mess to speak of and he could deposit his severed extremity in the gallon bag and place it in the provided ice bucket. During this part of the process, the feeling of being watched from behind the mirror was always extremely strong.

Something inhuman and horrible was watching him suffer and enjoying it. Some invisible, malevolent watcher that did not want to be truly known but craved to be sensed just enough that he knew his pain was bringing someone else pleasure.

Griffin only had the will to keep living so that he could provide for Mr. President.

Then came lunchtime. Griffin was always starving after the morning's work, and you don't want to try to stitch your own hand back on with an empty stomach. Depending on how much Griffin had succeeded or failed at adhering to his budget, this is when he would either eat his peanut butter and jelly sandwich in the employee break room, or head across the street to the strip mall with a few different dining options.

Griffin was no Rockefeller, so his choice of lunch was dependent on whatever deals were available at the various chain restaurants through their convenient phone apps. Griffin kept the notifications on from every one of those apps to see if they were running any promotions or discounts at a glance. Just before lunchtime, he tended to be incapable of thinking straight enough to search for coupons due to the fact that he had just severed his left hand with a carbon steel cleaver and was experiencing a level of pain that distorted his perception of reality on an almost psychedelic level. But if he had the notifications on and checked them on the way to work, with attentive couponing he could often find a hot meal at a reasonable price.

A Waffle House stood alone, and in the strip mall there was a fried cricken joint, a sandwich spot, and a pseudo-Mexican place. When he went to the Mexican place he would try to be a bit health conscious by getting the tacos with black beans instead of their institutional-grade meat product. He would pre-order this meal for lunchtime pickup while he was on the bus so that he could pick up his food immediately upon arrival and minimize the amount of time spent among other customers while cradling the bloody stump of his left wrist, which sometimes drew questions from people unfamiliar with local industry.

The restaurants also had loyalty programs where enough repeat orders meant he would get something for free, like fries or a drink, and looking forward to getting enough points to get those treats was another one of the few things that kept him from self-immolating in protest against something or other, which wouldn't even make the news these days if he did do it.

But without the bonus sodas from loyalty programs, he often got just water to drink while out for lunch, then coffee from the break room back at the office before getting back to work. Around the coffee machine he always got a little bit of conversation with his colleagues, though for obvious reasons many of them weren't eager to chat much. He would sometimes see a new hire, pale and bleary-eyed from blood loss, and then he would exchange a knowing, pitying smirk with another veteran professional, also pale and dead-eyed from the grim acceptance of their certain fates.

Once fully fed and caffeinated, he was ready to get back to work.

Griffin had learned that there was a delicate balance to the nutrition required to reattach your own left hand, especially considering that you had to do it one-handed. The problem is that if you're hungry, or at least if Griffin was hungry, his hands would shake, which is not ideal when one hand is the surgeon and the other is the patient. But if he ate a big lunch he tended to get the early afternoon slump, which would require him to have more coffee to perk up, which would make him loop right back around to having shaky hands.

This is why Griffin limited himself to two cups of coffee per day: one in the morning, and one right after lunch. This was enough to mitigate the initial fatigue of sleep inertia and the post-lunch fog, but not so much that he went around feeling like his heart was going to explode from excessive caffeine consumption.

He often felt like his heart was going to explode, but that was more of a metaphorical feeling and for different reasons.

These were reasons why he tried to avoid simple sugars and go for complex carbohydrates and proteins whenever it was economically viable for him to do so. He felt the best on days when he had the black bean tacos for lunch, which kept him from spiking his blood sugar too much and provided enough smooth, constant energy to get him through the horrifically painful process of sewing his left hand back on.

Back at his desk, the rest of the day would usually play out on relative autopilot. He would sit down, fish his severed hand out of the ice bucket, extricate it from the plastic bag, strap down the stump, line up the hand with the wrist, grab the sutures, and get to work. During this part he would often listen to music to pass the time faster. He would change the playlist for the procedure depending on the mood he was in at the beginning. If he was a bit low-energy, whether from accidentally eating too heavy a lunch or losing a bit more blood than usual, he would listen to pre-wipe disco. If he was too jittery from coffee or nerves, he would play soothing ambient works to even him out and stay in the zone.

Once he had his hand and wrist stitched back together, Griffin noticed the sensation of being watched from behind the mirror would decrease, and he would plunge his hand into the tub of regenerative cooling gel. He did not know the chemical composition of the liquid, but it induced extraordinarily rapid healing over the course of a wildly exothermic chemical reaction.

A white-hot bolt of pain shot down his arm as the open wound submerged, and the frigid liquid rapidly warmed to around body temperature while bubbling and frothing like a child's science fair volcano.

At this point Griffin would be pretty dizzy so he would hit a button and Dave would reappear to give him a glass of orange juice and a cookie.

He would go back and do this five days a week and at the end of each week would get paid an amount of money that kept him from starving to death in the street, barely.

After work he would spend an hour on the bus staring out the window and listening to podcasts on such things as the mysterious life cycle of the eel. In the colder months, where our story will pick up, the sun would have already gone down by the time work ended, so Griffin would just watch the lights of the city go by. The business district actually generated tax revenue for the city, so it was better taken care of with such things as updated streetlights. From this, Griffin's journey home slowly shifted from the bright cool broad-spectrum bluish-white LED streetlights to the narrow-spectrum sodium-vapor orange streetlights that cast everything beneath them in Halloweenish tints of orange and black shadow.

The sky did not look like it used to.

When Griffin was little, before the blue LEDs could be manufactured again, the sky glowed orange at night. The incredible light pollution of the sodium-vapor street lamps was prominent enough to reflect back from the clouds above, which at night had the dim distant warmth of the smoke-diffused light of a forest fire in a dream. As the LED lamps slowly took over, the sky cooled off, the orange faded, and the Halloween orange and black was reserved for the worse parts of town. Griffin's part of town.

These were representative samples, generalizations, of the wasted life of this young man. Let us return to a specific example. One day in November, Griffin noticed more activity than usual as he approached his three-story apartment building. His second floor neighbor Wes Sweat, a compact bespectacled man, was for some reason carefully placing an enormous and pristine-looking television next to the trash cans in the little concrete courtyard out front that held the trash and recycling bins. The two third floor neighbors, both named Mohammed, though one went by Mo and the other by Hammy, were having an animated conversation in Arabic with occasional lapses into English when necessary to name other neighborhoods in the city, as well as to use the word "fucking." None of these people paid Griffin any mind as he walked past them, punched in the door code, and went inside.

Griffin checked the mail table off to the side of the vestibule and immediately saw a prominently displayed publication that appeared to be titled ***"HATE AND EXTREMISM"*** in huge block letters, clearly visible to his neighbors, which looked like he was enough of an enthusiast to subscribe to a magazine on the subject. Much smaller typography indicated it was reporting on the subject from an activist charity organization that wanted him to give them money.

Back inside the apartment, Mr. President looked up at Griffin from the couch, so Griffin went to drum on the orange cat's tummy for a minute until he was purring like an idling motor-cycle. Griffin delivered Mr. President his wet food dinner, which the beast attacked with crazed ferocity, and then scooped himself a slop pile of shredded braised cricken into a bowl to microwave, before eating from the bowl with his hands because he did not want to clean a fork after his dish brush broke where the handle met the head. Griffin followed the cricken with the indulgent luxury of a can of beans at room temperature eaten with a spoon while watching the tail end of the twelve-hour video of birds and small woodland creatures scurrying around that he had put on to entertain the cat in his absence. The gentle chirp of songbirds competed with a cat messily eating cloned liver chunks to be the dominant sound of the room.

## 2

The next morning on the bus, Griffin was seated next to a sleeping man in full tactical gear who smelled of pepperoni. Griffin was watching videos of men using rotary sanders to polish dairy cow hooves to a gleaming shine when the algorithm decided that the next video on his feed needed to be some success-win-entrepreneur-billionaire-mindset bullshit. It was a clip of two men with expensive, precise haircuts on a podcast called *Right Hand Man* that was all about cutting off your left hand in a single swift strike. These two men were interviewing a third man who was completely bald, with a goatee so precise he must've had it styled moments before sitting down, who was wearing small perfectly round gold-framed sunglasses with black mirror lenses and a Rolex on the stump of his left wrist. Rolex began speaking.

"Every day I'm my own boss at my business where I cut my left hand off in a single swift strike. I love running my business where I cut my left hand off in a single swift strike. Here's what

I do every day on my grind, on my hustle, at my business where I cut off my left hand in a single swift strike. First, what you've got to understand— and people don't talk about this— what you've got to understand is that you don't actually have to cut your own hand off in a single swift strike every day. See what I've done here?"

He held up the Rolexed stump, gleaming with the bloody shine of an unhealed flesh wound, and the men with haircuts nodded as one of them said, "I hadn't thought about that. Nobody is talking about that."

The bald man continued, "See, when you're as good at cutting off your left hand in a single swift strike as I am, you don't need to sew it back on right away. This is crisp, clean work. Surgical grade. My hand is on ice, and this quality of work gives me two, three days before I have to reattach. I learned that from Roderick Faust. And what's important about that is that I can confidently walk around, go about my business, go on podcasts, and the quality of my work speaks for itself and attracts potential clients who want to know how they can get on my level."

"It's quite the level," said Haircut Number One.

Bald Goatee Rolex nodded and began gesticulating with a hand that wasn't there to emphasize his speech as he said, "Then that draws them into the funnel, so they can peruse the products I have to offer in this niche. For example, at retail I have accessories that I endorse, the ones I personally use. This includes the whetstone, the full-tang Chinese cleaver I prefer for the task, the end grain butcher's block, butcher's block oil, the absorbent pads and most importantly, the porous self-adhesive medical tape

I use for realignment and the premium regenerative coolant gel that guarantees 100% reconstruction in moments."

"It's a great line of products," said Haircut Number Two. "I've seen you put in the work with all of those. Your setup is second to none."

Bald Goatee Rolex Stump smiled richly and said, "Well, that's just tangible retail and affiliate marketing. I also have information products. There's, of course, the book on the breathing and meditation methods that allow peak performance, which are harder to convey in video due to how internal and intangible they are, and then there's the video courses that demonstrate all the details of the method for peak performance, with commentary, multiple angles, slow motion, and extensive FAQ sections based on feedback from previous satisfied customers. And of course, my absolute premium product, in necessarily limited supply, is personal sessions."

"Personal sessions?"

"I cut your left hand off. Ten thousand dollars per session."

"Wow. That's incredible."

"Want a demonstration?"

The haircut goons laughed. "Are we going to have to pay for that?"

"Hey, nothing like free advertising. Earned media. Social proof. Demonstrate the value of my work, show your audience that my expertise is real and proven. You haven't gone yet today, have you?"

A haircut responded, "No, normally I save my session for after we record the show. Otherwise it would be a bit distracting."

"May I?"

"Oh, wow. By all means."

The bald man pulled a chopping block from offscreen, making sure to angle the brand name on the side toward the camera as he put it down on the table between them. He gestured to it and one of the indistinguishable haircut podcast men put his left hand down upon it.

The bald man unsheathed an enormous Chinese cleaver and said, "Ready?"

"Ready," haircutted podcast haircut.

The bald man brought the blade down through the podcaster's wrist in a motion so precise and fluid that it was as if he was cutting through nothing at all. Haircut screamed, his face a rictus of excruciating pain as blood poured from his left wrist, most of him falling to the ground while his hand remained on the table. The other two men smiled and nodded, one in pride, one in admiration, while the wounded man crawled back into his seat, made his way to the microphone, began applying a tourniquet one-handed, and said, "Unbelievable. You're genuinely the best at this. Thank you for letting me sample that for free."

The bald man beamed. "My pleasure."

Griffin bookmarked the video.

Griffin got to work a few minutes late, swiped his card, and jogged down the corridors toward Dave to pick up his supplies before heading to his room. Once situated, he couldn't help but contemplate what he'd just watched on the bus. He had been doing this professionally for a few years, but was still basically self-taught. He learned on the job, taking on faith that the regenerative gel would allow him plenty of chances to figure out his method. Despite how long he'd been at it, he never really looked into any guides or sought out any tips from top performers in the field. He just went in, punched the clock, did the bare minimum, and went home. But not that day. On that day he decided to have some pride in his work.

They say that if you have two hours to cut down a tree, the first hour should be spent sharpening the axe. Of course, Griffin's carbon steel Serbian cleaver was already razor sharp, but his mind and methods weren't. He took out his phone, found the video, and clicked the affiliate links in the description to fork over some cash and get the ebook on the breathing and meditation methods that guarantee top performance. The book was expensive, but it promised a return on investment in terms of efficacy and efficiency in his work, so he figured it was worth it.

*Maybe if I actually apply myself I'll get a raise*, he thought. *Maybe even a promotion.*

*Maybe I could be on the other side of the mirror one day.*

So, instead of working himself into a state of avoidant dissociation, he began to read. The book instructed him to imagine a circle that draws itself in a smooth continuous motion, then uncurls until it is gone, and expands and contracts with the length of the line. He counted this off in segments of five seconds, then began timing his inhalations and exhalations with the swelling of the circle in his mind. He could feel his pulse lowering. He was instructed to imagine the circumference of the circle as the circumference of his left wrist. He was instructed to imagine the unfurling line as the blade breaking the circle of the wrist, flowing smoothly through his flesh. He put the tip of the blade on the far side of his wrist. His heart rate low, his focus complete, as the circle was undone, so was his wrist, and he drew the blade towards him in one unyielding motion. He barely noticed it, but he knew it was the best work he had ever done. He put his hand in the bag, put the bag in the ice bucket, and admired his work. It looked perfect.

*Finally,* he thought, *some progress.*

Then it was time for lunch. Griffin was so excited by how well he had done with such a small investment of money and time that he decided to treat himself, so he went to the Mexican chain restaurant and got a cricken burrito bowl. He washed it all down with a crisp refreshing diet cola and sat awash in wonder that the promises made by the guru on *Right Hand Man* had actually imparted such clear and immediate benefits to his technique. He returned to the office with a pep in his step because he knew that with such a clean cut, reattaching his hand was going to be a cakewalk. When he got inside, however, the receptionist behind the front desk called out, "Mr. Batt? Griffin Batt?"

He felt certain that he was going to be praised for his initiative and performance, if not singled out for advancement. With this in mind, he nodded to the receptionist and walked towards her with a smile she did not return, waving the bloody stump of his left wrist as if he were waving hello, as a little office humor, which she did not laugh at.

"That's me. What's up?"

She was wearing a headset and making prolonged unblinking eye contact and yet she put a finger to her ear to indicate she was not talking to him as she said, "He's here."

A large pale man with dark hair and a grey suit appeared behind him silently before saying, "Come with me, sir," and due to the tone of the past six words he had heard Griffin was no longer convinced he was going to be rewarded. The man walked him down unfamiliar corridors, which nevertheless looked exactly the same as the familiar corridors, before finally leading him to a door that simply said "Administration" and gesturing for him to walk through.

Griffin opened the door, stepped inside, and saw a smaller man in a greyer suit sitting behind a midcentury metal desk that looked bombproof in its monolithic solidity. Old fluorescent lamps hummed in the drop ceiling overhead, providing the only illumination in the windowless room. There was, however, a mirror behind the desk, which made him shiver as he glanced at it, and it was in the mirror that he first noticed that the only things on the desk were a single manila folder and an insulated cooler box.

Gesturing to a metal chair on Griffin's side of the desk that would have looked at home in either a high school or a prison, the greyer-suited man said "Sit down, Mr. Batt." He sat down in the most uncomfortable chair he had ever experienced, which was somehow hurting his knees to the point of distracting from the throbbing in his stump.

The greyer-suited man stared at Griffin with an unreadable blank expression for thirty seconds as his heart began to pound a bit harder and a little more blood shot from his wrist as a result. He tightened his right hand's grip around it to stifle this. Breaking eye contact, the greyer-suited man opened the manila envelope and started slowly paging through Griffin's personnel file with measured bureaucratic sluggishness. After the longest four minutes of his life, the greyer-suited man looked up at him again and spoke in a droning monotone that implicitly conveyed that he would never raise his voice because the things he said were inarguable facts.

"Do you know what we pay you to do, Mr. Batt?"

His eyes did not move at all as he said this, and Griffin pondered whether it was a trick question before answering, "You pay me to cut off my left hand every morning and reattach it every afternoon."

The greyer-suited man exhaled through his nostrils and droned on, "In most reductive possible terms, yes, I suppose that is how you might describe your work to a small child, but your definition is lacking in nuance and specificity. For example, do we pay you to do anything else?"

"Pardon?"

"Do we pay you to purchase and read books on company time?"

"Oh, no but I— that book was on breathing and meditation exercises that would allow me to perform my responsibilities with greater efficacy and efficiency, saving the company time and resources in the long run. And I paid for it out of my own pocket, so it wasn't a misappropriation of funds or anything like that. I don't know how I would even get any funds to misappropriate beyond my paycheck. I don't... I don't usually see anybody else who works here most of the day except for Dave when I pick up the day's vat of regenerative coolant gel."

The greyer-suited man stared at Griffin for another ten seconds, expressionless, eyes unmoving, and repeated, *"Do we pay you to purchase and read books on company time?"*

Griffin struggled to choke out a meek "No."

"Furthermore, do you understand the specific criteria under which you are contractually obligated to 'cut off your left hand' as you so simply put it?"

Griffin began sweating profusely as his body sent a hot red rush of shame to his face while he murmured the only answer he could think of.

"I'm supposed to cut off my left hand in a single swift strike."

"The precise language is that you are to sever the sinister extremity in a single swift strike, yes. So you are aware of your responsibilities. So would you care to explain why, after ostensibly studying to perform your responsibilities with 'greater efficacy and efficiency' as you put it, you would instead cut off your left hand in a solitary sudden slice?"

"I don't understand," said Griffin.

"Now, single swift strike implies that there would be one continuous, fluid chopping motion, yes? You understand that strike indicates a chop, coming down from overhead with great force?"

"Oh."

"Meanwhile, your supervisor's report from today says you touched the tip of the blade to the block on the other side of your wrist, then drew the blade towards you in an abrupt motion where the blade never left the chopping- and may I emphasize CHOPPING- block. A solitary. Sudden. Slice."

"I got the job done, didn't I?"

The man's unwavering blank face finally broke and showed a moment of disgusted contempt for Griffin for the fact that he would dare suggest something so foolish.

"No. No you did not, Mr. Batt. What do you believe is the result your employers are seeking from your actions? What is your purpose here?"

"I... I suppose I figured that they... wanted me to cut my left hand off as quickly as possible, and to reattach it as cleanly as possible."

"Wow."

"Wow?"

"That's... how long have you worked here?"

"Three years."

"How did you make it through the interview process?"

"...I have a master's degree in economics."

"Well, I'm sure that will help you in the competitive job market these days. Unfortunately, we are going to have to let you go."

Griffin's ears began to ring as his vision drew to a pinpoint, and he was fairly sure it wasn't from excessive blood loss this time. As his senses blurred from the distortions of emotional anguish,

Griffin could barely hear what the greyer-suited man said next, and had to ask him to repeat himself.

"Please collect your personal effects. Hastings here will escort you from the premises."

"My personal effects?"

He scooted the insulated cooler across the desk towards Griffin, who looked inside to see his left hand in a plastic bag floating in ice water.

"Don't I get to reattach it before I leave?"

"You want to finish out the day after you've made a mockery of what we do here? You really think you deserve free regenerative gel, courtesy of Roderick Faust? We'd just be throwing money away."

"I would like to reattach my hand."

"Your generation really does think the world owes you everything on a silver platter, don't you?"

Griffin stood up with the cooler and began to turn towards the door when he heard the greyer-suited man say, "You don't get to keep the cooler."

Griffin gingerly extricated the bag containing his hand from the sloshing ice inside the cooler, then looked up at him again.

"Can I at least get another plastic bag to hold some ice?"

"Mr. Batt, get the fuck out of here."

3

On the way home, Griffin decided to go to a movie theater to distract himself for a bit and clear his head before he would return to Mr. President and plan his next moves. While passing through the city center between his workplace and home, he got off the bus early, which the driver seemed to be even more grateful for than usual due to the blood dripping from his wrist. He walked across the bright brisk parking lot towards the theater, where at the concession stand he asked the bored teenaged girl manning the counter at 2 PM on a Wednesday for a large soda cup just filled with ice. The young woman, whose hair was the same light brown as Griffin's, said he wasn't allowed to bring in other beverages and just use free ice to cool them, so he held up the bag containing his left hand and said it was to keep it cold. The young woman made a gasping yelp of surprise and disgust and handed Griffin a 96 ounce bucket of ice.

As he dropped his hand into the bucket, the clerk asked if he was going to go to the hospital, to which Griffin just shrugged and said maybe later and asked for a ticket for whatever movie was playing next. Soon he was heading into the theater to watch the new entry in the *The Ape That Kills People* franchise. Overall, pretty good movie. On the way out he picked up some fresh ice, and when he stepped out into the chilly twilight he remembered that the sun was setting at around 4 PM these days.

Griffin got home when it was full dark, as per usual, the way lit by flickering orange street lamps that indicated he was nearing home. Upon reaching his block, he discovered that everyone else in his building had moved out since the day before. He didn't know if they had done it all while he was at work, or if he just hadn't noticed until the process was complete, because in retrospect the behavior he saw in the courtyard yesterday made sense. Either way, he wasn't terribly surprised to find every other window above his lit up like a dollhouse showing empty white rooms with cleaners visibly mopping up inside. As he approached the building and stepped into the pool of light surrounding the courtyard, a woman with her hair tied back looked out the window at him in confusion as if she wasn't expecting anyone to still be living there, but she didn't say a word and quickly got back to cleaning.

He found the door code still worked, and there wasn't anything posted on his door telling him he was being evicted, so he went back into his apartment, threw his left hand into the fridge, popped a can of cat food open one-handed, dropped it into Mr. President's bowl, and collapsed on the couch.

A few weeks prior, he had been interrupted as he sat eating his dinner by a dripping sound coming from outside his door. He was alerted to it when Mr. President perked up from a dead sleep beside him to stare at the front door with wide eyes and a low growl. Griffin went to check it out, and by the time he got to the door saw that there was already water coming in from underneath, so he opened it to find a bubble of latex paint on the ceiling in front of the doorway slowly growing, like the building was growing a cyst. Water dribbled through steadily, so he put a stockpot underneath the drip and decided to ask his neighbors if they knew what was going on.

He hurried upstairs to knock on Wes Sweat's door, who answered, "What's up, Griffin?"

"There's a huge leak in the hallway ceiling. Is anything going on with your apartment that would cause that? Go look, and I'm going to go upstairs and check on Mo and Hammy."

"Alright man," said Wes Sweat as Griffin was already bounding up the stairs to the third floor, where he knocked on Mo and Hammy's door only to find it was answered by a man who looked unnervingly like Griffin did. Not identical, but similar enough in build, skin tone, and genre of face that he could have served as an excellent stunt double. Griffin stammered in confusion for a moment.

"I, uh, I— Hello. Where are Mo and Hammy?"

The man opened the door not quite enough and smiled slightly too broadly. "The rental hosts? I haven't seen them since I checked in."

"I didn't know they were doing that. In this building? They were doing that? Okay. There's a leak downstairs in the hall. Can you check if anything in the apartment might have somehow caused that? I'll be right downstairs. Thanks."

Griffin headed back down in time to see Wes Sweat peeking his head out the door and saying, "Nothing leaking in here. No water pressure though."

Not breaking stride, Griffin responded, "Great. Cool. Awesome. I love that for you so much. I'll keep looking for the source."

In front of his door, the stockpot was already full, so he emptied into the bathtub and put it right back. Staring at the gurgling ceiling cyst, he tried to take a moment to put aside his growing indignity and figure out where it was coming from. The simplest answer was, of course, directly above where the leak was, but that was just the underside of the stairs, and there was no apartment there to leak from. This required, of course, going to go examine the stairs with unprecedented attentiveness.

Griffin quickly noticed that there was a small door on the wall above his hallway ceiling, below the stairs leading to the third floor, raised up to be almost impossible to reach from the stairs directly. Standing on his tiptoes on the railing and leaning over while holding onto the edge of the steps overhead, he managed to reach a latch and pop it open. He found that Wes Sweat's water heater was apparently hidden in a strange reddish chamber that seemed to be aggressively not up to code. The heater looked bulged, and the lower rim looked like it had burst open. Despite the size of the hole, there was a relatively thin stream of water pouring out steadily, and upon closer inspection this was because there was some sort of solid gunk that had apparently both caused, and then jammed up, the hole. The light was too dim to get a good look at the details of the mess.

Back inside his apartment, he saw another ceiling cyst growing over the middle of his floor and preparing to begin dispensing its contents. He put a bucket underneath it, stabbed it with a pen to relieve the pressure, and called the fire department.

In a few long minutes, a squad of enormous burly men rolled up in the platonic ideal of a big red fire truck, as any four year old boy would have loved to see. They came in loud and stomped up the stairs to where Griffin indicated the source of the water, and while they did this Griffin stood in the hall near the building's front door where he could half-see both the ceiling cyst dripping into the stockpot and the firemen rummaging around in the water heater compartment. One of the firemen who had been sticking his head into the compartment emerged, turned to his colleagues and said "It's a TTL. Call the guy."

The same fireman came down the stairs and said to Griffin, "We turned off the water to these so there's no more coming out for the moment. Whatever water is already in the walls and ceiling is still going to have to make its way out, and there's nothing we can do about that, so keep an eye on that stockpot there. Should probably clear out by the end of the night. We're having a guy come in in a minute since we're not exactly plumbers, and he's gonna take care of some detail work. We'll hang around until he gets here."

"Thank you."

Griffin went back inside his apartment to comfort Mr. President after his big scary day of encountering uncontained moisture. About fifteen minutes later he went out to check the stockpot, saw it was full, dumped it out, put it back, and as he did so saw at the front door of the building a fireman was letting in a slight, dark-skinned, extra-medium sized middle-aged man in bifocals and an olive jumpsuit with a receding hairline cut short and slicked back. He was holding a J-shaped farrier's knife that Griffin recognized from the hoof care videos he'd been watching. The fireman shook his hand and they nodded to each other before both going up the stairs. With the cyst-obscured view from his door, Griffin could see them from the knees down as they stood in front of the heater compartment panel until the fireman gave the jumpsuit man a boost and his feet vanished upward as he had apparently crawled inside entirely. A fireman handed something up to him, and a hose soon unfurled from the compartment, which the firemen led all the way out into the front courtyard.

Griffin closed the door and stared out the peephole to keep an eye on what was happening. He couldn't see anything clearly, so he put his ear up against the door instead and heard a faint, rhythmic scraping, followed by the sound of another gush of liquid and the voices of the firemen exclaiming in nonverbal disgust. Returning his eye to the peephole, he saw jumpsuit man's feet re-appear from the ceiling as he settled back on the stairs with the help of the firemen. The man paused for a moment, pulled the end of the hose down from above, then started towards the front door of the building again, and the firemen followed. Thick boot stomps echoed in the direction of the exit, followed by the creak of the opening door.

Griffin assumed they were all going outside, their work complete, so he turned away from the peephole, but as he did there was a knock at the door. He opened it to find the man in the olive jumpsuit with the round little glasses standing much closer to him than he expected, as the space that the man's head would normally occupy under basic standards of door-knocking etiquette was occupied by a throbbing cyst of stretched latex paint. Griffin stepped back with a start as he saw how close the man was— his nose was nearly touching the door, and the toolbox he held in front of him was already over the threshold.

The man cleared his throat and said, "Good evening, sir."

"Good evening yourself. What can I do for you?"

"You know the upstairs water heater popped a leak?" As he said this, the stockpot behind him dripped at a volume that indicated it was nearly full again.

"I am aware of this problem. Yes."

"Has there been any trouble with your own water heater?"

"No. But I haven't really checked tonight while this has been going on, come to think of it."

"Is it in-unit?"

"Yes."

"May I see it?"

"Go for it."

Griffin opened the door wide and waved his arm past the bathroom to the utility closet. The man nodded and proceeded to the closet door, which he opened before ducking inside to examine the half-size water heater. He put down his toolbox, pulled a light from inside, and began a detailed inspection.

Griffin asked from behind him, "So what went wrong upstairs?"

"The recent rains deposited a lot of sediment into the water supply, which, when abruptly introduced to half-size electric water heaters, overwhelms the internal heating mechanisms by causing the sediment to absorb heat intended for the water, as well as induce surges in internal pressure that can break the seal at weak points along the lower rim."

"Ah. Is that going to happen to mine?"

"There's probably been some buildup in this. Have you noticed your water taking any longer to get hot than usual?"

"Come to think of, yeah, it takes a little longer than it used to. I figured it was just because it's starting with colder water this time of year."

"I'm going to need to drain it, which- ah. Hmm."

"What? What's up?"

"There's no drain in the floor here. Not up to code. Same as with the ones upstairs."

"Shit."

"Not a problem. We can extend the drain hose to your bathtub."

"Oh, great."

"Pardon me."

The man excused himself and walked outside, then returned a minute later with another length of hose, which he affixed to a threaded nozzle at the base of the heater. In doing so, he knocked his toolbox over with the hose, spilling some items out, but quickly put things back inside and righted it. With the hose properly attached to the heater and the path cleared, he handed Griffin the other end and told him to take it into the tub, point it towards the drain, and hold on. Griffin followed the instructions, sat on the edge of the tub, got in position, and said, "Ready."

The hose jerked in Griffin's hands and a steaming brown-red slurry shot from the end of it. His hands quickly grew uncomfortably hot as scalding water shot through the hose, pumping out a stunningly thick and dirty sludge. Griffin wondered how in the world his showers and cooking water came out clear with all that in the tank. After a minute or two of the hose loudly, forcefully discharging what looked like straight hot shitty rust into the tub, silence returned, until the man said, "Wow."

Griffin hadn't realized how close the man was standing to him as he had been so transfixed by the filth, and the slight jolt of surprise resulted in him slipping slightly and dunking his left hand- firmly attached- into the tub to stabilize himself. He reflexively pushed back out in a fraction of a second, but his hand was already red and throbbing.

Griffin said, "Ow. Hi. You snuck up on me. I'm okay."

"Looks like we were just in time. Hopefully this is all it needed."

"God willing."

"Your hand okay?"

"Yeah, I think so."

"Well, I believe that concludes my business here today. I'll close up the valve and get everything back in working order and in an hour or so your heater should be full and working normally. If anything else like what happened today happens again, don't hesitate to call." He extended a card to Griffin, which he took without reading. "And you should run your hand under cool water. Have a good evening."

With that, after doing what he said he would, he walked out of the apartment, and Mr. President slowly crawled out from beneath the couch to release a miserable howl.

"I know, buddy. The scary men are gone. It's just us now."

The day after that, Griffin went into work as usual and cut his left hand off in a single swift strike and sewed it back on and fully reattached it with the regenerative coolant gel. When he returned home and went to wash off his stress sweat, he found that he had no hot water and the heater was leaking, despite what that guy had said, but by the time he discovered this he was already fully nude and dripping wet so he toweled off and got in bed to warm himself.

In bed he skimmed through videos of potters spinning cups and bowls and vases on their wheels, he watched glassblowers make their baubles, he watched metalworkers spin custom commissioned buttplugs, and he watched videos of farriers helping the ailments of horses and cows and donkeys by scraping away layers of keratin to free trapped stones and clear abscesses. He watched a farrier hold a cow's hoof between his knees and fearlessly cut away at it until the gnarled filthy painful lesions had been cleared away and what remained was smooth and gleaming and clean and the cow could walk again. Meanwhile, Griffin had an ingrown left big toe nail that he could not quite manage to extract and it was really starting to bother him.

He had intended to shave his armpits in the shower. Besides his scrotum, they were the only parts of his body he shaved, because it helped his antiperspirant work better. Without the hot water of the shower to ease the razor's path, he decided to use the electric trimmer instead. This went mostly without incident until the last pass over the left armpit, where the blade snagged skin and drew blood. Griffin splashed cold water on the wound to ease the irritation, then filed a maintenance ticket to have the water heater fixed by the property management company.

The next day, a sweaty, mumbling man came to look at the heater, and after five minutes of poking around he told Griffin that it was irreparable and would have to be replaced. Two days later he returned and carted the whole tank away without draining it again, spilling a great deal of water across the floor in the process.

A few days after that the swelling in the floor began.

At first it was just a slight irregularity in the hardwood floor between two planks, a line of wood leading from just outside the closet that held the heater and towards the bathroom.

In the following weeks, Griffin fell back into his mindless routine of going to work, cutting his hand off, sewing it back on, returning home to eat rice and beans with the occasional splurge on cricken or hard seltzers, and either watching streaming TV shows with Mr. President on his lap or playing video games with

Mr. President beside him before going to sleep and repeating the process.

On weekends he dedicated more of his time and energy to video games and hard seltzers. He felt a deep hollow void in his heart that it seemed nothing could possibly fill, and regularly prayed that he wouldn't wake up, and Mr. President would eat his body before somebody came to ask him to pay rent and noticed the smell, whereupon they would rescue Mr. President and give him a loving home with big clear windows overlooking a wide open space occupied by plentiful birds.

One evening in late October, soon after his heater had been replaced, he got home from a productive day of cutting off his left hand just in time to avoid a torrential rain storm. The sky began to fall almost as soon as he got through his front door, and soon there was a newly formed river running down his street that began to work its way under the front door of the building. He heard the water running in the hall and opened his door to see how bad it was, and he found that all the water was luckily pouring down the basement stairs before it could reach his door, resulting in a waterfall cascading down the steps. Griffin did not venture into the basement often because it was unfinished and held only a few utility meters and spiderwebs between the grimy floor and the ceiling. As he stuck his head out to look at the indoor waterfall, he was struck by the strong smell of sewage wafting up, then retreated back inside his apartment to comfort Mr. President.

Griffin felt so tired.

The morning after that, he opened his bathroom door and noticed it had difficulty passing over the swell in the floorboards where the door now scraped over the rise. He assumed that the combination of the water heater tank spilling and the heavy rains were responsible for the warped wood. He assumed it would get better on its own.

The next morning it was worse, and he nearly sprained his ankle as he stepped on the swell he'd forgotten was there while making his way to the bathroom in the moments after waking up. As he sat on the toilet, staring out the open bathroom door stopped in place by the swollen hardwood, Mr. President sauntered up and sat inside the boxer briefs around his ankles. While in this position, he filed a maintenance ticket with the property management company to come and take a look at the floor.

The next day, the same mumbling man who had spilled the heater came back and told him that he must be mistaken, because the floorboards had always been like that. Griffin said that he used to be able to easily open his bathroom door all the way, and the man said that was interesting, and left.

Griffin kept hoping it would get better and it kept not getting better. This continued until the day he came home to find every other apartment empty and the cleaning woman glaring at him from the window.

On that day, Griffin heard persistent thumping from upstairs, and when it stopped he watched through the single stripe of undiffused window as the cleaning crews exited the building and dumped several large black trash bags in the front courtyard. He realized, then, that for the very first time in his adult life in the city, he was entirely alone in a building. Needing to make sure that this was actually the case, he went upstairs and knocked on the doors to see if anyone was there to answer, and nobody was. To his surprise, the doors had been left unlocked, so he went exploring within the hastily-abandoned units. As he tentatively stalked through empty rooms, his heart pounded with the giddy exhilaration of getting away with something, a feeling he hadn't known in too many years, until he was standing in the same spot that he had seen the cleaning woman standing in earlier. He looked outside at where he had been standing and saw the vague figure of somebody looking at him from the shadowed sidewalk. The man staring back was too dimly lit to make out in detail, but from the age, build, and skin tone, the guy looked like he could have been Griffin's brother.

Suddenly paranoid, Griffin ran out of the apartment and back down into his own, where his adrenaline got the better of him as he tripped on the swollen floorboards and scared poor little Mr. President, who scurried under the bed as Griffin slammed into the ground. He lay on the floor for a minute catching his breath and gathering his composure, though he felt convinced that someone would soon be pounding on his door to arrest him for illegally entering the other apartments.

Nobody came.

Once he calmed down he realized that his brief adventure had left a large fresh trail of blood that would make what he did extremely obvious to anyone who saw it, and he needed to clean it up. He figured that the landlord would be able to figure out the source of a trail of blood that appeared after the cleaning crews left and led directly to his door.

He'd only been home for about ten minutes.

He applied gauze to his left wrist, tied it on with tape, and put the whole situation into a yellow rubber glove that hung limp and empty. The other glove actually got his right hand in it, though, and so he used it to grab his bucket and put the mop in the crook of his left elbow to go upstairs and destroy the evidence.

Ten minutes later he returned to his apartment, fresh blood coming up easy enough, and yet again forgot about the bump in the floor, which he tripped on, spilling the bucket directly over the bump, and he went to catch himself on the wall, but forgot his hand wasn't there, so he landed on the ground again in the enormous spreading puddle of dilute bloody water.

His rice cooker sang a little song to let him know it had completed its task, but it would coast on warm mode for a while. Griffin got up from the soaking floor, used the mop to halfheartedly push the remaining water into the bathroom, and threw his clothes into the tub, where he turned on the shower to wash them and himself at the same time.

After the shower he changed into black sweats and a worn out old t-shirt, figuring it was not the time to put on any clothes he would prefer not to get covered in blood. He popped open the rice cooker, letting the fragrant steam escape into the room, and went to open the cabinet to grab a plate, which he again failed to do because he did not have a left hand, which he was still not used to and really needed to get fixed ASAP. He poured seasoned vinegar over the rice and sat down in front of the tv with the entire machine clutched to his torso as he proceeded to eat it unadorned with a soup spoon. On the TV he loaded up a ten hour compilation of burl lathing woodwork videos set to royalty-free bossa nova music. Mr. President hopped up next to him, sniffed at his stump, meowed in concern, and curled up next to his leg, waiting for the moment the rice cooker would vacate the lap so he could usurp its throne.

After wolfing down a pile of almost completely unadorned white rice, Griffin decided he needed to relax from his very bad no good day before he even considered starting to apply for work or solve problems of any kind. He had no friends and his life had contracted to a pinpoint and the only thing visible through the pinpoint had vanished. Also, because of the whole hand thing that just kept on being a major problem, he couldn't play anything that required any quick reflexes in terms of actual button presses.

In the greatest epiphany of his recent life, he found the solution. Deciding it would also be a good idea to get some exercise in to lift his spirits, Griffin taped the motion sensor controller to his left stump and loaded up *Real Pro! Boxercise Motion*, wherein he followed the instructions onscreen to deliver rhythmic combos of jabs, hooks and uppercuts while pleasing sounds played and cool lights flashed whenever he did something correctly, which was the most positive reinforcement he had received at any activity in months. If not for Mr. President he would throw himself off a building.

After tiring himself out, he had a strong craving to have a quick drink or twelve, but figured that it would be a bad idea to consume a great deal of a blood thinning vasodilator with a large open wound. By the time one part of his brain finished making that argument against it, he had already consumed six ounces of freezing cold vodka and the room was starting to spin.

4

Griffin awoke the next morning unsure of when he went to bed or what time it was at present, but it wasn't like he had any appointments to keep today, so he laid in bed for a while, trying not to let any thoughts enter his pretty little head. Mr. President, who had taken up residence on his chest, was very pleased at this development, at least until he got hungry and started pawing at Griffin's face. This caused Griffin to stagger up and out of bed, meander towards Mr. President's bowl, and fill it with kibble while the cat exclaimed in delight. On the way to the bathroom he managed to trip over the bump again, remembering its existence a fraction of a second before his toe caught it, but this time he managed to catch himself with the other foot before he fully ate shit. He realized it was still getting bigger.

After he pissed he decided to check the utility closet to see if the new water heater was somehow leaking into the floor already, but upon inspection it was still appeared as pristine and intact as day one. Upon a more thorough examination, there was still nothing wrong with the heater, but he did find the curved farrier's knife that the man with the round glasses and the olive jumpsuit must have mistakenly left behind after knocking over his toolbox in there.

Griffin put the knife on the counter and tried to see what would happen if he stood on the bump with all his weight, and the answer was almost nothing. The boards squeaked a little, but there was otherwise no discernible effect whatsoever.

It occurred to him that with so much accumulated water, bloody and otherwise, having seeped through his floorboards, there might be visible water damage in the basement, and he might see some way to address the damages from below before anybody had to come and start cutting floorboards out.

First, though: breakfast. Griffin was mildly hungover and needed food to help even things out, so he headed to the fridge to check the inventory. The fridge contained a block of tofu, two 16-ounce cans of cheap beer, a nearly empty half-gallon of soymilk, one small bottle of orange juice he'd taken from work when he'd been full after lunch, a cucumber, partially cut, with the exposed end shriveling, a small container of braised shredded cricken, a pickle jar with one whole dill pickle floating alone in green brine remaining, his severed left hand, mustard, and a squeeze bottle of mayonnaise. Griffin ended the pickle's misery, washed it down with soymilk, shot some mayo straight into his mouth, opened a beer, and tried to think of what he could do to get his left hand reattached.

Without the job, he didn't have free access to regenerative cooling gel, and his health insurance had ended upon termination, so he had to either finance the reattachment directly somehow or immediately get a new job that gave him extremely good health insurance. The meager funds remaining in his checking account would vanish in seconds without the strictest discipline.

He decided to start a GoFundMe first, since that could coast along while he was looking for work. He had never had to do that before, but got most of the page set up pretty easily once he changed his phone keyboard to accommodate one-handed swipe inputs. After that, he managed to set his phone up on a tripod in front of the diffused windows, washed his face til he looked much less hungover, and tried to record a video pleading for help, primarily from strangers on the internet who would think he was hot.

The video started with a medium shot of Griffin from the chest up, wearing a blue broadcloth button down shirt buttoned up as far as he could get it one-handed, trying to look the precise level of needy to elicit sympathy rather than disgust and contempt. It's the reason why characters in network television crime procedurals who've just seen their children cut up into tiny bits are always far more calm than they would be in reality. Actual desperation, accurately displayed, repels people. You have to strike a sweet spot. Depict emotion but don't get too emotional. Look sad but be hopeful for the inevitable help you will surely receive from the benevolent audience. Be grateful in advance. Thank them for their generosity before they've given, so that they feel compelled to donate so that their self-image will match the praise they've already been given.

The classics.

In the video, he began to speak.

"Hi, my name is Griffin Batt. I'm 28 years old, and I've spent the past three years working as a sinister severance specialist. What that means is that every day I would cut off my left hand in a single swift strike, and then reattach it. It's dangerous work, but somebody has to do it. Unfortunately, my employment abruptly came to an end yesterday after I was let go right after my lunch break, before I had an opportunity to reattach my hand with the company's supply of regenerative cooling gel."

At this point he raised both arms into frame, showing one stump and one intact hand holding the other severed appendage in a plastic bag.

"Now, obviously, I am in the process of looking for new employment, which hopefully won't take too long as I have a master's degree in economics. But at the moment my priority is reattaching my left hand, as I do not have a personal supply of regenerative coolant gel. I've got plenty of professional experience reattaching my left hand, but without the gel it would take weeks for the limb to reattach fully. I would go to a hospital, but my health insurance ended as soon as my employment did, and the last time I went to a hospital and told them I was experiencing issues with my left wrist, they punched me in the gut and called me a sissy. I am not sure that man was a doctor. So I'm just looking for enough cash to get a single-use container of regen gel. Of course if this works, once the funds come through and I reattach my hand, I'll post photos of the successfully reattached limb to prove the money went where I said it did."

Griffin had recently read a story about a man who had a successful GoFundMe campaign to pay for heart medicine, but one of the people who donated had suspected him of fraudulent misuse of funds because the man who got the money had posted a picture story showing him eating sushi at a restaurant, so the guy who donated showed up at his door and cut him in half with a sword. Griffin wanted to make sure that didn't happen. Keep receipts and all that.

"And as further incentive to donate, plus to prove I'm following through on my claims, anyone who donates over $25 will get a set of feet pics. Anyone who donates over $50 will get to request a custom themed set of feet pics, and to anyone who donates $100 or more, I will show hole. Thank you for your time, and I appreciate you so much. Have a good day."

With that posted, Griffin started putting together his resumé and looked for jobs befitting someone with a master's degree in economics and his work experience. He did not find any. He did find an endless stream of demeaning, low-paying jobs where the listings contained numerous red flags for every aspect of the company culture. Fortunately, he had plenty of experience in those environments. After a couple hours of scrolling through listings while experiencing ever-increasing severe despair, he decided to check the progress of the GoFundMe campaign.

He had made one hundred and eighty five dollars and received a stunningly disproportionate number of comments without donations, some of which follow:

**GenerousGiver77:** Kids these days want everything handed to them on a silver platter. Back in my day if your employer cut off your left hand, you thanked god you still had a right hand.

**HitlerMussoliniFranco88:** >cutting off your left hand

**PUSSYDESTROYER666:** Here's $50! I want you to put mustard on those little piggies

**FifaPlayer80085:** YOUR MOM GOOD. SHIT MAN

**Minneapolis_Beardo:** I have donated one dolar to your cause. I have informed my church group as to your struggles. Thank you for sharing your truth

**LightRaySweetAngel:** I hope you fuckig die

**HORSE_CRIMES:** I've always been confused as to what the purpose of cutting off your left hand in a single swift strike and sewing it back on was, like in terms of economic activity and value generation, but at this point I'm too afraid to ask.

That last comment struck Griffin as strange. While death threats, white supremacists and foot fetishists were par for the course in terms of posting anything online and getting replies, that comment from HORSE_CRIMES was the first time he could remember seeing anyone question why it's important for some people to cut off their left hands in a single swift strike and then reattach them. He didn't see anyone questioning the economic utility of lumberjacks cutting down trees, fishermen catching fish, or burger flippers flipping burgers, but now for some reason cutting off your left hand in a single swift strike confuses people? The limits of stupidity and naiveté on the internet knew no bounds.

It then occurred to him that there was probably an internet community of amputee fetishists and they were surely always on the lookout for fresh content and new faces. It was a mismatch of content to market to try to appeal to foot fetishists in the first place, but feet pics were just the first place his mind went when he tried to think of ways to make fast money online by exploiting the sexual spectacle of his still relatively nubile young body. The only problem was the inherent contradiction of making people see him perform sexually specifically to fund a way to fix the thing about him that they get off to.

Considering this, he decided not to disclose the reason he was selling amputee erotica to the enthusiast sites where the market for such things remained. They could probably figure it out, though— ever since the advent of regenerative coolant gel, attractive first-world amputees were increasingly rare, as what used to be an irreversible lifelong affliction could now be fixed pretty quickly as long as the limb in question was cut or ripped off instead of crushed or otherwise destroyed, and the kinds of people who worked jobs that got their limbs crushed in machinery tended to be the rough-living types who weren't in high demand as the subjects of pornography.

Griffin quickly set out to find an amputee fetishist on a gay hookup app, and found one almost immediately by making his username contain certain keywords that indicated what he had to offer. Within an hour, a medium-tall, semi-hairless Dominican man with an extremely crisp hairline and a nice smile responded, indicating his interest in Griffin's condition, so Griffin asked to see his cock. It was pretty smooth and photogenic, and large enough to look good on camera but not so big as to present major difficulties in practice. Griffin told him that if he wanted to hook up there was one thing he had to do, so the man agreed to let Griffin suck him off on camera at 2 PM on a Thursday as long as his face was never shown.

While waiting for the man to arrive, Griffin put down a tarp, set up his phone on the tripod near the window again, and struggled to get it to precisely the right height to show his face while he was on his knees. It would have been easier if he had both hands, but most things would. He applied a fresh dressing to his stump with new gauze and tape to look presentable to the guy and to his audience on camera. He had quickly discerned that the general preference among amputee fetishists was for healed stumps, indicating a permanent condition, as the fetish was for the absence of limbs rather than the presence of bloody open wounds. He figured it was best to cover the exposed flesh as best as possible to appeal to the broadest possible audience within the narrow niche of perverts who would pay for that kind of thing.

When the man arrived and buzzed his apartment, Griffin put Mr. President in the bathroom to keep him from witnessing what was being done to provide for him. The cat made a little honking chirp as he was dumped in the tub and mewled in confusion as his owner stepped out and closed the door. Griffin greeted the man at the front door wearing only a white and grey striped tank top and running shorts, and the visitor in turn was already out of his coat, which he held by his side, and was wearing a short-sleeved olive henley tight over his pecs, light brown captoe shoes, and tight jeans that emphasized the bulge of his cock. He smelled like sandalwood and vetiver, which would make it easier since Griffin wasn't particularly attracted to him. The guy wasn't ugly, but the extremely precise fresh and clean look didn't really do it for Griffin, who liked his men a little more scruffy and rugged.

Griffin walked him over near the window where the light was better and got them situated in front of the phone camera. The man started to get a little antsy in anticipation looking down at Griffin on his knees, though Griffin was just leaning over to check that the framing on the video was solid, and when he was done checking the phone and looked back up at the guy he could tell that the guy's eyes were locked on his stump and the guy was hard as a rock under his jeans. It took Griffin about thirty seconds to get his face in proper exposure and focus, then he hit record and started undoing the guy's belt with his right hand.

Griffin made sure to keep his stump in frame as much as he could while getting the guy's jeans down and fishing his cock and balls out of the front hole of his trunks. From what he could see in the phone, he was looking pretty good, his hair gleaming, his eyelashes uncommonly thick. He then proceeded to jack the stranger off into his mouth, working the shaft with his hand while sucking the tip until the man put his hands on the back of Griffin's head and pulled him forward, putting himself deep in Griffin's throat. Soon enough Griffin felt the telltale throbbing of an impending orgasm and the man's moaning gasps increased in intensity so he pulled his head back to let thick hot ropes of cum shoot across his face, arcing over his cheeks and down to his chin, while still getting enough into his open mouth to satisfy the viewers who like that kind of thing as well.

After the man finished, he asked if he could piss in Griffin's mouth, and Griffin said he could but would have to wait a moment so he could have a clear point to cut the video before the man started pissing, so that Griffin would have two different video deliverables depending on the fetish market he was selling to. The man agreed, so Griffin made a big show of wiping the cum from his face with his good hand and sucking it off his fingers and swallowing it for the camera, and once he felt like he had a good finale frame for the non-piss version of the video, he told the man to let loose. A thick stream of pale clear well-hydrated urine erupted from the man and into Griffin's open mouth, where it bounced off the back of his closed throat and spilled out onto his tank top and to the tarp until Griffin began swallowing as much as he could, which was relatively easy given how hydrated the man was.

Once the man's bladder was empty and Griffin was kneeling in a puddle of urine, his eyes and hair sparkling with droplets, Griffin took the man's cock deep in his mouth once more and sucked hard enough to cave in his cheeks and pulled back til he came off with a loud wet pop that would play well as a sexy finale audio cue, right before he winked into the camera and blew a kiss to the audience with a hand that wasn't there.

The man zipped up his pants, thanked Griffin, gave him $300 he didn't ask for, and left.

Once the man was gone, Griffin stripped out of his tank top and shorts and wrung them out onto the tarp. In the bathroom he found Mr. President lapping water out of a puddle in the tub, so he went to the bed and shook a bag of treats to draw the cat away without any risk of getting piss or cum on the precious beautiful creature. Once Mr. President was safely out of the way and munching on his treats, he carefully picked up the tarp by gathering the corners one by one into his right fist to keep the liquid in the middle as he dragged it over to the bathroom to empty it.

Unfortunately, on the way over, Griffin had an accident with the lump on the floor. He did manage to successfully step over it without incident, but it turned out that dragging a piss-heavy tarp over the lump was a bad idea that resulted in a slight snag yanking one of the corners of the tarp from his fist, dumping most of the contents directly onto the ever-growing water damage lump, which was great for Griffin, and he loved it, and he didn't even crave death every waking moment of every single day even a little.

He rinsed off the tarp, toweled up the piss, then stepped into the shower with his soaked clothes and the towel in his hand, and at some point this transitioned to him laying limp in the tub as the water ran cold over him, since he had been in there long enough to fully drain the half-size electric water heater that had been occupying far too much of his mind recently.

Once the cold was unpleasant enough to overpower his complete lack of motivation to move, he set up his FanService page, edited and uploaded the two different versions of the video with different titles and tags, and posted teasers to various enthusiast forums. Mr. President kept pawing at him and mewling as if to comfort him throughout the process.

Thanks to the help of several hundred thirsty perverts, within two hours he had plenty more than he did in the morning, which made him slightly wonder why he had bothered having a job before at all. Then he remembered that his haul would likely be much lower if he still had his hand, as the market for gay amputee piss drinking pornography was much more of a low-supply high-demand niche than the oversaturated market for plain ol' prettyboys sucking dick.

Luckily, that porn cash was more than enough to cover a single batch of regen gel, and even if it wouldn't be in his account for a few days, it meant he could put it on credit without getting completely crushed by debt. He placed an order with a delivery shopper service to pick up the gel from the nearest pharmacy, then lied down to nap until it arrived. Mr. President launched himself onto him as he got settled, landing directly on his solar plexus with the force of a shot put, and started purring loud while Griffin struggled to regain his breath. Once the cat stopped moving they both fell asleep quickly, as it had been such a tiring day on an emotional level, and woke up to the sound of the buzzer letting him know that somebody was at the door.

He tipped the driver by effort, not by percentage of sale, since it was a relatively big ticket item that wasn't hard to carry very far. He was getting dressed to answer the door without having his dick out when he heard the delivery man knock, put something down, and walk back out the front door before he could answer.

At the door he found a single enormous economy-size vat of hair gel.

He checked the app he'd ordered through and found a series of messages he had missed while asleep.

Fred: They do not have

Fred: What do you want

Fred: ???

Fred: I get other gel

Fred has finished shopping for your order.

Fred has checked out.

Fred is on his way with your order.

Fred is arriving soon.

Fred has delivered your order.

5

The nearest place that sold regenerative coolant gel and actually confirmed they had it in stock was a 45-minute walk away. The bus ran perpendicular to it from where Griffin lived, growing no closer at any point, so he had to hoof it. He put on a navy peacoat against the cold, since the sun was already making a hasty exit from the sky and a chill was setting over the city. This was fine, as the slight vasoconstriction of surface-level blood vessels was better in terms of his wrist, and going for a walk to clear his head seemed like a fine way to spend an hour and a half after everything else that had been going on.

The destination, Faust Medical Supply, was a wholesale store that primarily sold directly to pharmacies, clinics, and hospitals, but it turned out that they would let you just walk in and buy anything that didn't require a prescription. They certainly didn't encourage it, since they were wildly out of the way and anybody with any other option would go to a dedicated retail location, but if you were willing to go into the ominously sparse industrial zone at the edge of town, you could get whatever you needed.

Street lights flickered on with insistent quiet humming as Griffin made his way out there. Right about at the border of the odd interzone between the residential and industrial areas, he found a building containing a small fish market he hadn't known was there before. Under a streetlight in front of the fish market, there was a busted open fire hydrant with two men standing around it. One man was holding a fish and an enormous square Chinese cleaver, with which he was rapidly scaling and cleaning the fish while occasionally dipping it into the frigid water rushing out of the hydrant, and the other man was holding neither of these things and doing nothing but watch. Once the man who was doing things finished doing them, he pulled a black plastic bag out of his back pocket and deposited the fish into it with no other packaging.

The man with no fish or cleaver handed the man with a fish and a cleaver a few paper bills, so the man with the fish and cleaver handed the man with no fish or cleaver a fish, so then there was one man with a fish and one man with a cleaver as two separate people, redesignated, their transaction complete, so they each silently nodded at each other, turned 180 degrees, and walked in opposite directions. The man with the cleaver walked into the fish market. The man with the fish walked into the darkness, vaguely towards the residential areas, where he would presumably cook the fish soon.

Further out towards the industrial zone, the streetlights grew fewer and further apart, leaving Griffin to wander through darkness longer and longer between each pool of sodium vapor clarity. Eventually, he crossed the tracks and the density shifted to light spilling from the dim high windows of warehouses and factories. Somewhere around there was the Bear's Head lunch meat factory, which as far as Griffin could tell ran 24 hours a day, judging by the scents of various lunch meats that wafted through the area at all times, and by the men on the bus that he used to take to work every day who looked like they'd just finished a day of hard work and smelled strongly of pepperoni. At the same time as the aroma of low-sodium chipotle roast cricken loaf reached him, an enormously large fat rat scurried through the light, looking halfway between a small dog and football, likely towards the meat factory whose dumpsters kept him in such a luxuriant weight class among rodents.

Soon the smells of meats were behind him, replaced by the scent of distant hot plastic and burning hair, accompanied by the thrum of unseen machinery somewhere within the district. He got lost and meandered for a bit as his phone's GPS was having trouble pinning down his location, and so was he. Eventually he saw a building with a gleaming LED sign standing out amid the dim orange ambient light. The sign said Faust Medical Supply. He walked in.

Inside, it looked like the bright sterile shelves of a pharmacy at the scale of a big box warehouse store. There was one person visible through a window into a small office near the entrance, so he knocked, heard some kind of murmured sound of affirmation through the door, and entered. Behind a semi-messy desk containing a large laptop surrounded by various inputs and receipts sat a man of about his age, a little shorter than him. Compact, lithely muscular, angular east Asian features. The man wore a short-sleeved white button down with a navy tie, horn-rimmed glasses, and a nametag that said "Jun." His hair was dark and lustrous and had been clearly cut short and clean a while ago and was in need of it again soon- just scruffy enough. He could have been out of a shampoo commercial.

Griffin was so entranced by this man's hair that he took a moment to react when the man started talking to him without looking up, saying, "Can I help you?"

Griffin continued staring at the hair, not hearing this for about four seconds, until the man glanced up.

"Sir? Can I help you?"

Griffin blanked on what to say and instead just held up the stump of his left wrist.

The man nodded. "Ah. Prosthetics or regeneratives?"

"Regeneratives. Gel, max speed, high coolant, single use."

"Aisle H4, rack 28."

Griffin continued staring at his hair.

The man said, "Sir?"

"Can you help me find that?"

"Of course. One moment."

He clicked a few times on the laptop and stood up. Griffin could tell that the man—Jun, he supposed— actually looked at Griffin's face as a person instead of just an interloping customer, which he hadn't seen in a while, and *smiled warmly*, which was even rarer.

Jun said, "Follow me, sir," and gestured behind Griffin as he started walking towards the door. As he began to follow, Griffin turned and noticed a bulletin board he hadn't seen on the way in. It was covered in bland business clipart and text that advised him to seek opportunities in Faust subsidiary companies, including Faust Logistics, Faust Fertility, Faust Collections, Faust Dynamics, Faust Financial, Faust Direct Sales, Faust Munitions, Faust Distributed Household Management, Faust Culinary Solutions, Faust Food Service Supply, Faust Insurance, Faust Snax, and Faust Media Distribution, to name the few he could discern before Jun opened the door and beckoned him out onto the floor.

As he walked through the door, Griffin gestured to the bulletin board and asked, "Are all these Faust companies, like, always hiring? I just got laid off from Faust Medical Solutions."

Jun released the door, trotted back in front of Griffin, and said, "For the most part. Some more than others. The food ones need a constant supply of hired gun line cooks, but from the looks of you I'm not sure your knife skills are up to the industry standard. Snax and Munitions basically just hire factory workers, and I genuinely have no idea what Dynamics does. Logistics is good money but requires being away from home for weeks on end when you're driving the trucks or out on the boats or wherever they end up sending you."

"Well then I couldn't do that one either. I got a cat at home who needs me. Can't leave the little guy alone all day wondering where I am while some cat sitter drops off kibble and cleans his litterbox for me. That's my son."

"What's his name?"

"Mr. President."

"Great name for a cat." He smiled at Griffin as he said it, and for a moment Griffin stopped wanting to die. A forklift whirred by in the distance, briefly visible between the columns and aisles. Without thinking, Griffin went to brush his hair back over his left ear in a cute flirty way, but he had forgotten he didn't have a left hand, so he just sort of waved his stump near the side of his head for a second. A hot rush of blood made him blush in embarrassment over that dogshit maneuver, but Jun seemed to find it charming and gave a cute little raised-eyebrow smile. In the aftermath of that moment, their eyes stayed locked as they walked, and a couple precious seconds ticked by as Griffin tried to think of anything clever or charming to say until Jun broke eye contact, glanced over Griffin's shoulder, and said, "Here we are."

Griffin's heart nearly beat out of his chest as Jun leaned toward him to reach over his shoulder to the shelf and Griffin forgot to turn around and look at the regenerative coolant gel products, because in that moment Jun's face seemed more important than reattaching his left hand. Griffin felt like they were about to kiss when Jun pulled back and presented him with the tub of gel he'd gotten from the shelf.

"This one's rated to the thermal load of the reaction required to reattach a hand in under a minute. Where's the hand?"

Griffin reached into the pocket of his peacoat for the bag with his hand.

It wasn't there.

"Oh my fucking God. It's not there. Oh my God."

"What? Where's the last place you—"

Griffin was already running back the way he came, scanning the floor for wherever he may have dropped his hand while distracted by Jun's eyes, what a fool he had been, stupid, stupid, and he heard Jun running to catch up with him, and in seconds they were back out in the dark streets of the industrial zone, Griffin trying to remember the path he took as he wandered around in that brief period of being lost, trying to remember where he was when he was last completely certain his hand was in his pocket, when he realized he didn't even bring it.

It was in the fridge back in the apartment.

He stopped in his tracks and turned around and Jun slammed into him and they both stumbled.

Jun, already more invested in Griffin's well-being than any customer service worker had ever been, asked "Did you find it? Where was it?" and then hunched over to put his hands on his knees and catch his breath.

Griffin, now also gasping with one hand on a knee and his left forearm against the other, had no choice but to admit, "I never had it. I left it at home. I forgot. I forgot because I was distracted."

Jun looked up at Griffin while catching his breath and Griffin could tell from the wrinkles around his eyes that Jun was smiling because he knew why Griffin was distracted.

On the way back through the warehouse, the two men were a bit giggly. Griffin found Jun quite attractive, as you may have surmised, despite the drab corporate outfit which he was presently fitting into *precisely*. All Griffin knew about Jun was that he worked at Faust Medical Supply, thought Mr. President was a good name for a cat, seemed to find him attractive even with no left hand, and cared enough about his well-being to run into the street after him to help him find his severed appendage.

Good enough for a crush, he supposed.

They got back to aisle H4, rack 28, to find the tub of regen gel right where Jun had left it on the floor before he started to run. Griffin stammered, "So, you, uh, you, you were saying—"

Jun laughed. "I've completely forgotten what I was saying."

"I think I asked if you were hiring," said Griffin as he bent down to pick up the gel.

Jun started walking towards the office and said, "Oh, here? No, we're not. But- right, the other Faust subsidiaries. What did you want to know?"

"Which ones are hiring, don't require me to travel, and won't be absolutely horrible to work for?"

"Oh, they'll all be absolutely horrible to work for. That's the only game in town."

"Well then, which ones won't require me to cut my hand off on a regular basis?"

"On a regular basis? Direct sales, Financial, Media Distribution, and Insurance."

"And which ones won't require me to cut my hand off at all?"

"Direct Sales, Financial, and Insurance."

"Which would you recommend?"

"To my understanding, Direct Sales is pretty much always hiring because they have a lot of turnover, but their potential for advancement scales pretty much directly with your sales numbers. Insurance is more stable, but there's only so far you can go with that."

"Why the turnover?"

"Because you have to cold call random people and try to sell them things. They hate it, most people who try to do it hate it, everybody involved is pretty unhappy to be participating in the whole situation, and you are subject to a constant stream of angry strangers who are mad at you for even talking to them."

Griffin held up the stump and said "Honestly, that still sounds pretty easy compared to what I was doing before."

"Ah. Sinister severance specialist?"

"Yeah. Got fired yesterday at lunch. Hence the, uh, this."

"I see. Let's get you checked out with the gel so you can go take care of that. And since you're so curious about other Faust opportunities, even after Faust just fired you, feel free to call me if you have any more questions." At this, he took out a business card, wrote something extra on it, and handed it to Griffin, who at that moment learned that this man's full name was Jun Saito-James, and that he had just been given an actual phone number.

Griffin tried to think of something cool and sexy to say, but when he looked up into Jun's deep brown eyes he blanked and could only muster, "If it helps, I have a master's degree in economics."

*6*

When the bandages came off his stump, Griffin saw that the precision of the cut that got him fired had resulted in a perfectly even scab forming across the entire cross section of the wound. He laid out his tools for the task and hunched over the counter next to the sink. The tub of regenerative coolant gel sat within the sink basin, its seal broken and lid removed, ready to fulfill its reason to exist. Griffin held a wooden spoon in his teeth. An enormous volume of paper towels covered the counter, held down by a wide cutting board, atop which sat a needle, sutures, medical tape, Griffin's severed left hand, and the small sharp knife he mainly used to cut up potatoes. The knife wasn't quite so sharp as his company issued cleaver, but it was more nimble and precise for the task of gingerly removing the scab to re-expose the flesh beneath without cutting away any more tissue.

The blade worked under the scab easily, and after a few minutes of careful knife work while putting deep tooth marks into the spoon, he managed to precisely excise the scab in one un-broken piece, leaving only exposed flesh which promptly started trickling blood again. It had somehow only been about 34 hours since he cut it off, so it was still pretty fresh as amputations go.

Then he finally did what he had thought he was going to spend Wednesday afternoon doing: sewing his hand back on. It was a bit weirder than he anticipated because his hand, while always on ice before being reattached, was usually only like that for an hour or so. Thirty-four hours of disembodied refrigeration affected the texture a little bit. But pretty soon he had it tightly attached at four points equidistant around the circumference, which was enough to switch to taping it to expedite the process. Once it was taped, he checked the alignment, confirmed it was good, braced his teeth on the spoon once more, and plunged his hand into the freezing cold regen gel.

The gel began bubbling and frothing and thinning out as it heated up, and the spoon cracked in his mouth at the fresh assault of white hot searing pain coursing through him. He had remembered it hurting less at work, but 34 hours of an unhealed major wound caused his brain to run out of whatever natur-al anesthetic neurotransmitters it could have used to mitigate the burning, and Griffin used all his conscious will to keep his hand submerged even as the primal animal instincts of his brain screamed at him to pull his hand from what was surely molten lead, and he wasn't sure it was working it hurt too much it hurt too much it hurt too much it hurt too much and then it was done, and Griffin realized the spoon had fully broken, and he spit splinters to the floor as he pulled his hand from the now warm watery cloudy pink fluid.

He was dizzy.

He grabbed the bottle of orange juice from the fridge and chugged it, then took the small container of shredded cricken, sat on the floor, and ate from it with his right hand as Mr. President chirped and mrowled alternating between concern for his human's health and interest in a pile of cricken. Griffin kept eating until he was a little less lightheaded.

Griffin put the container of cricken on the floor beside him and Mr. President's vacant orange eyes lit up like a twelve year old boy getting mozzarella sticks after laser tag as he ran up to shove his face into the pile of protein. Griffin's left hand was still mostly numb, but as blood began to flow back into the appendage, pins and needles started to make their way through skin and muscle, the electric buzzing pain of reawakening that strengthened with every movement he made, so he decided to just lay there on the floor with his hand motionless on his chest until he regained feeling and it stopped hurting.

He woke up in that position the next morning, right there in front of the sink, with Mr. President splayed out across his chest, having apparently wiggled his way under the hand to be closer to Griffin as he slept. While slowly awakening, Griffin tested his hand by gently skritching Mr. President's empty little head, and found that it still felt a little bit off. He was aware of the sensory input from the hand, but it felt like it was getting filed in the wrong part of his brain, and he realized that somehow texture, pressure and temperature were registering slightly separately and milliseconds out of sync, like when the RGB lights of an old projector don't quite line up.

Mr. President yawned, stretched, and begrudgingly hopped off Griffin as he made his way back to standing up, and in the process his stiff human spine popped, making a noise like a hardcover book being dropped on a potato chip. As he stood he realized that the tub of coolant gel was still in the sink, the pale pink liquid inside now even cloudier with the residual blood and trace biomass floating in it. The tub was too big to easily rotate within the sink, and it didn't seem like he would be able to pour out a container that large into the sink without risking it spilling everywhere, so he figured out another plan. He definitely wasn't *supposed* to just dump it down the drain in general, but it had been used and sat out all night at that point, so its efficacy was likely negligible at that point and it probably wouldn't cause any horrible effects on the sewer gators. And either way, the tub was bigger and easier to pour things into.

Griffin then discovered, to his great surprise, that it was harder to lift heavy open tubs of liquid out of sinks with a just-reattached hand that isn't quite sending or receiving signals correctly than it was to lift heavy closed tubs of liquid into sinks with no left hand at all. Focusing on keeping his grip tight no matter what other feedback errors returned from his nerve endings, he slowly extricated the tub of gel from the sink and began to walk it over towards the bathtub, where he could upturn it all at once without anywhere near as much concern about splashback.

Of course, in attempting to do this moments after waking, he forgot about the huge lump in the floor, caught his foot on it, and spilled some gel directly onto the lump, causing him to loudly yell fuck words, which made Mr. President run and hide under the bed. Luckily, his muscle memory now somewhat practiced at keeping him from completely falling over on the lump, he managed to make the rest of the way to the tub without incident, so he poured in the gel, turned on the shower, and let the water thin it out to the point that it could drain easily. He knew he was definitely not supposed to dispose of it this way— there had been some kind of procedure at work, he was sure, though it wasn't his purview. He just left the tub on the table when he left and the cleaning crews had taken care of it before his return every day. Certainly there was a proper method, and he knew that they sold the depleted stuff to be used in some kind of industrial process. He just wanted to be rid of it, though, so down the drain it went.

Once the shower was running, Griffin turned to take care of the spilled gel and found much less of it than it seemed like there should have been. Then he saw it— the floorboards were now so warped that there was actually a visible gap between them at the apex of the lump, and some of the gel had apparently gone straight through. The rest he mopped up and wrung it out into the bath.

It was now about 8:15 AM on Friday, and most days at this time he would already be heading out the door into the grim November chill to ride the bus with Bear's Head factory workers returning from the night shift. On this day, though, he could afford to relax a little bit. For once. His brief excursion into homegrown amputee watersports had continued to sell throughout the night, and he actually had enough money to make it through the rest of the month without having to panic if he couldn't find another job right away.

Once that limited niche was tapped out, though, he wasn't going to have anything else to sell to them, so he was going to have to go legit again soon one way or the other. But for once there wasn't a crazed rush, and the relief of being without urgency let him fall back asleep until 11, and when he woke up his hand felt closer to normal.

Then he needed a drink because, well, you've just read what his week was like.

He went to the liquor store and splashed out a bit by actually purchasing a couple bottles of cheap liquor instead of just one dirt-cheap bottle. Once supplied with vodka, coffee liqueur, and diet cola, he mixed up a Colorado Bulldog and settled in to binge-watch the new season of *The Contestant!*, a meta-gameshow about one man's journey to compete on as many game shows and reality shows as possible.

In the first episode of the new season he'd been dropped onto a remote island with no clothes and only an enormous bowie knife, where he had to find love among other sexy singles struggling to survive on the island who had not been informed of each other's locations but would be forced to compete for dwindling resources in an ever-shrinking circle with a border patrolled by men with paintball guns. The Contestant himself was one of those faces you felt like you saw everywhere, blandly handsome but with striking blue-grey eyes. The teaser opening for the episode showed brief clips of The Contestant biting into a live softshell crab like a sandwich, jumping off a waterfall into a lagoon as paintballs missed him by inches, and performing CPR chest compressions on an unresponsive, soaking-wet nude man while a wailing, sobbing woman stood over them crying, and he looked up at her and asked her what she did for fun on the weekends. The title card *ROMANCE ARCHIPELAGO: BATTLE ROYALE* appeared in huge block letters, with the chyron *Get Married Or Die Trying* in a stylized cursive font beneath it.

Then he woke up again, hazy, head aching, because instead of water he had only consumed double-strength mixed drinks so far that day, and it turned out that could have adverse effects. He stumbled down the cracking sidewalk to the corner store at the end of the block to get some coconut water, and when opening his wallet to pay for it he saw Jun's card in there. That was as good a lead as any towards new employment, or, you know, other things, so once he'd consumed enough liquid to clear his head, he called the official number on the front.

Jun answered, "Faust Medical Supply, this is Jun speaking, how may I help you?"

"Hi Jun, this is Griffin Batt. I'm calling to seek more information about employment opportunities at Faust Direct Sales."

"Sorry sir, you've got the wrong number. This is Faust Medical Supply. I can-"

"No, I know, but this is the number you gave me?"

"Pardon?"

Griffin realized he had never given Jun his name and they hadn't talked long enough for him to recognize his not particularly distinctive voice.

"Oh, I'm the guy who has a master's degree in economics, and, thanks to your help, two fully attached hands."

"Oh!" Griffin could hear the smile in his voice. "Well, I'm glad to hear our fine products met your needs. Always glad to hear from a satisfied customer."

"Glad to be satisfied," said Griffin, before cringing at what he had just said and silently making a face of confused panic until he heard Jun laugh again.

Jun said, "Let me get you the information on our direct sales sister company. Just a moment. Ah, it says here to type the phrase Faust Direct Sales into literally any search engine and then click the link to the website. Can I help you with anything else today?"

"Yeah, can I buy you a drink after work?"

"I thought you'd never ask. Hello Horses at eight?"

Griffin smiled. "Great. See you then."

Griffin had pursued an education in economics in the hope that he'd get some financial stability out of a job doing something like equities research, but in the course of developing the skills to be competent at this job, also discovered that he found it so boring that it had a powerful sedative effect. During the course of his academic career he had handled this problem with the daily use of stimulants ranging from pharmaceutical grade amphetamines to the military-grade antinarcoleptics they used to give to fighter pilots in the war.

Unfortunately, in the course of trying to find subjects within the field that didn't cause him to frequently involuntarily lose consciousness, he discovered the only jobs actually available to people in the field of pure economics outside of academia or extremely in-depth securities analysis were largely in writing reports for think tanks on why the free market was actually extremely good, and cool, and your friend, so you should probably deregulate anything concerning whether it's okay for children to work sixteen-hour days on oil platforms. He didn't want to do that, so. A brief period of pursuing employment in securities analysis had resulted in such extreme stimulant abuse that the subsequent breakdown and burnout made it clear that there was no going back.

The preceding paragraphs summarize some things Griffin told Jun on their first date getting drinks at the bar called Hello Horses. In response to this information, Jun sipped his daiquiri, then said, "So instead you got a job cutting off your left hand?"

"Yeah. Pays the bills. The extortionately high bills."

"I still have no idea what the point of cutting off and reattaching your left hand every day is," said Jun.

Griffin ignored this, not wanting to get into a dry explanation of the market any more than he already had, and diverted the conversation, asking, "So what did you study in college?"

"Ceramics."

"God, I envy any profession that actually has something solid and real to show for its efforts at the end of the day. How'd you end up in corporate medical supply sales?"

"Nobody's willing to pay for ceramics at a price that includes the overhead of somebody paying off student loans and rent in a first world country. Every line of ceramics sold at scale is either mostly made by machines or done by people in countries where the cost of living is measured in fish hooks."

"I suppose I've gotten pretty good at turning off the part of my brain that knows these things just to get through the day."

"Yeah, it's awful. I can't make a living making the kinds of useful and beautiful objects that every single person I know uses every single day, so I have to sit and review spreadsheets about warehouse inventory so that I can get health insurance good enough that if I get hit by a car, they only charge me a million dollars out of pocket instead of just shooting me in the head with a captive bolt pistol and harvesting my organs."

"I hate it when they do that."

Jun laughed at that, and Griffin didn't want to ruin the mood so he smiled back because he was pretty sure they were going to have sex later, and, judging by the way Jun bit his lip, he was definitely a bottom.

Griffin and Jun were stumbling through the front door of Griff's apartment, making out so hard they were blind to their surroundings, and *wouldn't you know it* but Griffin forgot about that fucking lump again because he was drunk and horny, so Jun tripped on the huge lump outside the bathroom and fell to the ground hard before they even got any lights on, which pretty immediately ruined the mood.

Griff had been walking in backwards, being somewhat familiar with the lay of the land, kissing Jun hard, when between kisses Jun just sort of fell away to the side in one smooth motion so abruptly that, for a moment, the half-drunk Griffin had no idea where he'd gone. Then he looked down at the dim form of Jun on the floor, lit only by the TV playing bird videos for Mr. President across the room. Jun was groaning in pain. Griffin flipped the lights on so he could actually see how bad it was and found Jun was lying next to the somehow now-even-higher ridge on the warped boards that had clearly cut the side of his head under his thick beautiful hair in some capacity. He was moaning in anguish and his blood was soaking into the ground around the lump.

Griffin knelt down and said, "Oh fuck, you're really bleeding. I'm gonna check the wound, okay?" Jun nodded his assent so Griff ran his fingers through the blood-soaked hair til he found where the wound was, just below where Jun parted his hair, and said, "Do you want to go to the hospital?"

From between gritted teeth Jun choked out, "No! Absolutely not, how fucking rich do you think I am?"

"Okay, I'm going to clean this, stitch it up, and you're going to be okay. Okay? I'm going to give you some lidocaine first so it hurts less. I'm so sorry about my fucking floor. Just hold still."

Jun nodded again.

Griffin grabbed supplies from the bathroom, put on gloves, smeared the anesthetic-infused antibiotic ointment on around the wound, then grabbed the remaining needle and sutures from the kit he had used on himself the day before. Griffin carefully sutured the bleeding wound, which was a bit tougher under a full head of hair that was still actively oozing blood and also he was a little bit drunk, but he got it done and said *I'm going to clean it one last time and this part is going to fucking suck okay?* and Jun nodded, so Griff poured rubbing alcohol over Jun's head and Jun groan-screamed as its astringent sting coursed through his wound.

Griffin took a breath. He put gauze over the wound and started to wrap the whole area and used medical tape to keep it in place, then helped Jun onto the couch once the bleeding was fully under control.

Griffin asked, "What do you want to do? Do you want to go home? Do you want to rest here?"

"I want to rest here for the moment, yeah. Do you have any painkillers?"

"Ibuprofen, weed gummies, and more alcohol if that counts."

"That counts. I'll take it all. Fuck, my head hurts."

"Okay, hold on." Griffin grabbed the ibuprofen from behind the bathroom mirror and gummies from his nightstand and when he turned back to Jun he witnessed Mr. President's round orange body crawling into Jun's lap, apparently aware that he was unwell and in need of comfort, despite being a total stranger.

"Hello sir. You must be Mr. President," said Jun.

"Meow," said Mr. President.

Griffin poured a glass of water and handed it over with four ibuprofen, figuring it was best to be generous with the first dose in a situation like this. Jun gulped it down and returned his attention to Mr. President, who was impatiently headbutting his hand and purring in demand of skritches. Griffin turned around, grabbed the rum from the freezer and lime juice and syrup from the fridge, and shook up a quick daiquiri for Jun.

When Jun sipped it his eyes lit up and he said, "That's just about a perfect daiquiri."

"Thank you."

"Wait, did I even ask for a daiquiri?"

"No, you just asked for any alcohol as a painkiller."

"You remembered my drink order from the bar and made it unprompted?"

"Yes."

Jun started to smile wide but winced when it seemed like making his face move that much was somehow pulling the stitches. He dialed it down to a smaller grin and said, "You're sweet."

Griffin smiled back. "Thank you."

Jun anesthetized himself with a gummy and a few more daiquiris, which Griffin made for them both while matching the bleeding man across from him drink for drink. Pretty soon Jun was snoring on the couch with Mr. President curled up on him, intently purring as if to aid in healing somehow, while some ancient network television comedy played softly on the television. Jun obviously hadn't felt up to deep conversation or sex, or even anything that would cause him to make too expressive of a face and pull on his stitches, so he requested to watch the most generic warm bath of an unfunny old multi-camera sitcom Griffin could find.

They sat on opposite ends of the couch, each with their back against an armrest, their feet meeting in the middle, a towel-wrapped pillow between Jun's head and the wall. Some combination of plenty of drinks and the abrupt introduction of physical harm and medical care had put them into a zone of oddly intimate comfort with each other, which for the moment was devoid of sexuality but full of fondness. Griffin figured once Jun was healed they could revisit the possibility of seeing through the original plan for the evening, but for the moment, sitting there watching Jun resting with Mr. President on his chest was the nicest he'd felt in a long time.

Then he heard a floorboard creak. He heard it again a moment later, and when he looked over, he saw that the lump in the floor was visibly throbbing as if it had a heartbeat.

2. 7

Griffin grabbed a flashlight and his phone and decided it was probably time to try to report the thing to the property management company again, since it would be much harder for them to claim that nothing was wrong now that it was throbbing. He thought this might indicate some kind of imminent plumbing disaster, so he took a short video of the lump in which the background audio was the laugh track of the tv show playing across the room, so it seemed like the studio audience found a pulsating hardwood lump absolutely hilarious. Realizing that a plumbing leak into the basement would likely actually require them to send immediate help, Griffin decided to go down to document the damage to send in with the service request.

He put his shoes on and grabbed a hat and a surgical mask because the last time he checked, the basement was a dusty mess of cobwebs, which he preferred to keep out of his mouth and hair. So he headed out his door, across the hall, and down the stairs into the musty darkness, where he opened the door to see the electric meters on the right wall under the one light bulb in the whole space, which seemed to extend across the entire building uninterrupted by anything but support columns. His flashlight's cold blue beam illuminated a circular sliver at a time, with the dark around it seeming all the deeper for the contrast.

He figured if there was a plumbing problem, he was more likely to find it faster by looking for moisture on the ground, so he slowly scanned the dirty floor looking for dark spots of gathered water. He proceeded to the area where he estimated the lump should be and quickly found the moisture, which was a rusty red just like what had come from his last water heater when he and that plumber guy had drained it into the tub.

Griffin moved his flashlight up to the ceiling to find the source and was unprepared for what he saw.

He screamed.

He dropped the flashlight and picked it back up and pointed it at the thing while shuffling backwards because he wasn't sure if it was dangerous or not and couldn't process what he was looking at.

On the ceiling of the basement, in exactly the spot that corresponded to the throbbing lump on his floor, there was a large keratinous stalactite growth, slowly pulsing, looking for all the world like an enormous conglomeration of infected hooves.

Not knowing what else to do, and realizing it was just going to keep hanging there, he took a picture of it with his phone to send to the management company, then headed back upstairs. He sent in the updated service ticket while sitting next to Jun, who was still out cold beneath the cat. He grabbed his phone tripod, rubbing alcohol, rubber gloves, the farrier's knife, and an additional flashlight. He took another shot of vodka to get some more courage, because this was no time to even consider sobering up.

Down in the basement, he set up the phone on a tripod to film with its light on, both for extra visibility and posterity, while he parked one flashlight directly underneath the thing to shoot light straight up, with the other flashlight in his still-strange-feeling left hand and the farrier's knife in the right. With enough light on the thing, he could finally get a decent look at the whole of it all at once, and in that moment the knowledge of hoof care he'd osmosed from watching all those farrier videos rose to the surface with perfect clarity.

The thing was about four feet in vertical length, two feet thick at its widest point, and all over was a pale yellowish-white dirtied by the plentiful ambient dust of the basement. He squirted rubbing alcohol onto the thing near the top and smeared it down with the glove like a squeegee to see what it looked like beneath the grime. It was mostly uniform in its opacity, thickly white, but there was a small dark spot visible near the tip. From the videos he'd learned that dark spots indicated cavities within the horn, and that indicated infected tissue further inside that had closed over, resulting in abscesses that filled with pressurized pus until the animal was in extreme pain. Not that this was an animal, as far as he could tell.

In his drunken daze, he began to carve out around the dark spot with the farrier's knife, since he knew the cavities usually widened as they went deeper and he would need some room to work. He dragged the curved knife across the surface and slivers of horn fell away like enormous toenails, but eventually he reached the point where the infected cavity began, which he knew because it sprayed him in the face with a high pressure burst of hot bloody pus. His hat and mask caught most of it, but his eyes got a direct hit from some of it, which was enough to cause him to scream while pulling the mask off and vomiting up everything inside him before rushing upstairs to rinse his eyes in the sink for a full five minutes before he started to feel clean again.

But he knew from the videos that the job was not done.

He went back down.

He felt an odd sense of purpose.

There was a clear problem: there was this thing.

He could help.

The thing was bad, and he could carve it away until it was better.

He couldn't remember the last time he'd done anything that seemed so immediately rewarding, despite how grotesque it was.

He put on another mask.

Back down in the basement, there was still bloody pus bubbling and dripping from the tiny opening he had created, but with the initial high pressure relieved, the viscosity of it was keeping it from draining any further. He had to keep going. He sprayed the area with rubbing alcohol to thin the pus so it could flow a bit better, then cut away a chunk to find that, yes, the wound channel did increase in diameter upstream. He cut and cut and cut and cut and there was the rhythmic sound of slices of keratin falling to the ground and the drip drip drip of bloody pus continuing to drain, and before he knew it there was what appeared to be the origin point of the abscess. He knew from the videos he had to clear away as much of the damaged tissue as possible so that what was left wouldn't suffer from the creeping rot contained in the infected horn, so he excavated a wide circumference to give himself room to reach the deepest parts of the infection.

After a few minutes of this, he unearthed what appeared to be some kind of cystic sack, but filled with a clear fluid instead of bloody pus, so he cleaned the surrounding area with a few more sprays of alcohol and sliced the sack open. The fluid inside was water-thin and drained almost instantly, but there was still something within the sack, a solid mass obscured by the membrane, and it was moving.

He took a deep breath, regretted it instantly due to the smell, and inserted the knife into the opening in the membrane and worked it around the edges until the sack fell away, revealing another thing he was unprepared to see.

His hand.

Griffin Batt stood there for a full minute, silently regarding the grotesque mockery of his own left hand, slightly underdeveloped, the only thing left at the core of the wound channel, clearly the cause of all the infected tissue below, squirming.

It seemed to be trying to grasp blindly for something.

It was not supposed to be there.

None of it was supposed to be there.

He gripped the knife firm and prepared to do what he did best.

He started cutting away at the base of the hand and it reacted, flailing until it felt where his knife was coming from and ineffectually trying to swat it away in panicked desperation, trembling and clenching as blood poured from its base, and soon it was pale and limp as he cut it free entirely. There was an umbilical-cord-esque piece of tissue where the cystic sack attached to the horn, and he cut that out too, then scraped around the inside of the cavity until everything was gone and sprayed it with alcohol to reveal the smooth, white, healthy horn that remained.

If you were to look at the floor without knowing what was going on, you'd likely assumed that Griffin had brutally murdered someone and disposed of every part of their body except the hand. He dumped the rest of the bottle of alcohol into the mess to dilute it and hoped it helped somehow.

When he checked his phone on the tripod, he realized from the timestamp on the video that that process had taken a little over an hour, and despite how horrific it was, he had been so focused that it hadn't seemed more than 15 minutes to him.

He hadn't had that kind of flow state in years.

Every hour had been an eternity as long as he could remember.

He went back upstairs, threw the hand in a plastic bag in the freezer, showered, and fell asleep in his bed, feeling oddly proud of himself.

Jun shook him awake and said, "Hey, just wanted to let you know I'm alive."

Griffin barely knew what was going on and it took him a second to remember why there was a handsome man with a massive bandage on his head standing over him, but when he did, he said, "Oh, great. I was hoping that would happen."

"Me too."

"Are you heading home now?"

"I don't have to right away, but I'd prefer to change into some clothes that don't have any blood on them."

"You can borrow a shirt. Let me take a look at you before you go."

"Oh, you're always welcome to take a look at me." He grinned, then winced. "I forgot not to smile."

"Never forget not to smile, Jun."

"I got hit in the head pretty hard. I forget things now. It's my new thing."

"I'm sorry to hear that."

"Sorry to hear what?" Jun smiled and winced again. "Fuck, I should stop trying to be clever."

"Yeah."

They just looked at each other for a moment, trying not to smile, looking exaggeratedly serious, until Griffin cracked and said, "Wanna do this again sometime, but, y'know, without any head wounds?"

"I would love to. Just be sure to get your floor fix- huh." Jun was looking at the lump on the floor, which had shrunk dramatically since last night, and was now just a bit of residual warping in the boards from the initial water damage. "Wasn't that bigger yesterday? When I tripped and smashed my head on it?"

"Yeah, I mostly fixed it last night while you were asleep. Wanted to make sure you didn't accidentally almost kill yourself again on the way out."

"Thanks. And thanks for, you know, sewing me back together and taking good care of me. Let me know how I can make it up to you."

"Well, I have- hmm. Actually, there's something I need to tell you." There was a pregnant pause as Griffin tried to figure out how to say what he needed to say, and Jun looked worried as it went on.

"What?" said Jun.

"I promised some weird shit to people who donated to help reattach my hand and now I need you to help me take good photographs of my feet and my asshole."

Jun recoiled. "You're a foot guy?"

"No, no, I just figured they'd be easy to raise money off of."

Jun exhaled and the smile returned to his face. "Oh, thank God. Yeah, take your pants off."

# Part Two

# Hand to Mouth

8

In the second episode of the new season of *The Contestant!*, The Contestant was on *American Gladiators*. Unlike the old version of the show, where steroid-juiced and spray-tanned goliaths battled it out with giant foam-covered q-tips in utterly non-gladiatorial bouts of competition, the reboot series was just outright gladiatorial combat. Since the advent of regenerative medicines, liability insurance on reality television had become much more lax with what was allowed, since as long as the brain was intact and the limbs weren't crushed, just about any flesh wound was not just survivable, but reversible. Sure, it was an unremitting nightmare of human suffering, but what a show.

A fun fact about the original gladiators of antiquity is that they were supposedly pretty chunky. Dad bods abounded because if you know someone's going to swing a blade at your bare flesh, it's just stupid to have the distance between your skin and vital organs be as short as possible. A sturdy insulating layer of subcutaneous fat helped in both blunt force shock absorption and in allowing combatants to get shallow cuts without damaging underlying tissues. They would still bleed visibly and look extremely gnarly in the process, but in practice it was usually more like those hardcore wrestlers who throw each other through piles of fluorescent light tubes or thumbtacks and hit each other with running weed whackers.

Anyway, The Contestant was in real gladiatorial combat, his hair hidden beneath a centurion helmet through which his scared blue-grey eyes were visible, his torso covered in plate, his neck protected with a titanium band, and his limbs free to move. A chyron labeled his opponent as Styx. The Contestant was wielding a trident, and he had clearly lost a bit too much weight from his time on *Romance Archipelago: Battle Royale*. Styx was bigger and thicker, clearly with the layer of protective blubber gained from training specifically for this show instead of the nightmarish gauntlet of every single one of them. Styx, his face fully hidden under an iron mask, held the classic combination of sword and shield. They were under the hot sun on red sand, every effort clearly having been made to look as much as possible like the modern conception of what gladiatorial combat must have looked like, and sweat was already pouring from The Contestant, darkening the sand beneath him. He was being pushed steadily backwards by the brazen offense of his opponent, despite the greater reach of his trident. Styx clearly had time to truly learn how to use his weapon of choice, and effortlessly deflected the clumsy thrusts and jabs of the trident with his shield. The crowd in the stadium was on their feet and roaring, evenly split between enthusiasts for *American Gladiators* and followers of *The Contestant!*

As they approached the wall of the arena, Styx took advantage of The Contestant having nowhere left to go, and after ducking a wild stab from the trident, rushed in and plunged his sword into The Contestant's lower thigh. The Contestant screamed and fell, immediately sobbing hard, snot and tears running down his face, eyes red and panicked, and began crawling away from Styx, who now lingered over his prey with absolute confidence in his victory. Styx lifted his chin to the crowd and raised his arms, eliciting deafening cheers and boos in equal measure. He took his sword and used it to gesture to The Contestant's left arm, drawing more boos. He paused, considering this, and pointed the sword at the already wounded thigh of the man who was weakly pushing himself backward with his remaining good leg and arms. The sand under The Contestant grew dark and thick with blood and sweat and tears and snot. The crowd cheered at the sword pointed at the wounded leg, and in a showy, exaggerated motion, pulling back farther than necessary, striking a pose at the moment before reversing his momentum, Styx brought his sword down and cleaved off The Contestant's leg just above the knee. With a final animalistic shriek of horrified pain, blood running from him in a river and the color draining from his face, The Contestant fell limp. Styx put his arms out in resplendent bravado, rotated himself for the viewing pleasure of the crowd, and bowed. A title card onscreen declared **STYX - WINNER - BROUGHT TO YOU BY FAUST FERTILITY: YOUR LEGACY STARTS WITH FAUST.**

A calm voice implored the audience not to worry about The Contestant. The Contestant was going to be just fine.

Griffin changed the channel and decided he should probably start looking for a job.

The next step in the process was to look for openings he could apply to. Jun made Faust Direct Sales sound like it was pretty much open to anyone who could walk in the door and speak English, and Griffin felt pretty confident about doing both of those things, so he opened up the website and went to their optimistically-named "careers" section to look for an application. He found the page, submitted his resumé, then filled out an additional form that required him to manually type out the entire contents of his resumé into separate text fields that didn't allow copy-pasting. He hammered out a quick cover letter about how he had a life-long passion for exchanging his time, labor, and dignity for small amounts of currency over the course of his one experience of the incomprehensible cosmic miracle of life, but phrased in a way that sounded better than that.

A few seconds after he submit, his phone rang. He answered and was greeted by a pleasant young woman's voice saying, "Good afternoon. I'm looking for Griffin Batt."

"Speaking."

"Hi, Griffin. My name is Clara. I work for Faust Direct Sales."

"That... that was an extremely fast response time."

"Well, our system flagged you as an ideal candidate because of your experience as a sinister severance specialist."

"Oh, wonderful. I wasn't sure if that would be seen as a transferable skill to this line of work."

"It's not the direct physical skills, but the work ethic it represents. Clocking in and doing that difficult, vital work every day. May I ask why you left your previous position?"

"I mean, my passion for the work was as strong as ever, but that kind of work is rather physically demanding and it was starting to catch up with me and affect my performance. I figured it was better to call it and move on to greener pastures of my own volition before my body made the decision for me."

Griffin felt her nod before she said, "I understand. Not a line of work to grow old in. Do you have any experience in customer service or sales?"

"No. Wasn't that clear on my application?"

"Haven't read it. Could we do a quick test of your phone skills and etiquette? It would be a simple simulated conversation where you would play the part of yourself as a Faust Direct Sales representative and I would play the part of a customer you've cold called. That sound good?"

"Oh yeah, no problem. What am I selling in this test run?"

"Don't worry about it. Just try for a cordial opening as you try to get a lead. Now go for it."

Griffin cleared his throat and paused for a few seconds to delineate the beginning of the scene and then switched to his most pleasant and charming tone to say, "Hi, may I speak with Clara?"

He was met with a long, dead silence followed by a gruff, clipped, "Speaking."

"Hi, Clara. My name is Griffin and I'm calling on behalf of Faust Direct Sales. Would you happen to-"

"How about I stomp your goon ass if you ever fucking call me again, you piece of shit?"

"...Pardon?"

"What if I punch you in the back of the head so hard that you die? You've already told me your name and where you work. Do you have any idea how easy it would be to come down there and smash your face into paste? I know where that fucking call center is. Maybe I'll be waiting in the parking lot with a piano wire for your pencil neck."

"I- that's quite alright, ma'am. How about I take you off our list so you don't get any more unwanted calls?"

Clara lapsed back into her normal voice and said, "Pause. The instincts and tone are pretty good, but the one thing you can never do at this job is offer to take them off our list or to hang up first. You haven't even gotten to the point of starting the actual pitch for the product."

"What product? You told me to just focus on opening."

"I know what I said. Despite that, let's try again. And remember what you can't do. Now go again."

Griffin gave another delineating pause. "That's quite alright, ma'am. Would you happen to be interested in any of our fine products?"

Clara's voice became deeper and rougher as she said, "I am going to find out where you live and shit in your mouth. I'm going to drag you to the sewer and slit your belly open and make you watch the rats grow fat on the feast of your entrails. Your body is my canvas and my art is pain. You will forget the feeling of sunlight. You will beg for mercy as your pitiable flesh is unmade by teeth and acid and the rats will not understand your pathetic pleas and I will understand them and I will ignore them and smile and drink your tears from your mother's skull. There is nothing to save you now— I have made up my mind. I have made up my mind that the rest of your life will be an eternity of misery and despair where the sweet relief of death is as constantly tantalizingly visible and totally unattainable as the horizon. The horizon on a clear night in the middle of the ocean, the dim and distant stars only proof of void above, the pure black of the water only proof of unending cold and pressure and inevitable drowning, the horizon only existing as the invisible line where the stars are overwritten by the heavy alien darkness of the water. And you, you will bob in the waves there in that dark, cold and scared and alone and wishing it could all end, never getting your wish, feeling your entrails floating around you, your intestines tangling your hands as you struggle to tread water, and you sink into the cold void below and water fills your lungs and every cell of your body screams out in terrified desperation for air and yet you live. You live as the water bears down heavier and heavier and heavier until you are destroyed under the pressure and dispersed through the indifferent infinite waters and yet, somehow still awake, still alive, you feel every molecule of what was once the shameful pathetic wretch known as 'you' float to their own individual oblivions. I. AM. **NOT. INTERESTED. IN. YOUR.** *PRODUCTS*."

"No problem at all, ma'am. Would you like to sign up for the Faust Credit Card?"

Snapping back to her normal voice, Clara said, "You're hired. When can you start?"

The call center office was full of cubicles that were somehow both beige and cold grey under fluorescent lights that flickered between medical green and nicotine yellow. They went on so far, and there were no windows. Clara turned out to be the actual supervisor, not just a voice on the phone delivering threats, and was perfectly cordial and professional when not channeling the mind of a homicidal maniac to test a prospective hire's mettle. She was about five foot five with vaguely mediterranean features most obviously in the form of stunningly voluminous tightly curled hair thrown over one shoulder, though she had the same blue-grey eyes as Griffin.

She led Griffin across the floor through a long line of cubicles packed with workers in headsets, some starting to pitch a product before abruptly stopping as they were clearly starting to get yelled at, some making noises of polite agreement through strained smiles, some openly and fully sobbing. One guy was screaming that he was going to kill himself and everyone else there in a cleansing fire while a pack of security guards made their way towards him with a look of almost bored familiarity with that type of thing. As they tackled him and his screams were replaced with the sizzling snap of tasers, Griffin and Clara reached a cubicle with an empty chair that she gestured for him to sit down in. He did.

"Alright, Griffin. This will be your station. At the moment we're selling Tag Killer, a skin tag removal ointment. It also works on moles, early stage melanomas, and really any kind of surface-level nonstandard tissue growth pattern on the skin. One important thing to mention in the disclaimer, if they express interest, is that it should NOT be used on or near tissue that has been treated with regeneratives within the past year, or it'll dissolve it back down into a raw slurry of amino acids and lipids and the like. Any questions?"

"Yeah. Do we know if the people we're calling actually have skin tags or unwanted moles or skin cancer, or are we just taking shots in the dark and hoping to find somebody who not only has this problem but is also cool with talking about it on the phone with a stranger who's obviously trying to sell them something?"

"The latter. I'm sure there's some way to buy user data from search engines to find out who's searched for things that seem to indicate they have those conditions, but the going rate on data like that would cost enough that the method of just calling everybody and asking directly is cheaper per sale. And it turns out that most people really don't want to talk about their most secret skin conditions with total strangers who want money from them, but you know what? You know what, Griffin?"

"What?"

"I believe in you. Good luck." And with that, she gave him a little two-count drum on the cubicle wall, flashed a smile that did not reach her eyes, and walked away. Griffin turned to the desk, put on the headset, and activated his workstation. The screen revealed a monochrome, obsolete interface that seemed to be older than he was, and very well might have been a relic of the first rebuild systems post-wipe. Everything was rendered in painfully bright oscilloscope-style kind of green lines. The only things visible on the screen were a long list of names and a button that said CALL. Griffin selected the first name, one of those stereotypical pre-war old lady names, and clicked the button.

As it rang, a call script replaced the column of names and the CALL button was replaced with an INPUT PAYMENT INFORMATION button. There was no option on the screen to end the call. Griffin's heart rate picked up as the ringing continued, and he felt a kind of fear he wasn't expecting, given his past work experience and the composure he managed at the interview. When the voice of an elderly woman responded, he hesitated for a moment before launching into the script. In his most inoffensive customer service voice, he asked, "Hello, is this Olivia Huston?"

"Yes."

"Hi, this is Griffin for Faus-"

"Griffin was my husband's name. He passed away."

"Oh, I- I'm sorry to hear that."

"I loved him so much. I still love him so much. It never stops. Every day I wake up without him next to me, the hole in my heart and soul grows larger and deeper."

"I'm sorry to hear that, Ms. Huston."

"Mrs. Huston. Either call me Mrs. Huston or Olivia."

"I'm sorry to hear that, Mrs. Huston. Uh, that being said- let me start over. I'm calling on behalf of Faust Direct Sales. Do you have a moment today to talk about Tag Killer?"

"I've got plenty of time to talk, even if I don't know how much time I have left on this Earth. And what is Tag Killer?"

"It's a revolutionary new topical skincare product for the removal of skin tags, raised moles, or melanomas." Griffin paused, then mumbled to himself, "Why don't they list that first?" before continuing, "It makes your skin smooth, insofar as it will be devoid of unusual growths."

"My Griffin was the smoothest man I've ever known. Every inch of him below the eyebrows was gleaming and hairless. He looked like a bronze statue come to life. I would lick the sweat from him whenever he came in from working in the yard on hot days. He never used any such products. The only treatments his skin would get were from working up a good honest sweat and me licking it off him. And I stayed good and youthful for a long time with the routine consumption of his sweat and the facial application of his hot white cum."

Griffin stared into space while considering how to proceed before deciding on saying, "So would you like to try Tag Killer now that you no longer have access to that?"

"Hmm." About a five second pause. "No." She hung up.

Griffin looked around and saw Clara making her way back down the cubicle aisle with a fresh mug of coffee billowing steam. He gave her a thumbs up over the cubicle wall and twisted his mouth into a smile that didn't reach his eyes either, which caused Clara to stop in place to return the gesture, but the inertia of the coffee carried it forward over the lip of the mug and down onto her shoes, at which point she looked down, then back up at Griffin, and flipped her thumb downward, never changing the look on her face.

Griffin turned back to his station and pressed the call button again and was told to go fuck himself and hung up on before he even heard any ringing.

The rest of the morning passed in much the same way, in the form of a series of instantaneous rejections, and Griffin fell into a rhythm of getting told to fuck off. The immediate and impersonal nature of it was a soothing relief compared to the slow and directly dehumanizing humiliations he had endured recently.

At noon he went to ask Clara what she usually did for lunch and she said he should come with her to the Waffle House across the business park. In the parking lot, an EMT crew was visibly in the process of loading two sheet-covered bodies into ambulances, and the cook was leaning against the wall outside, smoking a cigarette and checking the action of his standard issue Waffle House pistol. As they approached, the cook saw them coming, checked his watch, said, "Oh fuck, lunch already?" and threw the cigarette straight down to smash underfoot before holstering his weapon.

Inside, they both got burgers and hashbrowns and were eating together in the unexpectant silence of colleagues who truly do not give a shit about their work or each other. Griffin noticed her watching him eat, and she noticed him noticing and opened her mouth, which had no cheeseburger in it at that moment, to ask, "You know you can eat with both hands, right?"

"What?"

"You've been eating with only your right hand and keeping your left below the table. I couldn't figure out what looked off about the way you were eating but you just aren't using your left hand at all, are you?"

"Oh. Huh. I didn't realize I was doing that. Yeah, I guess my body sort of forgot it was an option to use my left hand during a workday lunch."

"You mean you would eat lunch with your hand still off?"

"Yeah. And worse, my last job fired me right after my last lunch break, so they didn't even let me finish out the day to reattach it. Had to get gel myself and reattach at home."

"I thought you said you decided to quit on your own."

"Oh. Right. Well. You've already hired me. No takesies-backsies. Please. I hope."

She laughed. "I'm not going to call headquarters and tell Roderick Faust himself that you've slipped through the filters on a lie. Don't worry about it."

"Oh, I'll worry about it as much as I please," said Griffin, and he carefully gripped the burger with his left hand.

The afternoon passed much the same way as the morning, and as he was subject to an unending barrage of verbal abuse he fell into a trancelike state, barely present in his own body, becoming merely the delivery mechanism for a script. The day ended, he left his station, and he took the bus home, watching the lights outside switch from cool blue to piercing orange. He texted Jun and asked if he wanted to meet up for a drink later and his left hand went numb for a moment as he typed.

When he got home, as he entered the building he saw a masked man carrying a knife and wearing a blood-spattered jumpsuit pounding on his apartment door.

9

The man turned to face Griffin. He was wearing something between a full hazmat hood and a welder's mask, a head-engulfing opaque polyhedron with one shinier tinted see-through section around where the eyes would be, spatters of blood across it all. The knife in his hand was small and curved in a J-shape, dirt-smeared crimson soaking his gloves. Griffin was shaking, frozen where he stood. His heart was pounding. A sharp pain shot through his left hand at every heartbeat. He reached back behind himself to try to open the door and found his hand wouldn't close on the knob.

The man in the mask turned and faced Griffin and said, "Don't worry. I am not going to hurt you."

Griffin did not believe him. Griffin, in his panic, was sending his increasingly numb left hand frantically scrabbling blindly against the door while keeping his eyes locked on the masked threat. Griffin pressed his back against the door while the figure walked towards him calmly, pausing dramatically to pull its mask off, though as it did so Griffin was already turning away and starting to beg, "Please, if this is about the fundraiser, I already took the photos of my feet and my asshole."

Mr. President began to audibly meow from behind the door when he heard Griffin's voice, which continued, "I'll show you my feet and my asshole right fucking now! I just haven't had time to edit the photos so they really pop! I promise you'll get your money's worth! You can see, right, you can see I really did spend it on reattaching my hand! I'm not a fraud! *Please! I'll put mustard on my fucking asshole! PLEASE DON'T KILL ME!*"

The figure stood without its mask, the one light in the entryway behind its head, its face in shadow, and said, "Sir, I have no idea what you're talking about. Sorry I look terrifying right now, but it comes with the job. Don't you live in that unit?"

Mr. President's meows became frantic howls. Griffin looked up.

The man who had fixed the water heaters above the stairs when the firemen were here. About five foot eight, dark skinned, little round glasses with a low-strength prescription, receding hair swept back into a patent leather shine. The man who had helped drain Griffin's water heater into the tub a little while back. That's who it was.

Griffin was abruptly flush with embarrassment as he said, "Yes. That is... that's my apartment. I live there. Hello again. Sorry I overreacted. Hello sir. How are you doing."

The man used his left hand to peel the filthy glove from his right hand and offered the exposed clean appendage to help Griffin back up to standing. He said, "How's the new heater holding up?"

"It stopped working like right after you left. Didn't explode though."

"Ah. Well. I tried. So. You're the one who filed the ticket about the teratomalith in the basement?"

Frantic meowing continued. Griffin blinked. "The what? Hold on." He leaned to yell around the man towards his door, "I'm okay, Mr. President! I'm okay!"

The meowing calmed and quieted. To the man in front of him, Griffin repeated, "The what?"

"The big disgusting growth thing hanging from the ceiling."

"Oh. Yes. That was me. I did that."

"I see. When I got here to work on it, it looked pretty significantly different from the photo you attached to the ticket."

"Is that bad?"

"Not in this case. It actually looked a lot better than the photo. Are you the one who worked on it already?"

"I guess so. Yeah, I mean, I took a whack at it when I was a little buzzed because I wanted the swelling in my floorboards to go down, but... yes. That was me. I did that. Is everything okay?"

"Yeah, it's fine. Honestly? You did good work. I was prepared for much worse when I got here, but you took care of most of the hard parts, so thanks for that."

"Oh. Thank you. And you're welcome. And... what?"

"Can I ask, what was in the cystic core?"

"The what?"

"The cystic core. The initial growth point of the mass usually has some abnormal fully developed tissue within it. When I was cutting the whole thing apart, I never found one. So I figured you must have gotten it. What was in it?"

Griffin remembered the hand was still in his freezer. He considered this, considered lying, and said, "A hand."

"A hand?"

"A hand."

The man in the round glasses glanced at Griffin's hands, then back into his eyes, and said, "When you were panicking at my approach earlier, didn't you say something about reattaching your hand?"

"I may have."

"Hmm," said the man.

"Hmm what?" said Griffin.

"You poured used regenerative gel down the drain, didn't you?"

"...I may have."

"Don't do that again."

"Okay."

"I'll spare you any more grief and won't tell management what caused it. Just don't do that again."

"Okay."

"Have you ever cut a teratomalith before?"

"That's the word for the big weird gross flesh toenail hoof thing? Terror-dome-alicious?"

"Teratomalith," said the man.

"Teratomalith."

"Yes, now you have it.."

"Then no, I didn't know they existed until I found this one. How often do you deal with these?"

"Too often, but— pardon me. Where are my manners? What's your name?"

"Griffin. Griffin Batt."

"Griffin, that was genuinely good cutting for somebody who has never done this kind of thing before. You ever consider getting into this line of work?"

"To be clear, I didn't know that 'this line of work' existed until this conversation."

"Would you like to be in this line of work? Demand is always rising, and it's hard to find good cutters these days."

"Thank you, but I'm good. I just started a new job today."

"A new job doing what?"

"Call center."

The man made a face for a half second and chuckled and said, "In case you ever change your mind, here's my card." He unzipped the jumpsuit, reached inside the breast, and produced a small shiny card that said,

BRANDON PEARL

PEARL PLUMBING

TERATOMALITH REMOVAL SPECIALIST

There was a phone number below that information. Griffin took the card, nodded, pocketed it, and said, "Thanks for clearing all that out, Mr. Pearl. Now if you'll excuse me, I have a cat to feed."

Mr. President was happy to see Griffin, having thought that he was in grave danger moments earlier, and the moment the door was open he dashed out and circled Griffin's legs in a figure eight pattern while chirping, almost tripping him with every step, but Griffin had gained plenty of practice in maintaining his footing despite the best efforts of weird little lumps, be they hardwood or cat, and made his way inside. On the television, birds pecked at little piles of seed carefully placed by the videographer, and as he took off his coat and went to get a can of cat food, he realized that Mr. President's weird little chirps had started imitating the sounds of the birds he watched for entertainment.

Griffin cracked open a can of food and went to place it in Mr. President's dish, but the deeply round cat barreled towards his hand at such speed that it knocked the can fully out of his hand and upside-down onto the floor. Mr. President began eating loudly, and Griffin sat and watched.

"I had a big day, little guy," said Griffin.

"MYAM MYAM MYAM MYAM" said Mr. President, involuntarily, by eating too fast.

"First day at the new job went pretty well. An old woman told me about licking sweat and cum off of her dead husband. Don't worry, he wasn't dead at the time she was doing that, and as far as she told me it was all his sweat and cum, so that's basically fine. Didn't get the sale, though. Then I think about three hundred other people told me to fuck off, or go fuck myself, or go fuck myself and die, or just hung up on me, and only one person screamed a racial slur that doesn't even apply to me. Didn't get to talk to my other coworkers much, but my supervisor is surprisingly nice when she's not threatening to kill me. Don't worry, she wasn't serious when she did that."

"MYAM SCHNARF GRRRRRRWWWLL" said Mr. President.

"I even ate lunch with both hands, which felt pretty weird once I realized it was an option, but it was pretty nice, actually. My hand's starting to feel a bit weird, though. I can't remember the last time it was attached this long. Like obviously it never felt GOOD cutting it off and reattaching it every day, but it became so routine that it just being there throughout the whole work day feels wrong somehow."

"HWEK. HWEK. HWEK. HWEK."

"You okay there, Mr. President?"

Mr. President threw up the entire contents of his stomach onto the floor, sniffed it for a few seconds, and continued eating the remaining fresh food.

"Jesus, buddy, I know I fed you this morning. I'm gonna get this cleaned up and then I'm gonna go get a drink with Jun, okay?"

Mr. President looked up and said, "Brrt. Mreh."

"You want a different video?"

"Ekk. Ekk ekk ekk."

"I'll put on a different video. Maybe some videos of actual other cats so you remember how to meow normally."

"Ekk."

Griffin walked into Hello Horses, still fairly subdued at 7 PM on a Monday night, to find Jun already waiting for him at a small table across from the bar with two daiquiris already in front of him. Jun was backlit with searing bright magenta, while the soft light on his face danced across the spectrum, slowly making its way around the circumference of the color wheel. Jun smiled when he noticed Griffin's approach, and in the moment he did so he was goblin green, which accentuated the bags under his eyes in a less flattering way than usual. By the time Griffin got to the table, he and Jun were both under a deep blue, mixed with the magenta into classic bisexual lighting.

"Hey, handsome," said Griffin as he sat down.

"Hey yourself. How was your first day?"

"Pretty good. No blood loss at all. And the parade of verbal abuse was impersonal and repetitive so I got used to it pretty much immediately. There was one woman who went on a strange tangent about me having the same name as her dead husband who she used to lick the sweat off of, but otherwise pretty uneventful."

"Did you manage to sell anything?"

"Oh, no, didn't come close to selling even once. From what I can tell that's pretty much normal. My supervisor Clara, the one who interviewed me, said that I had a better first day than most. Most people don't sell anything on their first day either, but they also cry at least once. Turns out Clara was right and I actually am well suited for this work, at least in terms of emotional resilience. Learning to sell is easier if you're not crying, so I figure it'll be pretty easy to pick up. Now that I've got another job, it's nice to have a new skillset to pursue."

"Wait, are you going to stop looking for another job?"

"I got the job."

"No, I know. But it's a call center job."

"What's your point?"

"You keep mentioning you have a master's degree in economics."

"For all the good that's done me."

"You realize you can keep looking for something better even if you have a job, right?"

Griffin face dropped and his eyes drifted into a thousand-yard stare way off behind Jun.

Jun leaned in after a few seconds and said, "Griffin? Did that... really not occur to you?"

Griffin's eyes refocused on Jun. "Uh, no. No it didn't. I don't... I don't know why. Once I crashed out of finance I just—I never thought I would work my way up to anything like that again. Being the kind of person who could do those things wasn't a possibility anymore, so... I just stayed with the same thing until they fired me. And I found another thing and I guess I figured I would stay with that as well. Because it was something rather than nothing."

"You can do other things. I'm pretty sure you're not stupid. You're just settling for way less than you could because you don't believe in yourself."

"But you work in medical supplies as, like, what is the job title, warehouse manager? Isn't that pretty unambitious?"

"Okay, a couple things. I'm forklift certified. I'm OSHA certified, for whatever that's worth anymore. I'm about as good at it as you can be for that kind of field, and I'm proud of the work I do. For how cavalier people are about injuries these days, I think it's straight up a good thing to make sure that medical supplies are getting where they need to go as efficiently as possible. I'm not going to win any awards, but you and I both know it's a few steps above call center direct sales."

"Okay. Yeah. I get it. You're right."

"So why don't you keep looking for another job?"

"I think I was offered another job like an hour ago, actually."

"You were offered a job between leaving work and getting to the bar without looking for it? Do I have to teach you how to spot a scam? It's probably some MLM scam."

"No, when I got back to my apartment to feed Mr. President before heading over here, I ran into this maintenance guy who saw the stuff I did in the basement to fix the lump in the floor. Said it looked way better than he was expecting and gave me his card."

Jun perked up. "That's great! Why don't you take him up on it? You can still keep looking even with that, but I'm sure it'll be better than call center sales."

"I'm not sure it will be. I still pretty buzzed when I went down to fix it that night. I don't know if I'd have the stomach for it sober."

"It can't have been that bad. What did you do?"

"Extremely bad. I went down to the basement and I... I'm not sure how to describe it. I took a video, actually. I could show you. It's extremely bad."

Jun squinted and cocked his head. "Show me."

Griffin pulled out his phone, tapped into his media library, found the dark video, handed the phone to Jun, and said, "It's like an hour long so you can just scrub through it with your thumb to get the gist."

Jun took it and began to watch. His squinting skepticism of how bad it could be faded and his eyes gradually widened. The audio of the video was completely drowned out by the music in the bar, which was presently *You Spin Me Round (Like A Record)* by Dead or Alive. Jun's left thumb moved across the screen slightly to the right, further down the playhead, his eyebrows shifted slightly upward, and his right hand inched to cover his mouth. In this position, he leaned in closer to where he held the phone on the table between them, then abruptly sat up straight with the phone held at arm's length. He glanced from the screen to Griffin's eyes and back again with an otherwise unchanging expression of shock and disgust.

Jun brought his right hand down to yell "WHAT THE FUCK IS THAT?" before putting the hand back to his mouth with disgust winning the war over what expression dominated his face, dropped the phone, and ran to the bathroom. Griffin picked up the phone and saw the video was at the section where he had just been sprayed in the face with pressurized bloody pus and was in the process of vomiting onto the floor.

He had figured that was probably going to be the part that did it. He glanced over at the bartender, a sturdy looking pale man in his late thirties with a mop of black hair who was giving him a *what the fuck did you just do* look, as bartenders tend to do to patrons who cause their date to run from the table in urgent need of emesis. Griffin tried to assert his innocence towards whatever accusation was being silently leveled at him through an odd combination of a shrug, a stutter, and pointing at his phone, before getting up from his chair to walk up to the bar and say, "I had told him the video was extremely gross but he didn't believe me and insisted on seeing it."

Jun had already made his way back from the bathroom. The bartender turned to him and said, "You okay, Jun?"

"Yeah, Jerry, I'm fine. He didn't do anything wrong."

Griffin said, "I told you it was bad."

Jun nodded. "He told me it was bad."

They returned to the table.

"Okay, yeah, maybe don't take that job, Griffin. And no offense, but I am going to need some time to let that image of you getting sprayed in the face fade from my memory before I come anywhere close to kissing you again. And you're getting the next round to help that memory fade faster," said Jun, before taking up his daiquiri and downing half of it in one gulp. "And tip well. You scared Jerry. And then keep looking for a better job so you can tip Jerry even better next time."

"You encouraging me to improve my life is just a scam to get Jerry bigger tips, isn't it?"

Jun laughed. "God. I really DO have to teach you how to recognize a scam." Down went the other half of his daiquiri. "Seriously though, what the fuck was that thing?"

10

The rain started while Griffin was at work. It began while he ate lunch with both hands in the break room, and the murmur of drops hitting the roof of the building blended with the cacophony of hundreds of voices speaking at once in the same room at all times and became a single edgeless wall of soft sound through which words would occasionally surface. He returned to his desk and the increasing patter above was transmuted by the endless drop ceiling into the soft whoosh of the white noise machine standing sentry outside the door of a therapist's office. He put his headset back on and the narrow hiss of no signal in his ears overwrote the growing sound even more. He got back to work.

"Hi, may I speak to—" Griffin turned his eyes to the name on the screen for the first time, confident in his ability to cold-read names of any length and origin, but this name made even him pause for a second to practice it in his head before saying, "—may I speak to... Schvantlfeim?"

A deep masculine voice with a thick inscrutable accent responded, "Yes. I speak."

"Hello sir, my name is Griffin and I'm calling on behalf of Faust Direct Sales. Do you have a moment to talk about Tag Killer?"

"You say Dog Killer? No need. Am."

"Pardon? No. Tag Killer. Tag Killer is a revolutionary topical treatment for skin tags, moles, skin cancers, or any—"

"I kill your dog. I give good price."

"I don't— I am the one offering goods. I did not call in search of services. Did you say you'd kill my dog? For a good price?"

With a marked tone of pride, Schvantlfeim said, "Yes. I best dog killer of steppe."

"Please say you mean you were a veterinarian, where you were from?"

"No. If bastard wild dog threaten home, if eat chicken, if attack child, I kill dog and solve problem. I take rock, I throw rock through dog head. My service quality. Much demand."

"So do you have any interest in Tag—"

"When come to city, find no work. Business fail. City people treat dog like child. Cherish. Protect. Even when see starved dog of wild, they say, rescue. I offer kill, they say, no. No, Schvantlfeim! I best at what nobody want! Now look for work. Veterinarian, do not hire. Before when kill dog people say, Schvantlfeim, thank you so much, thank you for killing bastard dog what ate my daughter. In city those who kill dog, crying child beg for dog back. What to do?"

"I'm sorry to hear that, sir. Would you like to hear more about Tag—"

"You hire? You hiring?"

"I... yes, there's usually job opportunities here, but we do telephone direct sales. There is no dog killing of any kind at this job."

"Is fine. I work hard. Name of place?"

"I'm calling from Faust Direct Sales."

"Faust."

"Faust, yes."

"Good. I apply."

"Okay, we look forward to hearing from you. In the meantime, are you interested in hearing about Tag Killer, a revolutionary new—"

"No. Thank you. No. Have good day."

Schvantlfeim hung up.

Griffin hit the CALL button again and took a deep breath. The phone rang.

A voice answered. "Hello?"

"Hi, am I speaking to Dylan Rösch?"

"This is he."

"Great, this is Griffin calling on behalf of Faust Direct Sales. Do you have a moment to talk about Tag—"

"How about I kill your fucking dog?"

Griffin almost laughed at that, having grown so used to verbal abuse but still so capable of being surprised by fun little coincidences. He dislocated his mind from his body and let it go wandering off while his mouth kept making various appropriate sounds until he got hung up on. When he briefly returned his mind to his body between calls, he noticed a slight headache, which he attributed to the stress of whatever stream of violent invective he had just been listening to, which was true in part, but was also partially from the shifting barometric pressure as the rain gradually made its way from drizzle to deluge. He went for a glass of water to clear his head and passed Clara, who was on the phone, saying, "And how do you spell that, Mr. Feim? Oh, that's not the- I see. When can you start?"

After work, which he already mostly did not remember, having now figured out the level of dissociation ideal for mentally enduring it, Griffin stepped outside the building into the dark and was met with the unrelenting roar of torrential rain and the distant growls of thunder from other parts of the city.

The bus home moved slow through the rising water. The shifting lights beyond the bus window illuminated nothing and blurred into fragments snatched from the air by falling drops thick as chains. He had been soaked to the bone in the time getting from the office door to the bus stop. He shivered in his seat.

The long subtle incline of the city was never more clear than when water needed somewhere to go. Once there had been dirt to soak it up and now there was only concrete and pavement and sewers designed centuries ago and so all the water slid downhill in a journey that seemed to perfectly follow his bus route home, and by the time he'd arrived in front of his building, Griffin was ankle deep in water anywhere he stood in the front courtyard. At the front door he saw the water was already leaking underneath into the hallway and he had no choice but to let it in along with himself. The door opened and the water poured forth in front of him, where it luckily fell down the stairs into the basement before it made its way to his apartment door. The smell of raw sewage came from the basement, clearly already backing up from wherever the basement was supposed to drain to.

Inside the apartment, Mr. President was howling at the noise, hungry and afraid. Griffin stripped out of his soaked work clothes and cracked a can of cat food while the sounds of birds on a sunny day came from the television. Outside the blurred window, there was a formless rushing roar and the distortions of street light through water danced across the film.

A wailing klaxon emitted from his phone's emergency broadcast system. It was a shelter in place order. The rains were expected to continue through the night without relent. He ate his rice and beans and looked at the window where he noticed there was a visible water line, even through the diffusion, beginning to rise from the bottom. A peek out the door of the apartment showed water crashing against the lower windows of the glass front door of the building, continuing to cascade down the stairs, where the basement's flooding was already up to the second step.

Griffin took in all this information and decided it probably wasn't good.

In the apartment he started loading his clothes into plastic trash bags and carrying them upstairs, where he put them in the tub of the abandoned second floor unit. The smell of mold and shit hit him every time he went out into the hall. Loading his water-sensitive items into bags and taking them upstairs took so little time that it was, in itself, depressing. After putting a few identification documents into a gallon sized plastic bag, it was time for the electronics, though he left the TV running for Mr. President, and the tranquil forest sounds centered him while he moved through his tasks in a haze, knowing what was about to happen and not wanting to accept it. Mr. President was sitting on the couch in a loaf, oblivious to the growing danger. Luckily, there was so little room in the apartment that his carrier never really got put away anywhere, and he didn't take it as a sign of impending vet visits. This was also partially because Griffin had been unable to take Mr. President to the vet in far too long, which crossed his mind as he picked up the carrier, and the thought of this failure sent a hot rush of shame to his face, but he pushed his feelings down and set the carrier on the couch. Mr. President got to experience one second of feeling suspicious before Griffin had scruffed him, and then he was in the carrier and it was getting zipped up behind him.

Griffin brought the loudly protesting animal, his cherished son, to the second floor apartment and set him down. He cracked the carrier and went back down for supplies.

The waterline was halfway up the front door of the building, and what was making it under the door was coming in faster. The waterfall into the basement was now crashing directly into roiling sewage that had made its way halfway up the stairs. In his apartment, he filled tote bags with canned goods, got his toiletries and some soap, and ran them up before heading down one last time.

Still not feeling that any of this was real, Griffin texted Jun a quick "I think my apartment is about to be destroyed in the flood" and then switched his phone to record video. He pointed it at the windows, where water was visibly up to his chest level and rushing past. He started recording, again said "I think my apartment is about to be destroyed in the flood," and at that moment the windows cracked. Less than one second later they burst inward completely and pale brown water rushed in.

"I was right," said Griffin, and the incoming water knocked him off his feet and slammed him into the kitchen counter, where he held on and pulled himself up, then stopped recording.

He sent the video to Jun, who texted back "what the fuck are you okay?"

"Yeah I got most of my stuff onto the second floor as fast as I could. I am also still standing in a mix of freezing rising filthy water and broken glass as I type this though lmao"

"Griffin," said Jun, "get the fuck out of there and get upstairs"

"Fine okay jeez don't worry I'm just probably homeless now," said Griffin.

In the hall he saw that the rising sewage from the basement was one step from reaching the level of the ground floor, and the front door of the building was shooting out water at the edges, so Griffin went upstairs and tore off his wet socks and pants before plugging in his phone. He felt a throbbing pressure behind his eyes and wanted to sleep forever. It occurred to him that if he hadn't been fired and met Jun he wouldn't have had anyone to text that to who would have responded. He wondered how it had been so long that he'd gone through the world entirely without personal connections, like he had been a secret, like Mr. President was there just to prove to himself that he existed outside of his own mind.

In the second floor apartment Mr. President was pissing in the bathroom sink. Griffin pulled a bag of pants and underwear out of the tub and threw it on the floor for a pillow. He took the other clothes out of the tub and put on several layers of everything. He covered his torso in threadbare white t-shirts under henleys under sweatshirts under an oversized hoodie and put on sweatpants as a base layer beneath his jeans. He took another t-shirt and wrapped it around his head like a balaclava, his eyes out the neck hole with the sleeves tied in the back. He shivered harder and harder and lay down with his head on the bag.

Mr. President appeared on his torso and he took the cat in his arms and held him close and whispered apologies. He said he was sorry he hadn't given him a good life. He said he was sorry he never got to see outside at all. He said he was sorry he couldn't take him to the vet more often. He said he was sorry, over and over and over, and begged the cat for forgiveness. Tears poured out of Griffin hot and thick, his face red and contorted as years of pain made their way to the surface. Somewhere next to him his phone was buzzing repeatedly and Mr. President was licking his hand. Griffin grabbed the phone and saw a message from Jun.

Jun said, "Please let me know if you are safe or if anything changes. Stay safe. Don't go anywhere. Get to the third floor if you have to. I'm trapped in my apartment too but I'm on the fourth floor. Send me a photo of you with Mr. President for proof of life as soon as you can. When the water clears you two can come here, okay?"

Griffin squeezed Mr. President against his face and took a selfie with his tear-streaked face and red swollen eyes pressed up against a very confused looking orange cat. He sent the selfie and the phrase "ok thank you im sorry" and then the sentence "i am going to try to sleep now" and he curled into the fetal position and shivered. He heard the sounds of crashing glass from downstairs again, as distant to his mind as if it were happening on a tv with the sound turned down, and Griffin fell asleep there on the floor of the abandoned apartment as cold filthy water flowed through what had until recently been his home. Mr. President crawled into the hoodie and purred and Griffin wept softly and slipped into sleep all at once, like a man falling through thin ice into a deep frozen lake.

Next to him, his phone buzzed on the floor, and had he been awake he could have seen the flash of the message preview that simply read, "Why are you saying sorry?"

In the morning Griffin awoke in the same position, still shivering, with a deep pit of hunger in his stomach. Every calorie in him had been shaken off in the effort of shivering hard all night. He wanted an enormous burrito, piping hot and so densely packed that it would burst like a cyst when he began to cut into it, but one look out the window showed the street was still more of a river, so he settled for a can of low-sodium black beans reheated on the thankfully still functioning stove.

The power was out, but his phone had soaked up enough charge before the grid failed that it was still going. He put it on low-power mode and sent another proof of life selfie to Jun, a high angle shot looking down on Mr. President as he ate his morning can of wet food.

"Oh thank god," texted Jun.

"I am so tired," texted Griffin.

"I didn't sleep well either worrying about you," texted Jun.

"Please send me a picture of your ass for morale," texted Griffin.

Jun sent back a picture of himself facing away from his bathroom mirror, his ass peeking over the sink and out from under a cozy cable knit cardigan that he had pulled forward in one hand to lift it up and away. His ass was small but perky with a faintly visible dusting of downy hairs and Griffin wanted to bite it.

"I would send you a picture of my cock but if I take off any clothes I will freeze to death," said Griffin.

"Get here and warm up so I don't need a picture."

"I don't know where you live," said Griffin, and Jun told him. It was near Hello Horses. Griffin sent a picture of the flooded street outside and said, "Do you have a boat."

"No," said Jun.

"Fuck," said Griffin.

"It's not as bad here. It already drained out. Looks like it all went to where you are."

"You might want to get a litterbox or anything that can be a temporary litterbox like an aluminum roasting pan as soon as possible. I don't own almost anything anymore and Mr. President has just been pissing in the bathroom sink of this apartment."

"Okay yeah I will get that as soon as I can"

It occurred to Griffin that he was still employed and that his workplace might not be flooded, so he texted Clara a picture of the street-turned-river and said he would be unable to make it in to work today. When he looked up from his phone again, Mr. President was sitting on the windowsill chirping, his head darting back and forth, fascinated by the water and the blinding light of external reality after years of watching shadows on a cave wall. A bird flew by, unaffected by the rains, and the cat's head whipped to follow it.

Griffin smiled, just a little.

## 11

Griffin spent all that day looking out the window with Mr. President, watching the water go by, too cold and tired to have a single thought in his pretty little head.

12

At some point during the next long night of shivering, the power came back on and the streets had drained enough that vehicles were making slow, tentative journeys through the water, local drivers working on sense memory of where the streets had been to keep them from going too deep. Just past the end of his block he could see there was still a small lake covering part of the neighborhood. Griffin changed out of the thick layers of clothes he'd been curled up in all night and grabbed his bags. He loaded up Mr. President, who voiced some objections at being dragged away from the unforgettable viewing experience of the second story window, into his carrier. The first floor had flooded up to the third step of the stairwell up to the second, and drained back down to just below the first step down to the basement. Everything reeked of shit. He didn't even open the door of what had been his apartment to check how bad the damage was. Bag on back and cat in hand, Griffin ventured out into the street to find an area high and dry enough that he could call a taxi and actually expect it to show up.

He blinked and he was in the back of a car. He blinked and he was buzzing an apartment building doorbell. He blinked and he was in a hot shower, leaving black footsteps on the bottom of the tub, seeing grime whirl down the drain. Then he was leaned against the wall, the shower a bit off of him, and Jun was scrubbing him down with a long soapy brush.

"Arms up," said Jun. Griffin complied and was met with a piercing acrid odor. "Oh my God, I think I understand what it means to smell fear now. You smell terrified. Keep the arms up, I'm not done scrubbing."

He blinked and he was floating in warm water, his knees drawn up in the tub that was slightly too short for him, his skin scrubbed red and smooth.

He blinked and he was dry and lying on his side, limp and naked, unable to move, his left hand thrumming from the heat and feeling like it was in three places at once. Mr. President was sniffing him, evaluating the strange new smell of Jun's soap. He seemed to approve and curled up next to his head.

He fell into deep sleep all at once, like a tired man laying in someone else's bed with his own cat.

Griffin awoke to the smell of boiling potatoes.

He looked around, his long term memory functioning properly now, and took in Jun's bedroom. There was a large pair of windows letting in dim blue light, the last rays of a late November day, and an open door through which he could see Jun at the stove, poking away at something that was bubbling steam, his figure outlined against the warm light of the stove lamp. Old Japanese jazz was playing softly. Mr. President was curling himself around Jun's shins, clearly desirous of whatever food was available to beg for. Jun was wearing the cable knit cardigan and navy sweatpants. Griffin was still nude under the covers.

"Hey," said Griffin.

Jun turned around, wooden spoon in hand. "Hi. You sleep okay? You alright?"

"I think so. I must be better. I barely remember getting here."

"Your body got here six hours ago. I think your mind just now caught up. You were nearly catatonic and it was all I could do to clean you up and throw you in bed."

"I'm so hungry. What are you cooking?"

"Mashed potatoes and gravy are on the stove, and there's green bean casserole in the oven. Turkey's defrosting."

"What? What is it, Thanksgiving?"

Jun cocked his head. "Yes. Thanksgiving is tomorrow."

"Oh. I completely lost track of time this year. In the midst of everything going on." Griffin wasn't lying about this, but any implication that he would have had plans if not for the unfortunate events of his past month was a stretch. Griffin had spent last Thanksgiving splitting a rotisserie cricken with Mr. President and soloing a bottle of cheap brandy. He had spent the

Thanksgiving before that eating several chili dogs and a case of light beer.

"I can see why it slipped your mind," said Jun.

"Can I have some mashed potatoes? All I ate yesterday was cold canned beans."

"It's still just hot chunks of boiling potato. There's leftover curry in the fridge, though. I just realized I don't know if you're vegetarian. It has meat in it. Does that work? That sound good?"

"Yes. Yes, please."

Jun put the wooden spoon aside on the counter and pivoted to the fridge, where he opened a container, ladled a pile of brown slop into a bowl, and popped it in the microwave. Griffin got out of bed and realized his cock was out and went looking for his clothes. There was a little stack of folded garments by the door smelling freshly laundered, so he put them on and stepped out of the bedroom. The living area presented a couch across from a tv, then a table dividing the space, then the kitchen nearest the front door. The microwave beeped and Jun retrieved the bowl, put it on the table, and pushed it across to Griffin, who sat down and stared into the steaming bowl of carrots, onions, potatoes, cloned beef, and brown sauce. It smelled better than anything Griffin had ever cooked himself.

Jun had turned his attention back to the stove when Griffin quietly said, "Why are you being so nice to me?"

Jun turned around and looked Griffin in the eyes. Griffin was on the verge of tears. "I'm not sure I understand the question. Your apartment just got destroyed in a flood. You and Mr. President needed somewhere safe to stay."

"No, you know what I mean. You barely know me."

"Okay. Well, I know you were willing to help me and patch me up when I got hurt without hesitating for a moment. I know you didn't get disappointed and mopey that we didn't keep hooking up after I got hurt. I know you went to fix the thing that hurt me while I was resting. I know that it was so disgusting that you threw up while doing it and I threw up just looking at the video and yet you did it anyway. I know your cat seems really happy and well cared for, and you put on videos for him to watch while you're away. I know I think you're really hot and just really easy to talk to. I know you need to eat that curry."

Griffin fought back tears and dug a spoon into the curry, bringing a piece of falling-apart-tender beef to his lips. He said, "What else do you know about me?" and then stuck it in his mouth so that he wouldn't be expected to say anything else while chewing.

"Hmm." Jun looked out the window as he pondered this. "I know you were listening close enough to know my favorite drink and made it without me asking for it specifically. I know that when your cat approaches in your sleep, you stick out an arm to draw him towards you without waking up. I know you have absolutely zero standards for how people are supposed to treat you."

Griffin just chewed and nodded, and they looked into each other's eyes for a few seconds, understanding something, until Griffin turned his eyes down to search for a particularly hearty chunk of meat or potato.

"This curry is really good."

"Thank you. It is exactly the recipe on the back of the box of curry mix."

Jun went around the table, took Griffin's face in his hands and kissed him. Griffin kissed back. Jun said, "Do you have plans for Thanksgiving?"

"No, I don't."

"I'm doing a friendsgiving thing tomorrow. Having a few people over. Stay and be a part of it."

"Okay."

"Finish your curry."

"Okay."

"Then just rest. I'll keep cooking."

"Okay. Thank you."

Jun returned his attention to the stove, where he began the process of mashing the boiled potatoes. Griffin ate and watched him cook. Jun would occasionally glance back to make sure he was eating. Jun liberally applied butter and salt to the potatoes, and as Griffin was nearly finished with his bowl of curry, Jun brought him a spoonful of mash to try, which he blew on to cool off and guarded with a cupped hand beneath before wordlessly extending it to Griffin's lips. Griffin opened his mouth and took in the spoon and they locked eyes.

"Needs a little more salt."

"Yeah, thought so."

"I'm going to lie down again."

"Good. Leave the door open in case Mr. President wants to join you."

Griffin went back to the bed and crawled in, the warmth of the kitchen not making its way past the door. Mr. President chose to stay behind where it was warmer and brighter and smelled of food. From the bed, laying on his side, he saw Mr. President leap onto the table and begin licking at the dirty bowl where his curry had been. Jun turned and grabbed the bowl and said, "Hold on, I'm pretty sure that's poison to you. Let me get you some real food."

Mr. President voiced his discontent at this, but upon witnessing it Griffin felt something within him lessen its dreadful grip.

Jun shook Griffin awake the next morning.

"Hey there," said Jun. "Good morning. You ready to be conscious again?"

"Good morning. What time is it?"

"It's about nine. You slept for something around sixteen hours since you got here. I almost thought you were dead at one point because you weren't responding at all even when I was shaking you, but then you asked for five more minutes. Then you took ten more hours."

"Oh God."

"It's fine. I imagine you're hungry again."

"Every day, yeah. It keeps happening."

"Come on and eat. You'll get plenty more later but you look like you need everything you can get right now."

Jun helped Griffin out of bed and shepherded him into the kitchen. They were both still wearing the same things as the day before. Jun sat him down at the table and Griffin watched him cook.

"Coffee?"

"Yes please."

"Cream and sugar?"

"Yes please."

Jun poured two cups from a cheap little drip flask coffee machine into heavy-bottomed handmade mugs. He put one on the table, and set a small carton of cream down next to a box of sugar packets. Griffin stared at the beautifully crafted mug, its glaze a blue-green crackle, and tried to figure out what looked so strange about it, when it occurred to him that it was a clear day and this is what sunlight looked like indoors in the morning. He hadn't seen sunlight indoors anytime except for lunch breaks in years. He poured in the cream and sugar and mixed it and watched the color change in the light. He sipped the coffee slowly, gently letting his mind get up to speed. He remembered that his apartment had been destroyed and didn't feel much of anything about it. It occurred to him that this would likely require him to do some paperwork at some point in the near future, but that was another day's problem. He thought of the sensation of cold water rushing into the room and slamming into his legs.

Jun set a small mountain of hot pancakes in front of each of them and they ate.

After they ate Jun took out the turkey, seasoned it heavily, and loaded it into the oven. They bathed in turn, Griffin just wanting to relish the process of feeling clean on purpose. Wrapped in a towel, he emerged from the steamy bathroom into a bright den of deep savory warmth. He glanced towards the kitchen, expecting to see Jun there in his cable knit cardigan, but it was empty.

"Other way," said Jun.

Griffin turned to see him naked on the bed, reclined like he was expecting to be painted. Griffin dropped the towel, approached the bed, fell to his knees, and swallowed Jun all at once. He gasped, and they spent the rest of the morning getting to know each other better.

Thanksgiving dinner was scheduled more like a late lunch, and people began arriving at around two. Griffin and Jun had cleaned up all over again, Griffin fussing himself into the most presentable form he could manage after evacuating his home with garbage bags, ending up in a pair of corduroy pants and his most respectably uninteresting grey sweater over a white button down. Jun changed pants and shirt but remained in the cardigan as he went about the process of preparing the space. They cleared the coffee table into the bedroom so they could move the kitchen table away from the wall and lengthwise.

To Griffin's surprise, the first people to arrive were Clara, his supervisor from the job he'd occupied for two days, and her partner Bell, a Mexican woman with an adorably round face who looked every bit the grade school teacher she turned out to be.

Soon after appeared Michael and Poppy, the token heterosexual couple, both white, heavily tattooed and dressed in heavy metal band t-shirts.

Griffin moved through the interactions on autopilot, smiling and nodding, unsure of how to comport himself around so many people. His experiences of this holiday were comprised of screams and platters of food flying across the room as a child, and isolation as an adult. But he talked and people seemed to actually listen, which he was unprepared for. Clara, it turned out, had also gotten her job at the call center on Jun's recommendation a while back, and they'd known each other since college, where they had taken the same ceramics classes at one point.

Michael and Poppy, when questioned, could not for the life of them recall how in the world they knew Jun, but they had ended up at the same parties enough over time that one day it was as if they had always been there. Michael and Poppy had met as coworkers at an electronics store, and had also been hired on into the Faust family of companies through Jun's recommendation. Michael now did something involving video compression optimization at Faust Media Distribution, and Poppy was a scientist for Faust Food Service Supply. Last to arrive, almost late but immediately forgiven, were Alan and Chandler, two clean-cut men who Jun had also referred to jobs at Faust Insurance. While some couples look alike, what was notable instead was that Griffin and Chandler bore a remarkable resemblance to each other. While it was agreed that they both just had one of those faces, Jun was lightly teased about it by Chandler, before subsequently being praised as a pillar of the community for helping everyone find

gainful employment in these trying times, and Jun played it off
by saying he didn't need thanks because the cash bonus for every
person he recruited to any corporation under the umbrella was
thanks enough.

Everybody brought too much wine.

Griffin drank, and felt different than he usually did, in that he
actually felt more connected to the people around him, rather
than just more numb and alone. This was unfamiliar. People
asked Griffin how he knew Jun, and the story drew some questions about what the economic utility was of cutting off your left
hand in a single swift strike, to which Griffin said he'd rather not
get into dry economics on Thanksgiving. Much sympathy was
offered over the destruction of his apartment, which resulted in
more wine being poured, until Griffin was becoming one with
the couch, burdened by the weight of turkey and potatoes and
casserole. Somewhere in the night he had told jokes, and people
had laughed, and they had told jokes back to him, and he had
laughed. They told stories and he listened, he told stories and
they listened.

The night went on, blurrier and blurrier at the edges, til the
others were gone. Mr. President emerged from under the couch
and made a beeline for some turkey scraps on Griffin's plate.
Jun transferred some more turkey into a bowl on the floor for
the orange boy, loaded the dishwasher, put the food away, and
approached Griffin's reclined form on the couch.

"Get up. Brush your teeth."

"Nnnngh. Leave me here. Go on without me."

"Up."

"Did I say anything stupid?"

"No."

"Did they like me?"

"I think so."

"You think so?"

"I didn't take a poll or anything. I think so."

"That's good."

"I like you."

"I like you too, Jun."

"Get up."

"Fine. Be that way. Help me." Griffin extended an arm and Jun pulled him back to his feet. From the momentum of the pull, Griff closed the distance and kissed Jun again.

Jun smiled and said, "Brush your teeth. You smell like straight up red wine."

"There's a secret reason for that and you're going to be really surprised to learn what it is. It's that I drank so much red wine."

# 13

The next morning Griffin woke up early. He was spooning Jun, so he took Jun's shoulder and gently shook him awake.

"Hey. I have to go to work."

Jun nodded without opening his eyes.

"I assume I can come back here afterward and you'll actually let me in when I get here?"

Jun nodded again.

"Are you actually conscious?"

Jun nodded.

"What's two plus two?"

"A math problem."

"Great. See you later."

Griffin rummaged through his trash bags until he found his work clothes and got himself dressed in the cool early morning light. Mr. President was snoozing on the couch. Griffin fed him, gave him a little kiss on the head, and searched for the tv remote to put on bird videos until he started hearing actual birds chirping and remembered that Mr. President would get to just enjoy looking out the window for real today.

He was already out the door and on the street when it occurred to him that he had no real idea where he was, was unfamiliar with the neighborhood, and didn't know how to get to work from here, plus there was still flood grime all over the streets. It was a densely populated tree-lined zone of apartment blocks over street level storefronts full of convenience stores, laundromats, and small takeout Chinese restaurants with names like Jim Food King and Dumpling Garden. Rats the size of dogs were making brazen trash robberies in the pale morning light, the fearless oversized rodents making meals of mostly meat-stripped turkey carcasses they'd seized from dumpsters. Men with full-face masks and overdesigned tactical gear emblazoned with the acronym BHAPAS were chasing down the rats armed with tranquilizer dart pistols and nets.

With time on his side, Griffin started the long walk back to what remained of his apartment. It was an easy walk with a constant gentle downhill grade, and the flood lines on the buildings grew higher inch by inch for every block he passed. The sidewalks cracked more and more as he descended through greater water damage, though some of it had certainly already been that way and the flood had simply carried away whatever pavement could be lifted. The trees fell away slowly and then stopped altogether, and the blinding light of the sun off concrete and glass with no plant life to mitigate it let him know he was close, as well as the increasingly fortress-like appearances of each liquor store and fried cricken joint he passed. One block of apartment buildings had erected what he at first thought was a wall of sandbags, but turned out to be an entire building's worth of trashbags set out for collection at once.

He found what had been his home until recently, empty of everything familiar. The front windows were completely gone. In the hall by the stairwell, the smell of human shit was powerful. Something was dripping from the ceiling just outside the apartment door. Inside the apartment there was mud up to his chest height against the walls, particulate matter from uptown dust in small dunes against the walls, and assorted small detritus from distant trash cans. Reddish liquid dripped from the ceiling. A tangled mass of competing tumors of different kinds of tissues erupted from every drain in the place— something that looked like a knot made of cricket legs came from the kitchen sink, a mess of teeth gurgled in the bathroom sink, and hairy skin emerged from the shower drain. The utility closet door was open and the water heater was a shredded mess of sheet metal, pushed outward by a bleeding mass of pulsing flesh.

The TV was washed up against the fridge lengthwise. Though he had no intention of retrieving it, he pulled it away, and the freezer popped open to unleash an unbearable smell of rot. Despite nearly gagging, Griffin opened the fridge door as well, and an enormous rat ran out past his feet. The rat seemed to have taken care of the contents of the fridge single handedly, trapped inside by the weight of the tv, perhaps managing to crack the door enough to get sustaining gasps of putrid air when it tired of its feast. The rat turned to Griffin and screamed, and in a moment of thoughtless reaction Griffin grabbed whatever was in the freezer and threw it for the rat to distract it. Only after letting it go and seeing it mid-flight did he see that he had grabbed the teratomalith cyst's homunculus copy of his left hand. This didn't matter to the rat, who took the hand in its teeth and ran away to leap through the broken windows.

There was nothing worth salvaging.

On the way back out, Griffin looked up the stairs to see the panel that housed the water heaters for the upper floors had burst outward, pushed by a twisting mass of keratinous vines of hornlike growth, flecked with muscle tissue that connected and inserted at random intervals and twitched at nothing.

Griffin took pictures of the damages for insurance, which he hoped he still had, though he hadn't checked in a while. With that settled, he made his way to the bus, at least knowing the way to the call center from here. The path there started on the same bus as before, packed with men from the Bear's Head lunchmeat plant who carried aromas of strong salts and spices and cures. The tired man sitting next to him on the bus that morning smelled like maple ham.

Griffin walked into work a minute late, certain Clara would understand his tardiness now that she had had even more opportunity to see him as an entity that existed outside the constraints of the job. The windowless main area of endless fluorescent lights was just starting to fill up as hundreds of headsets met their designated heads, and the distributed murmur of the same script being read by an entirely out of sync choir was filling the whole place with white noise.

He made his way towards his station and passed Clara's office, where he saw Clara's silhouette of voluminous hair peeking out from behind the broad back of an enormous man. The man wore the most basic business casual outfit possible in the form of a pair of khaki slacks that were not loose enough to hide enormous quads, and a buttondown blue oxford shirt that threatened to rip at the shoulders under the strain of containing his deltoids. Clara was observing the face of this man with the fascinated face of a child seeing a grizzly bear at the zoo for the first time, until she noticed Griffin pausing in the doorway and her eyes flicked towards him for a moment. Tracking the movement of Clara's eyes, the man in the chair turned and revealed a face that was clearly into middle age, at the apex of physical solidity, well beyond youthful grace and smoothness yet well before the encroaching decay of sarcopenia. The man was horseshoe bald with dark brown hair, obviously dyed, as the smears of dye were clearly visible in the spill over the edges from his eyebrows and mustache, which were ample and walrusy. This dye job extended down into a thick bushy beard.

"Good morning, Griffin," said Clara. The man's eyebrows went up at this mention of his name. "This is... Schvantlfeim."

Griffin's eyes widened in turn. "I was not expecting you to follow through. Or be real. Hello."

Schvantlfeim was already shaking Griffin's hand in tall, powerful movements that almost took the whole rest of his body with them. "Griffin! You are who I talk to before? Thank you for job recommendation. I appreciate greatly."

Trying to peer around the incredibly wide Schvantlfeim, Griffin saw Clara wide eyed and shrugging with an expression that said *I also was not expecting him to be real.* Griffin decided to become an active participant in the uncomfortably protracted handshake just enough to signal that he would like it to end.

Clara cleared her throat. "Griffin, could you show him the ropes? Don't worry, he already passed the remote interview. Utterly unflappable against the worst I could throw at him. Just like you. Here's his station number. It's right next to yours. The guy who was there before died in the flood, so you can reset it to defaults and get him logged in."

"Oh. Okay, yeah, sure. I can do that. Come on, Schvantlfeim."

"Thank."

Griffin and Schvantlfeim left the office and made their way through the ocean of cubicles, the morning's growing noise of quiet conversations interspersed with crying all around them. Griffin led the way by a couple steps and said, "It's pretty simple, really. You make the calls, follow the script up until they inevitably cut you off or hang up on you, and if they just cut you off you try to veer back to the script. The only thing is you're not allowed to hang up first or give up trying to sell the stuff. What we're selling now is Tag Killer, like I was pitching to you before."

"And you are good salesman?"

"Oh, I've never sold anything and I've only worked here a few days, but apparently I have incredible call resolution speed. People hate my voice and tell me to fuck off so fast that it brings my average completion time down dramatically. I don't understand how that helps, since, again, I've never sold a thing, but I heard it's just a matter of persistence. You seem like you can probably manage a bit of rejection just fine.

"Yes. I patient and persistent. Once, back in steppe, a family say to me, Schvantlfeim, please, a dog eating our chickens. Dog come in the night and eat the chicken from coop. Dog clever. Dog never attack during daytime. So I wait. I wait perfectly still in coop with stone in hand. I stay through the dead of night until dead of night become dead of dog!" He bellowed a triumphant laugh. "We ate well of him."

"...Where are you from again?"

"The central steppe. No work there now. Since they cut cables and dropped satellites during the war, the steppe fell behind the cities. When they destroy highways and train lines and deleted internet first time, many community alone, return to nature. The dogs return to nature as well, but nature of dog is beast. Starving beast, fight like demon for food. When train line rebuilt, we return to cities, flee steppe, but life strange and hard here too."

"Yeah, here it's more a problem with giant rats than with dogs. I saw a rat eating a human hand this morning. Well, it was one of my hands, a copy of one, and I threw it to distract the rat, but still, the fact that I had to do that is wild. You make it through the flood okay?"

"Yes. My storage unit on hill."

"Glad to hear it. And here's your station, right next to mine. Just put on the headset, hit the call button, and start talking when they answer. There will also be a button to input payment information, but I've never gotten that far so I'm not sure how to use it. It'll probably be pretty self evident, just ask them for their payment information and type whatever they say. I assume. Hopefully you find out soon. If you do, tell me."

"Thank you, Griffin. You are good man."

"No problem, Schvantlfeim. Now I'm gonna get to work too."

Griffin sat down at his station, donned his headset, and got to work. He scanned the screen, hit the CALL button, and listened for the voice. A man greeted him.

"Hi, is this Peter Drayton?"

"It is."

"Hi, this is Griffin for Faust Direct Sales. Do you have a minute to—"

"I recognize your voice."

"Pardon?"

"Are you Griffin Batt?"

"...How do you know that?"

"I contributed to your GoFundMe to reattach your hand. I rewatched the donation video every single day since it came out, a few times a day. When are you going to send out those pictures of your feet and asshole?"

"Sir, I'm not— I don't— I just got my hand reattached and I've taken the pictures but I haven't had time to edit them to make them really pop and send them out. Plus the floods. Do you have a minute to talk about Tag Killer? It's a-"

"I only have time to talk about when you're going to make good on your pledge rewards and send me a picture of your feet covered in mustard."

"You were that guy?"

"I was that guy."

"I'll... I'll get them out soon."

"You better. Or I'll tell everyone you backed out on your word and you'll never get a penny of donation from anyone ever again. And now I know where you fucking work."

Peter Drayton hung up.

Griffin exhaled for a long time, then looked over at Schvantlfeim, who was leaning back in his chair with his feet up on the desk, smiling wide and speaking in a booming, jovial voice, "Of course! As many as you need. And how you like pay for this?" as he took down his feet, leaned back towards his station and clicked the INPUT PAYMENT INFORMATION button. "Ha! No, I do not believe I can take tips. Thank though."

Griffin took off his headset, stood up, and walked to Clara's office. Clara was busy typing something as he entered, and without looking, said, "What's up, Griff?"

"Hey. I have to quit."

"Have to? That's more than I usually get. Why have to?"

"Some guy recognized my voice and knew my full name and threatened to extort me over foot pictures and also I had already told him I work for Faust Direct Sales so he could know where to find me."

"Yeah, that'll do it. Let me know if you need a reference."

"Thanks. I think I have an opportunity lined up."

"Cool. Go get it. Are you staying at Jun's for the moment?"

"Yeah."

Clara smiled and said, "Good. Later, Griffin."

"Later, Clara."

At that, Griffin turned to leave the office, dodging a thin older man who was coming in at the same time, fully crying, who immediately yelled "I FUCKING QUIT, YOU ***BITCH!***"

Out through the door, Griffin heard Clara's voice faintly behind him, saying, "Okay. Let me know if you need a reference."

# 14

Griffin sat in a booth of the Waffle House and watched the fry cook load bullets one by one into a stripper clip for his standard issue WH polymer-frame semiautomatic. The sun was still low in the sky. He ate soft damp breakfast menu hash browns and drank from a paper cup of coffee. His jacket pocket bulged with extra mustard packets he'd requested for an upcoming photography project.

He texted Jun, "Hey, I've decided I'm going to go after that other job. The disgusting one. Some guy was threatening me about those pictures you took of me, so remind me to edit those to placate the people who donated."

A moment later Jun texted back, "Well I'm glad you aren't just sticking with the call center at least. Nothing wrong with blue collar work. And yeah edit those and then show me them again for no particular reason."

"Thanks. I quit the call center already because it seemed like that guy was going to come down here since he knew where I worked."

"Oh shit."

"It's fine. I went back to my apartment before work today and it's destroyed. I mean I knew that but it's destroyed by more of those things that I cut up that were growing out of all the drains and water heaters. I think the guy who I talked to is going to really need the help."

"Jesus. What the hell is going on with those. I fed Mr. President before I left btw."

"I also fed him before I left."

"He's tricked us. He is a glutton."

"He is perfect. When will you be back at your apartment? I don't have any way to get into the building."

"Around six. I'll make a copy of the key."

"Great. Okay I'm going to go call that guy. Later handsome."

"Later prettyboy."

Griffin tabbed from the text messenger to the phone's actual phone function. He got out his wallet, found the business card, typed in the number, and hit the call button. Falling back into the patterns he'd quickly learned from the call center, he went into a dissociative trance as he listened to the ringing on the other end of the line, until a voice responded and he remembered that he was doing this on purpose and probably wasn't going to be told to fuck off.

The voice said, "Pearl Plumbing."

"Hi, is this Brandon Pearl?"

"Yes sir. With who do I have the pleasure of speaking?"

"Hi Brandon, this is Griffin Batt. We met the other day when— well, we met the first time when those firemen called you to my building— but you said I had carved up that teratomalith in the basement really well and gave me your card."

"Ah, right. I remember you. You reconsidered?"

"Yes I have."

"Wonderful. Since the floods there's been more work than I can handle on my own and my last assistant turned out not to have the stomach for it. You think you do?"

"Yes sir."

"When can you start?"

"Right away."

"Tomorrow right away or right away right away?"

"Right away right away.

"Great. You got good shoes?"

"What kind of good?"

"Not fancy good. Boot good. Waterproof good."

"No I do not."

"You'll want something either very durable or, for today until you can get something good, very disposable. You got a knife?"

"Something tells me I probably don't have the kind of knife I need. I used the curved blade you dropped from your toolbox when I carved up the one in the basement."

"Oh, I buy those farrier's knives by the dozen for the detail work. Hard to sharpen that shape. No, I mean a big sturdy knife for the big stuff. There's teratomaliths all over the place since the sewers backed up and plenty of that stuff just needs to be chopped apart with an axe or a machete or whatever big knife you prefer using. I can get you a spare machete."

"I don't have anything like that at the moment, but I really know my way around a carbon steel Serbian cleaver. That's my weapon of choice."

"Oh, right, you were one of those guys. Wild. Okay. Tell me where you are and I'll come get you and we can swing by a couple places for supplies and then hit up the first job for the day. If you make it through the day and actually want to come back again tomorrow, you got a job."

"Do I need to know anything about plumbing?"

"No. Tell me your location and I'll be there as soon as possible."

A windowless panel van rolled up fifteen minutes later with Brandon Pearl at the wheel, wearing olive drab coveralls that looked freshly laundered and as yet unsoiled by any organic fluids. Griffin was standing outside the restaurant, drinking a lidded to-go coffee on the curb, his left foot tapping in a combination of caffeine jitters and first-day nerves. He approached the van as the passenger side window rolled down and a bundle of cloth shot out at him, which he caught in his free hand.

"Good morning, Mr. Batt."

"Call me Griffin. Good morning, Mr. Pearl. What's this?"

"Call me Brandon. That's some coveralls I think will fit you. Clean. Put them on now. Get into character."

Griffin put his coffee on the ground, spilled mustard packets from his pockets, donned the engulfing garment, and picked the coffee back up. He said, "It fits alright. Anything else?"

"Get in."

Griffin opened the door and stepped up into the van's passenger seat. He buckled in, then looked over his shoulder and saw the back was filled with a variety of standard plumbing tools alongside various means of damaging organic tissue, ranging in precision from scalpel to chainsaw.

"Where to?" asked Griffin.

Brandon shrugged and checked a message on his phone. "Oh, some circle of hell or another. Bear's Head plant had a backup. Not gonna be pretty."

"Is it ever pretty?"

"One time a sink exploded so hard that it shot the faucet out of a third story window, and when I got there to work on it, it had been blasting high pressure water out the window so long that there was a rainbow visible through the mist on the street."

"Oh wow."

"That's the only time it's ever been pretty. This is not a pretty line of work."

"Got it."

Brandon started to drive. As they pulled out of the parking lot and onto the street, he turned on the radio. A DJ was mid-sentence as the sound clicked on.

*—Second to none. We play only the best pre-war hits. Real vinyl records from before the wipe. Classics and oldies from the halcyon days. We dig up real records. No disc rot here at WROT. Only real music made by real people from the real good times. We're always on the hunt for the best big hits and deep cuts to get you up out of your seat when the needle meets the groove. Now enjoy another half hour of ad-free nonstop music.*

"Radioactive" by Imagine Dragons started playing.

The Bear's Head Factory was an enormous pre-war structure that sprawled over what would have been two or three blocks. It presented a fortress-like facade from the main street-facing side, with huge blank concrete walls going up twenty feet, topped with another ten feet of chain link that arched back over the sidewalk in an upside-down J shape. An adjacent streetlight offered a potential point of entry for an accomplished acrobat or rock climber, but this level of security was more than enough for the average passing pedestrian. From the street, there were a few shapes visible through the top of the chain link arcs, mostly unremarkable additional grey rectangles and one notable smokestack-type structure that never seemed to exude any smoke.

Brandon and Griffin pulled up to the back, where there was a bay of fourteen adjacent loading docks for cargo trucks behind walls of reinforced chain link. Behind them, across the street, was a separate employee parking lot, which was also lined in implicitly threatening chain link topped with razor wire despite having a fully open front with no closing mechanism that anybody could walk into without incident, as long as they had the presence of mind to use the large obvious opening instead of trying to scale the fence. At this time of the morning, there was a single refrigerated trailer emblazoned with the acronym BHAPAS, sans rig, parked at bay five of fourteen. As they approached, the entire fence began to rise between the solid thirty-foot pylons that held it. A middle-aged black man in a long white lab coat and hairnet with blue plastic covering his hands and feet ran outside and waved.

The worker came up to the van and said, "Brandon! Thank God you're here! Where have you been?"

"So sorry for the delay, Elgin. My former apprentice decided this line of work wasn't for him. Had to pick up another set of hands to lighten the load. This is Griffin. He's new to this but does good work." Brandon glanced over at Griffin in a way that signaled *you better not make a liar out of me, kid.*

"Griffin Batt. Good to meet you."

"Oh, meeting me is gonna be the highlight of your day. It's all going downhill from here. Pull around."

Brandon drove past the loading dock area and found his way to a pair of heavy double doors. He parked, turned to Griffin, pointed to the rear of the van, and said, "Choose your weapon."

"You got a bunch of those farrier knives, you said?"

"Yeah. Don't worry about that. That's detail work for later. Choose something big you think you'd be comfortable with.

There's a cleaver somewhere back there. Machete's easiest for big work, in my opinion. Whichever you want. Those sound good?"

"Yeah, I'll take them both, I guess. What are you going to use?"

"Machete and chainsaw. I do not fuck around."

Griffin looked at the chainsaw, then back at Brandon, and said, "Can you explain to me what I'm about to get myself into?"

Brandon unbuckled his seatbelt and opened the door. "Walk and talk, kid."

Griffin got out as Brandon opened the rear of the van and started rummaging for tools. "So," said Brandon, "you found that teratomalith growing under your apartment."

"I did."

"And what I hadn't told you is that the water heaters upstairs had burst because little ones of those things had grown in each of them."

"I thought you said it was something about accumulated sediment blocking the heating element?"

"I did say that, and I wasn't lying. I just left out that trace organic material in that sediment had mixed with regeneratives that made their way into the water supply after the rains, and that the resultant growth had punctured them from the inside."

"Oh. Jesus."

"Right. I had hoped that draining yours would prevent anything from growing in there, but it seems like there must have already been some plaque developing inside." Brandon handed Griffin a pair of tall rubber boots. "Put these on. Anyway, without springing for much better filtration further upstream in the system, it gets to be inevitable. Without a designated organics trap to get destroyed, like a circuit breaker, it all builds up in heaters or wastewater. The latter's not usually much of a problem until there's floods like we've had recently. Then it becomes... *much* more of a problem."

"How much more of a problem?"

"Well, you know how you had that one decent-sized TTL that you carved up beneath your apartment, and that was just from whatever organic material went down your shower drain combined with regeneratives through a single leaky pipe?"

"Yeah."

"This is a processed lunchmeat factory that makes all sorts of things. Ham. Cricken. Cloned beef. Torki. Some real animal tissue, some plant derived synthetics, some 3D printed clone scaffolding. They have industrial scale production and wastewater systems for their processing. That all got mixed with sewage backup when the flood hit."

"Oh God."

"Don't go asking for him. Put a mask and face shield on. Get ready for some shit. Make it through the day and you got a job. You want to have a job, Griffin?"

"Yeah. I mean, I like shelter. I like food."

"You might like different food after this. Come on. These guys are counting on us. Elgin! Open it up."

Brandon handed Griffin an enormous cleaver and machete, then hoisted out the chainsaw and a toolbox. Elgin opened the doors and a stench that was complex and multilayered hit them at once. So many different kinds of decay layered over each other that they blended into a harmonic choir of miasma.

Griffin pulled off his mask and threw up onto the ground as casually as he could, spat, then put it back on. Brandon laughed. "That coffee even soak in yet, kid?"

"I think so. Fuck. Okay. Let's do this. I'm fine. Let's do this. Holy shit. It smells so bad. Am I going to die?"

"Get your shit together, kid. Breathe. It's not gonna smell good but you'll get used to it pretty fast. Just keep the mask on from here on out, now that your stomach's empty. We can get you some peppermint oil if you don't get used to it."

"Okay. Let's do this."

"Yeah. Let's."

They moved through the doors and Griffin saw that they were in the middle of a hallway across from a door, and the way down the hallway in both directions had been sealed with thick plastic sheeting to keep the stench as localized and contained as possible. The door was to a stairwell, where the way up had been sealed off in a similar fashion. The only open path from the exterior double doors was down into the basement. Brandon led the way down.

Griffin had never seen anything like it in his life.

Downstairs there was a hallway, clearly designed for some sort of now-obscured industrial storage purpose from what remained visible of the original building, but most of the hallway was occupied by what appeared to be an amorphous mass of giant tumors, tangled branches of keratinous horn-like growths, and thin webs of muscle connecting the branches and tumors, twitching from sourceless nerve impulses. All of this was lit with the indifferent buzz of industrial fluorescent tubes, their shadows twisted through thickets of horn. The hallway was clear up to a point, and that zone showed signs of having been filled with similar material up until very recently. This had apparently been the work of the last couple of days. The nearest points of the gargantuan teratomalith were a mess of torn muscle, broken horn and bloody tumors, but not fresh— they were healing over from yesterday's wounds at the hands of Brandon Pearl and, presumably, the assistant who had chosen another line of work for reasons nobody could possibly blame him for.

Griffin choked out, "Holy fucking shit. Holy fucking shit. What do we do?"

Brandon said, "We keep hacking away at it. It's the worst I've ever seen, but because it's that bad, it doesn't actually take much skill or knowledge to deal with it. You just have to hack away at it, like you're cutting up a beached whale. As long as the cystic core is intact, somewhere in that whole mess, it will continue to grow and heal no matter how much we cut off of it. See, somewhere in the rooms off this hallways was an enormous amount of stored ham, pepperoni, cricken, torki, and who knows what else. Well, Elgin probably knows what else. But my point is, this thing has so much biomass to work with that we need to attack it faster than it can heal, and eventually we'll find the core, and once we cut out the core we won't have to rush as much because the rest of it will die. But that's probably not gonna happen today. You got me?"

"I, fucking, I, yeah, I— holy shit, man— I got you. So where do we start?"

"Start with what's in front of us. I'll take the right side, you take the left, and you let me know if you find any parts with thick bone growth, because the chainsaw can handle that better than the cleaver can."

Brandon walked forward, revved up the chainsaw, and lowered it into a thick branch of horn. He did not hesitate or gag. Griffin did both, but then worked up his courage, made his way to a mess of twitching muscle, and swung the blade. He remembered the feeling of cutting his hand off and felt an odd sympathy pain in his left wrist as a sheet of muscle separated from a branch of horn. A spray of blood shot from the wound and onto the face shield. The buzzing of the chainsaw stopped.

"Kid, did you not put gloves on?"

"Oh. No."

"Christ. Go upstairs, look in the back of the van, use the hand sanitizer and put on some gloves."

Griffin said, "You know I didn't know I was going to do this when I woke up this morning?"

Brandon looked unimpressed. "You know I did? Get the gloves."

Griffin got the gloves and returned to find Brandon with muscle and tumor and bone and horn in an unrecognizable grey-pink pile growing behind him. Griffin made his way around the pile and got back to where he'd first started chopping, then looked over at Brandon, who would have been unintelligible had he decided to try to yell over the chainsaw, but whose momentary glance spoke *do not make a liar out of me* with perfect clarity. Heeding this, Griffin raised the blade again and swung it hard, lopping off another branch, swinging again, taking away all the keratin he could, until the solid stuff was clear and the lower levels of muscle and tumor remained. He hacked away straight down the middle through twisted layers of skin and flesh and fat, blood pouring away freely, when from somewhere within the great monstrous mass he heard a deep inhuman guttural sound audible over the chainsaw, a long wet roar like a wounded, cornered tiger choking back blood.

Griffin yelped, dropped the knife and fell backwards.

Brandon said, "I think you hit a nerve."

"THIS THING MADE A NOISE. IT HAS A MOUTH AND LUNGS SOMEWHERE. IT YELLED."

"Well, it has something. Anything big and squishy enough will make noise. You don't have to be smart to make a noise like that. I've had parts of me that weren't my mouth make that noise when I was real sick. Come on, kid." Brandon extended a bloody gloved hand to Griffin. "Get up."

Swaying back up to his feet, Griffin said, "This thing isn't— is this human flesh?"

"I'd estimate this is pig flesh. This is probably all growing from the ham, at least this area is. Farther down the hall there's gonna be cricken, and I am absolutely not looking forward to that. But remember, *this is not smart. This is not a person.* This is an overgrown tumor in the basement of a lunchmeat factory, and last I checked, those don't have souls. It is perfectly fine to be doing this, at least ethically. I admit it is deeply unsavory. But it's honest work. Remember what Elgin said when we got here?"

"He told me it's all going downhill from here, and he was right."

"Before that."

"I don't remember, then."

"He said, '*Thank God you're here!*' Remember that?"

"Oh. Yeah."

"Think about that. Anyone ever say that to you when you were cutting off your left hand every day?"

"...No."

"Really think about it. Feels good to have someone be so relieved at your presence, doesn't it?"

"Huh. Yeah, that does feel nice," said Griffin, who was covered in a thick shiny layer of inhuman gore from toe to tip.

"It sure does, kid. Now earn it. Because he was saying that to **me**. He had no idea who you were. You keep going, you swing that knife right all day, the next time he says it, it'll be to the both of us. Imagine someone thanking the Lord almighty for the gift of your presence, your skill, your courage. You can be the one who earns that, or you can go back to cutting your hand off or answering phones or whatever it was you did before."

"Okay. You're right."

"I'm always right, kid," said Brandon, who revved the chainsaw back up to roaring and plunged it into a mass of quivering muscle, spraying himself with a fine red mist.

They continued like this for a while, once Griffin got over his disgust and got into the rhythm of it. He would swing his cleaver, chopping off chunks of this horrible thing and using the flat side of the blade to chuck pieces behind himself like he was throwing dirt with a shovel, and upon seeing what he was doing and thinking of it in that way, he considered the possibility of sharpening a shovel for exactly that purpose. Every once in a while he would hit a thick mass of bone or unusually dense horn and step back to shake out his aching hands while Brandon stepped forward to saw away the offending blockage. At intervals, Elgin and a team of men in BHAPAS uniforms would come down and shovel the gore into thick plastic bags and cart them away. After a couple hours of work, when their arms were shaky and their hands were numb, Griffin leaned against the wall and Brandon put down the chainsaw as Elgin and the BHAPAS men filled up another batch of bags. Brandon started shaking off his numb, bloody hands as he turned to Elgin and asked, "How's it going up there? This stuff mostly usable?"

Elgin nodded. "Mechanically separate it, put it in the enzyme bath, feed it into the bioreactor, still get some yield. Biomass is biomass at that point. Once it hits the scaffold, you can hardly tell the difference."

Griffin consciously processed this exchange a few seconds after it happened, at which point he looked over at Elgin and said, "You're still going to sell this stuff?"

Elgin shrugged. "Kid, bioavailable protein is at a premium these days. We can't afford to trash this stuff. After the enzyme bath, the filters clean out any contaminants, including trace re-generatives, and sterilizes it all before the amino acids get reconstituted on the protein scaffold. What comes out the other end is perfectly edible. It's not going to go to any of those fine dining places that brag about using real chicken or beef. If you've ever seen a place say it's using institutional grade meat product, it's probably this stretched out with some textured soy protein."

Griffin was suddenly relieved he had decided so often to get black beans instead of meat. He felt nauseous again, swallowed, and said, "Christ. I'm glad I usually go for vegetarian options or cricken. At least I know exactly where that comes from."

Elgin cocked his head. "Nobody really wants to know how the sausage gets made. How long you been at this, Griffin?"

Griffin looked at Brandon, who repeated his *do not dare make a fool of me* look back at him. Griffin stood up a little straighter and said, "Uh, Brandon and I met a little while back after the last batch of floods before this one. I cut up my first, uh, teratomalith not long after that. Brandon saw my work on that and tried to hire me on the spot."

"And you know where cricken comes from?"

Griffin blinked. "I think so. Crickets get liquefied and their protein is basically 3D-printed into a fibrous matrix alongside flavored coconut oil. Right?"

Elgin nodded again. "And you know why real chicken isn't sold at scale anymore?"

"No. Why?"

"Before the war they would keep those birds in tiny cages their entire little lives, stuffing them full of hormones and feed so they'd get as fat as possible as fast as possible. Then when they went to slaughter them they'd do it so fast and at such scale that every bird's meat might as well have been dragged through the shit of every other bird. Which wasn't great to begin with. Chicken is porous meat, and all of it, in store, was sold raw in a condition about as good as if it had been pulled out of a toilet and briefly hosed off. It was a nightmare. And the conditions in the farms were perfect for disease to spread at incredible speed, and it did. Birds got sick, infected each other, infected people, and millions of them had to be destroyed. Killed. Thrown away. Not sure what they did with the bodies, honestly, because what could they do with that much diseased biomass? That information is lost to us. So after the war, the wipe, and the die-offs, we decided to stop hinging our food supply on something so efficiently optimized to spread disease and collapse catastrophically. That's why you need a special license to sell it these days, why only the fanciest restaurants do it. Now, cricken hits the shelves fully cooked and shelf stable. Now Bear's Head Alternative Protein is perfectly safe to eat, fully cooked and shelf stable."

BHAPAS men shoveled more flesh into bags. Griffin tried and failed to hide the disgust he was feeling. He looked back at the enormous tumor from hell that he'd been hacking away at for hours and said, "It doesn't... it can't all be from stuff like this, right?"

Elgin laughed. "No, no. Of course not. This stuff doesn't happen every day. I would've preferred for all of this to go into their usual production batches of ham and cricken and the like. We can sell that for a lot more money. A lot of it is rats."

"You're fucking kidding me."

"I'm not kidding. You know, a couple years back I went on vacation to London. Horrible mistake, don't do it. I was expecting it to be like those ancient movies from before the wipe and it is way worse now. But I went to an interesting museum while I was there. There was an old prison they had there. You know how one of the terms for prison is The Clink? This was the original

The Clink. And because they truly did not give a shit whether prisoners lived or died, they didn't feed them. Prisoners had to beg for food from passerby on the street, and church donations of food for the prisoners were a matter of course for the locals who wanted to demonstrate their piety through charity to the poor bastards locked up in there. But when times were tough, people wouldn't give as much and prisoners would starve. But one guy came up with a system. There was plenty of stuff he couldn't eat, as a person, that the rats found perfectly suitable to eat. Minuscule crumbs and seeds and trash he couldn't eat if he tried, the rats would feast on that shit no problem. He'd keep rats around, bribe them with crumbs of whatever he could get his hands on, and they would return to him regularly, expecting treats. Then one day once they got big enough, he would smash their heads in instead of feeding them, and, let's say, harvest their protein, so to speak. He ate better than a lot of the other prisoners did."

"I don't care for any of that," said Griffin.

"And that's part of what we do here. I don't know if you've noticed but the rats in this town are *fucking giant*. They get enough trace regeneratives and hormones in with their trash that they become truly huge without us having to invest anything whatsoever up front to get them up to weight. And once they're through the mechanical separator, enzyme bath and filters- well, like I said, biomass is biomass."

"And now you know, kid," said Brandon. "You hungry? I need a break and some lunch."

Griffin watched the BHAPAS team shovel gore slop into another bag as he said, "Somehow, yes, I am hungry."

Soon they were back in the van, stripped of their filthy coveralls, sitting in a different parking lot, eating fresh drive-through bean burritos. They chewed in silence as the oldies station softly played the piña colada song. Griffin punctuated his chewing with long draws of diet cola from a massive cup, while Brandon slugged coffee from a thermos. In minutes they were crumpling empty wrappers and digging out the last bits of stuck food particulate from their molars with their tongues. Griffin's straw started to slurp at the last dregs in the cup.

Somebody said, "Alright. Come on. Let's get back to work."

Griffin was surprised to realize he was the one who had said it.

15

For the first time in his life, Griffin Batt felt a sense of belonging and purpose. That first day in the basement of the Bear's Head factory, he had felt something overtake him that he hadn't been sure was real: the desire to do a good job for its own sake, because the work needed to be done and he was proud to do it. It took them a few more days to clear out the basement. The section of cricken growth had been tough, what with the exoskeletal growth, but they made it through and found the cystic core containing a monstrous chimera blending the features of a fetal pig and giant cricket. It had been writhing inside the cystic sac when they found it, so Griffin split its head in half using a method you may be surprised to hear about. In a single swift strike, the abomination's skull was relegated to the past tense and it went limp, and at the same moment the remainder of the flesh in the place stopped its intermittent twitching and pulsing. Staring at the spilled brains of the pig-cricket-tumor-monster, Griffin felt a profound sense of accomplishment, reinforced and amplified by Brandon patting him on the back and saying, "Good work, kid."

Jun had been happy to hear about the work and the satisfaction it granted him, but was less enthusiastic about the gory details or the smell that first evening back. Mr. President had been absolutely fascinated by it, alternately licking Griffin and hissing at him. Jun had thrown Griffin in the shower and let him know in no uncertain terms that, were he to continue pursuing this line of work and intending to continue kissing Jun on a regular basis, he was going to need to bathe before coming home. So Griffin got a membership at a 24-hour gym near Jun's apartment and stopped in to shower before heading back. He kept at this regularly enough that he was eventually tempted to try the actual exercising part of the gym, and found to his dismay that it did actually make him feel better. Once the smell was dealt with, he was continually surprised by how well he and Jun got along, and kept getting along, and how easy it all was. After all, there were nearly five billion people in the world, and to think that getting fired while his hand was still severed led him to finding just the right one seemed like a miracle.

Mr. President would sit on the windowsill all day and watch birds fly by, contentedly chirping at them as ancient hunter instincts attempted to take control within his empty little head. When Jun and Griffin were home, the fat orange cat would endlessly run circles around their feet, headbutt their faces, and demand pets as much as possible, which he almost always received, until those strange times when his two dads would throw him out of the bedroom, close the door, and do something that involved repetitive thumping and sounds they never made while hanging out with him. Mr. President did not understand or particularly care for this, but they were always more relaxed afterwards, and he was happy his humans were happy.

Griffin even went out sometimes, as Jun's friends became his friends as well, and he got to know better the lives of Clara and Bell, Michael and Poppy, and Alan and Chandler, amidst various karaoke songs and bar trivia nights and board games, as thirty-ish friend groups comprised of couples had done for a century, each person a unit to themself, each pair an item, the whole group of couples a network of friendships of varying intensities. Clara and Griffin grew to be real friends, and she never did tell him how she'd done that thing with her voice on the phone that time during the job interview, but she swore it wasn't a voice changer.

Griffin even got around to editing and sending out the photos of his feet and asshole to those who had donated to help him reattach his hand, and nobody ever followed up on any of their threats about it. He used the very mustard he'd packed into his pockets on the first day working with Brandon for one particular custom set, and as he squeezed the spicy yellow paste all over his toes, he felt an oddly palpable sense of completing a chapter of his life.

Brandon Pearl took Griffin as his genuine apprentice, working his way to a real license to be a plumber. Luckily, there wasn't yet any certifying body for teratomalith removal work, so he let Griffin prove himself and his work ethic through that gruesome pursuit. Most of the work was smaller in scale, closer to the water heater explosions and basement ceiling growths that had resulted in their meeting, through every once in a while some industrial backup resulted in a week of nonstop teratomalith removals that thickened their wallets considerably. But it was on one of those routine days working on an apartment building boiler that had burst from a teratomalith that Brandon finally asked the question that Griffin had been avoiding asking himself for so long. They had found and extracted the cystic core, and just like Griffin's first, it had contained a human hand, slick with blood and pus and blindly reaching for nothing, and Griffin had cut it out with a deft pull of the cleaver. It fell to the floor with a soft wet slap, and as they stared at it for a moment, Brandon asked Griffin something.

"I've been meaning to ask you," he said, "what exactly is it about cutting off your left hand in a single swift strike makes money? How is that a job?"

Griffin didn't move at all as he soaked in this question. He allowed himself to sit with it and truly consider it for the first time, rather than just handwaving it away as the demands of the market. He just kept staring at the severed hand on the floor and after a long pause he said, "You know, I hate to admit it, but I have no fucking idea."

# Part Three

# The Handyman

# 16

# NINE MONTHS LATER

One thing Griffin had neglected to do in all this time was file for a change of address. He had canceled his internet subscription and ended all associated utility accounts shortly after evacuating his old place during the flood, and had started pitching in on Jun's expenses without his name ever actually being added to any of them. He had enough money coming in from his work with Brandon to allow him to put the regular contributions he made to the unchanging bills of rent and internet on autopay, which was a level of financial confidence he had never thought he could possibly re-attain. He and Jun and Mr. President built a happy little home together, but none of the records of Griffin's existence had been adequately updated to show where exactly this home was, and it was for this reason that things suddenly got much worse.

Since the floods and the evacuation, Griffin had, for obvious reasons, stopped paying rent on the old apartment once it had been rendered uninhabitable by being flooded with bio-hazardous waste and broken glass. If there had been other tenants in the building, maybe they could've come together to form a tenants union and attempted to file a class-action lawsuit to make maintenance demands of the property management company and stay in a hotel before returning, but the cavelike hovel held so little sentimental value to Griffin that he had abandoned it without a second thought and just stopped paying. Automated emails continued to come from Clearwater Property Management Company, alerting him that he was behind on his rent, and he would reply to these emails to say that the reason he was not paying rent was because the apartment did not exist in any legally habitable capacity due to an act of God, so he was not going to be paying for a soaking wet room with no windows that was imminently perilous to human life, which he also did not live in anymore.

These emails were unceremoniously responded to with automated replies informing him that the inbox was not monitored and he should send inquiries through the tenant portal. He did so, and got automated responses informing him that the rent was still unpaid, and stacking up, and they might have to move forward with eviction if he continued not paying. Brandon put him in touch with a lawyer about the situation and the lawyer said that, with the very obvious lack of a habitable apartment to inhabit, he was technically free to just not pay and leave. He took this advice, set his email inbox to instantly archive all emails from or mentioning Clearwater Property Management Company in a designated folder, and then let time pass while he lived his life in the steady and unfamiliar rhythms of growing contentment and stability.

Spring came and went, and somewhere in there the time passed when the old place's lease expired anyway, and he had certainly taken no steps to renew it, so by the time summer rolled around Griffin had all but forgotten about the whole thing. He hadn't checked the email folder to see their impotent attempts at rent seeking in months. He was more concerned with things like the glossy sheen of Mr. President's coat now that he could afford to take him to the vet to learn that he was basically healthy, just fat, and feed him the primo cat food made with cloned beef rather than Alternative Protein. He thought more about the little sparkle in Jun's eyes when he smiled at Griffin, about the way he would rest his cock gently between Jun's thighs as they spooned and drifted off to sleep, about the persistent gentle aroma of Japanese curry that wafted through the apartment fresh at least once a week and stuck around long enough after that it was now the smell of home to him. He thought more about the slow, steady thickening of his arms and legs, the widening of his shoulders and back, and the ease at which his body was packing on muscle even amidst the grinding arduous workdays of ter-atomalith removal. Jun had already been quite happy to spend his time looking at and touching Griffin even before he started hitting the gym, but the past nine months of growth, physically and emotionally, had made Griffin start looking like a man for the first time in his life. The lanky prettyboy of November had become a solid pretty man by August, and Jun couldn't keep his hands off him. Yes, amidst all this, Griffin wasn't concerned with the messages impotently demanding he pay the rent at his old apartment at all.

Maybe things would've gone a little better for him in the long run if he'd been paying just a smidge more attention. Or maybe, as it had been with his firing in unfortunate circumstances having led to meeting the man who would become his new home after his old home was destroyed in a storm that would have followed the same path of destruction no matter his employment status, things went exactly as they were supposed to in the eternal arm wrestling match between the silent hand of fate and the invisible hand of the market. Those little momentary mistakes that cascade into wildly different futures seem huge as mountains in retrospect, but they fall through the hourglass with the same level of pomp and circumstance as every other grain of sand.

August was the height of the rainy season. The unbearable heat of summer also caused a surge in violence throughout the city, especially on the days when the heat was so high but with such cloud cover and still air that the solar and wind arrays couldn't keep up with demand, and the rolling blackouts and brownouts would make air conditioning drop through swathes of the city all at once. As soon as this happened, whatever thin veil of humanity some people managed to hold onto while at comfortable temperatures fell away, and then knives fell, and then bodies fell, but also just some limbs fell, and this resulted in a dramatic increase in the use of regeneratives among the civilian population. The combination of widespread violence and heavy rains resulted in what Brandon called the "make or break" season of teratomalith removal work, as in "make a shitload of cash" or "break your mind and spirit witnessing the horrors contained in the sewers of this godforsaken hellhole town." Griffin, having handled just about everything the job threw at him with no significant problems to speak of, figured he was ready to make a shitload of cash.

It was all well and good being one of the main guys for property management companies to call to come fix calamitous water heater growths. It was better, in fiscal terms, to be the main guys to call for industrial TTL removal like at the Bear's Head Factory that first day. It was best of all, for wallet and career, to be the first name on the list when the city needed help. The men of Pearl Plumbing spent August on call, having been paid a retainer to ignore minor jobs so they could respond to teratomalith growths in the sewers at a moment's notice.

Griffin had invested into various work tools that were more his style. He had a long splitting axe for stubborn sturdy sections of bone or keratin, a large carbon steel Serbian cleaver in the style he had grown so accustomed to during his sinister severance days for the standard bits of butchery, a general-purpose machete, and an ongoing supply of disposable farrier's knives for detail work. While the farrier's knives were simply trashed when too dull to use, he took pride in the maintenance of his axe, machete, and cleaver, and wore the cleaver in a leather sheathe on the back of his belt during work days, with the axe hanging at his side. He would take them home to sharpen and oil the blades on a regular basis, enjoying the meditative nature of sharpening in a wholly different way than he had when he was doing it to cut off his own left hand every day. He would get his cleaver to a razor's edge, dab it with oil to keep it from rusting, and treat the blade of the axe with similar reverence. The evenings when he would sit at the table and clean his tools while Jun cooked, Mr. President lounged around, and Jun's jazz records played were the most gently contented moments of Griffin's entire life.

There was one evening in late May in particular that Griffin held in his mind when things got tough, a cozy cottage of a memory in which to take refuge, of just one of these times. In the memory, he had already finished sharpening the blades that sat in their sheathes beside the table in the living room, where Jun and Griff were tipsily dancing after dinner to "Sweet Agnes" by Masayoshi Takanaka, their breaths smelling of curry and sake, when Jun, apparently suddenly realizing just how much stronger Griffin was than just a few months ago, had abruptly jumped into his arms while they danced, his arms around his neck and his legs around his torso, and they kissed while Griffin held Jun up by his ass, and when they broke the kiss Griffin saw through the window that there was still some traces of sunlight, even after dinner, and Griffin, also taking the moment to revel in his newfound strength, bent down enough to put Jun back down on the ground for a moment before bending down even further, wrapping his arm around Jun's waist, standing up and throwing Jun over his right shoulder entirely, continuing to dance while laughing as hard as he could without falling over, then squatting down, scooping up Mr. President with his left arm, and dancing more, with everything he loved in the whole world held in his arms for a few beautiful fleeting moments.

Most days were less idyllic. Sometimes emergency work kept him out long after he'd rather be home and he'd roll in late, tired, with a stomach full of passable but ultimately unsatisfying cricken burrito, and he'd slide into bed next to Jun's sleeping form, at which point Jun would roll over to throw an arm over him and Mr. President would leap onto his torso with the grace and subtlety of a bowling ball. He tried to minimize these nights, but knew that August would be rife with them when they did hit, which is why he spent his free time with Jun as much as possible as Jun used some of his limited vacation days just to sprawl in his lover's arms.

The first half of August was unusually dry, which afforded Griffin a few rare opportunities to spend all weekend with Jun doing absolutely fucking nothing, the two of them lazing about in the voluptuous languor of late summer together, Mr. President modifying his loaf to maximize airflow over as much surface area as possible while Griffin and Jun took vodka bottles from the freezer to roll over each other's skin. Now that his heart didn't hurt all the time, now that he didn't constantly feel like there was a scream gripping his throat, Griffin was less inclined to get drunk for no reason, and they barely put a dent in the bottle all weekend, choosing instead to savor just how cold it could get. They ate sauced cold blocks of silken tofu with spoons. It was too hot to fuck, even too hot to cuddle, and they instead contorted themselves into strange shapes in front of the air conditioner, maximizing both exposed skin and small points of contact between them where they could relish the feeling of touching without too many of the burdens of excessive sweat.

A strange thing had happened that summer. Griffin had been sweating so constantly and profusely in his work that at some point he had stopped smelling of anything at all. It was as if whatever cellular waste products were usually being disposed of in sweat had simply all been dealt with, and where before his sweat had been thick, salty,  and redolent of the oils of his skin, it now ran as thin and clear and odorless as water. Jun, who had come to love the particulars of Griffin's scent, was frustrated by the sudden absence of it, and had taken to licking the sweat off of him as if in seeking a purer dose of the stuff. In the moments where Jun's tongue was exploring the ridges of his abs or armpit, Griffin would think of the first day at the call center and hearing about Olivia Huston licking the sweat off of her own Griffin in years long past, and he would laugh at the synchronicity of the memory as much as the tickling of Jun's tongue.

The mayoral election was coming up, which they heard about over the radio on a stuffy cloudy day while rubbing ice cubes on each other. Jun encouraged Griffin to finally get around to changing his address and his voter registration so he could do his part and vote. The race this year was populated by plenty of young politicians with good ideas about how to materially benefit the city, which meant that every decent thoughtful person would vote for a different one of them, leaving the outlying coke-fueled far-right maniac to soak up the remainder of the votes from the disaffected and the reactionary. But it was Griffin's civic duty to show up and vote for the guy he liked most, thereby indirectly dooming the city to another few years of rule from a notably unstable former cop who had once been caught on camera torturing a man for saying "sir" in an insufficiently deferential tone, and so Griffin decided to go ahead and update his voter registration and address.

The day he went to go confirm this at the post office, it was a relatively manageable 96 degrees Fahrenheit, so he took his IceCap out of the freezer and put it on his head, then wrapped a soaked bandana around his neck and set out on the walk. He wore a loose 50 SPF solar shirt. The bandana was bone dry on arrival but the IceCap was still cool, while the solar shirt was soaked with his odorless sweat. The clouds overhead were thick and still, pinning the city under its own stale air, offering ominous portents of rain to come.

The day after that the rains hit. Griffin still got a little antsy when it rained, a mild PTSD response he was trying to get over, but every time rain came and went without it pouring into Jun's apartment or destroying everything he owned, the easier it got. He tried his best to let the rain become an abstraction in his mind, because if he thought too hard about it he would remember everyone downhill still going through the types of things he had gone through whenever the rain got too strong, and focusing on the consistency and safety of Jun's apartment— hell, of *their* apartment— made him calmer and clearer. He had to be a little selfish and a little intentionally ignorant of the ways people were suffering so that he could function.

He thought about that sometimes. He actually helped people suffer less now. It wasn't as intimate as a doctor or massage therapist's means of lessening suffering, but it was no less real. He hadn't learned much about genuine plumbing in his time working with Brandon, save for the fact that every plumbing system functioned better when not blocked by large masses of hideous teratomalith growths, but he was now routinely receiving that kind of *Thank God you're here* response that Brandon had talked about back on day one. And as a professional, the more empathy he felt for the suffering of others, the worse he would be at lessening it. Understanding people, feeling their feelings, understanding their suffering, would all make him worse at what he did that actually helped them: swinging a huge fucking blade into those teratomaliths until they were cut up into manageable little pieces and able to be easily removed.

Remembering his old pain would slow him down. Understanding the pains of others would slow him down. Caring would slow him down. Every bit of understanding and care he held within him as he went to work would only cause more suffering for every moment it slowed him down, because down in the trenches there was only one goal: cut those things apart as fast as possible so you could get on to the next one. Nobody was going to remember his name, nobody was going to write poems about him, nobody was going to judge his bedside manner. They were going to say *Thank God you're here* and he and Brandon would lock in, grab their tools, and start cutting. Then the water would flow again, they would harvest whatever reclaimable biomass they could, sell it to BHAPAS, and they'd be off to the next job.

Caring was reserved for those he loved. He loved Jun. They said it regularly now. He loved Mr. President, but this had been constant even at his lowest, and was less novel. Notably, Mr.

President could not say it back. Mr. President would express it in as many ways as a cat could, with purrs and chirps and meows and headbutts and little reaches and cuddles, and all this was heartwarming, but it wasn't in the same genre as when Jun would say it back. Griffin would say *I love you* and Jun would say *I love you* and Griffin always noted that he never said *too*, that no matter who said it first neither of them ever said *too*, that it was never framed as a response or reaction, just another standalone fact not hinging on what had come immediately before it.

He and Brandon got along, as work friends do, as men do, facing in the same direction and with the same goal, communicating largely through nods and grunts and pointing. They did not share much with each other, but they did not need to. Brandon must have had some life of his own beyond the van and the farrier's knife and the chainsaw, but he never mentioned it, and that seemed to be a point of pride. *I'm not gonna keep you here any longer than you need to be just to pretend we're best friends,* said Brandon. *We're gonna get the work done and get the fuck home and live our lives away from this disgusting shit. You get me?*

Griffin got him.

*17*

On the second Monday in August, Jun was back at work. Griffin stood in the apartment, watching the rain fall, thick steady drops adding up to white noise. It was noon but the storm clouds darkened the city. There were no lights on in the apartment and distant flashes of lightning occasionally lit the room and were followed several seconds later with long rumbling roars of thunder. In the dim light, the brightest thing in the room was the screen of Griffin's phone, open and on a call with Brandon, set to speakerphone, as Griffin asked, "And what happened to the last guys?"

"They never came out of the tunnels," said Brandon.

"Did it flood while they were down there?"

"No."

"Did they find out what happened to them?"

"No. They just never came out of the tunnels. That's all I can tell you and past that I would just be making stuff up. They never came out of the tunnels. So now we have the contract."

"Did you know these guys at all?"

"We'd worked one job together when there was sort of an all-hands-on-deck situation that required dedicated real plumbing teams and teratomalith removal teams working in tandem when a school cafeteria flooded on a Saturday. Kitchen sink backed up somehow. Regeneratives got into a container of institutional grade meat product made of the BHAPAS stuff. Imagine a flood of sloppy joes made of giant rats made of tumors. Wanted it cleared out and ready to go by Monday. They seemed like they knew what they were doing in terms of the plumbing, but were pretty green in terms of the teratomalith stuff. And when I say green I don't just mean inexperienced. They got a little green around the gills just looking at it, too. Some people get so tempted by the money that comes with the contract that they don't take into account that they might well and truly not be built for this line of work, because they figure they're gonna manage to learn on the job, get used to it, develop their skills and become the experts in the field. And sometimes that happens. That's part of how I did it, now that I mention it. Nobody really starts out liking this kind of thing."

"I actually kind of liked it from the beginning," said Griffin.

"You showed me the video, Griff. You threw up and I don't believe it was just because you were that drunk. I believe you liked it more than you liked cutting your fucking hand off every day, but I think your scale of liking things is pretty off kilter if that's what you're judging everything else against. You don't like this shit that much. You like fixing things and feeling helpful and getting paid. Don't tell me you wouldn't rather rescue kittens from trees if it paid just as well."

"Alright. Well. How do we make sure we come out of the tunnels?"

"Number one, don't do anything stupid. I know you know this, but don't underestimate the sheer force of water. If water is flowing, even just a few inches, it can absolutely wreck you, whisk you away, and you're dead. You don't want that happening. You especially don't want that happening in the sewer. Keep your headlamp charged and keep backup batteries in your pack at all times. The first rule is, above all else, above money, is we come home at the end of the day. No stupid risks. Call in backup when needed. Just, you know, don't fuck around."

"Got it."

"A lot of what's now the sewers used to be the subway. It used to be the main way people got around before the war, but it started flooding so often and was so damaged during the war that they decided to make it an extension of the sewers to help mitigate flooding and sewage overflow events. So there's chunks of it that are a lot more designed for human use than the main sewers used to be. There's platforms, service walkways. There's also huge swathes of empty tunnel between those places. No longer any risk of getting hit by a train, but there's still the usual. Huge rats, toxic water, nightmarishly huge teratomaliths made from the combined organic waste of thousands wherever the flow happens to deposit sediment. You know, the usual."

"Of course. The usual."

"So be ready."

"I'll be ready. All my blades sharpened, batteries charged, everything good to go. Don't worry about that. I don't fuck around."

"I know. I appreciate that. They also got us maps of the sewers just in case, and I got some extra stuff to help for the big jobs, too. Just be ready for the call."

"You got it. I'll-"

Griffin's phone buzzed and the screen brightened to indicate another call coming in. No indication of a scam on the filter.

"I'm actually getting another call right now. Talk to you soon. Later man."

"Later kid."

He hung up and answered the new call from the unknown number with a curt, professional, "Griffin Batt, Pearl Plumbing and Teratomalith Removals."

"Mr. Batt, my name is John Smith. I'm calling on behalf of Faust Collections."

*Fuck. They're still trying?*

"If this is about my old apartment, it got destroyed in the floods. The lease was no longer legally binding when the apartment ceased being habitable and became imminently perilous to human life. There was no attempt made to place me in a more suitable unit or repair the property. All valid rents have been paid in full. The debt you bought is worthless."

"You think so?"

"I know so."

"We'll see, Mr. Batt. How's Jun doing? Mr. Saito-James?"

Griffin's heart rate began to speed up.

"Is this a threat?"

"No. Just a friendly inquiry about the indispensable lynchpin of Faust Medical Supply. We at Faust Group Companies love to check in on our colleagues. Make sure they're doing well. Make sure they're not getting involved with degenerates who don't pay their debts."

"Here's a counter-proposal, John: how about you fuck off to hell, eat shit, and never call me again? You're not getting a dime from me."

"How's Mr. President?"

"How do you—"

"I have your information. I know all about you. So why don't you pay us what you owe before we have to do anything else with that knowledge?"

"You are *never* getting anything from me, and if you try, it will not be worth the trouble."

"Sure. Say, are you going to turn on any lights in the apartment or are you just going to slouch there in the dark?"

Griffin scooped Mr. President off the windowsill and ducked down away from the glass.

"What the hell is wrong with you?"

John scoffed. "Nothing's wrong with me. I pay my rent. Well, mortgage. Like a person should. Like a *citizen*."

"Go to hell."

"I'm sure you'd love the company. You can pay your debt through the Faust Collections portal by typing in your full name and phone number. Or I can talk to you again soon. Have a nice day, Mr. Batt."

The line went dead.

Griffin held Mr. President in his arms as he leaned against the wall under the window. He reached up and pulled down the accordion blind, then called Jun.

"Hey there, prettyboy," said Jun.

"Hey, handsome. Listen, some maniac debt collector just called about me not paying for the rest of my lease on the old place and he brought up you and Mr. President and he mentioned how I was standing in the apartment as we were on the call. And I mean HOW I was standing. This was like thirty seconds ago. I don't know how he knows all this. I'm huddled under the window right now so he can't see me."

"What the fuck? Seriously?"

"Yeah. So. Be careful. I don't know what to do here yet. I haven't had a moment to think about it and my heart's been pounding ever since he mentioned your name."

"What's going on in the apartment that he mentioned?"

"I'm kind of standing in the dark watching lightning strikes."

"Griff, there is no way he could see that from outside. An unlit interior on a dark rainy day? No fucking way. They might be watching from your phone cameras."

"Oh god. Shit. You're right. Can debt collectors get that kind of surveillance now?"

"Seems like they can do whatever the fuck they want."

"It was Faust Collections, by the way. He brought you up as if he was checking on a colleague under the same corporate umbrella."

"Oh, fuck that. Listen, I'm going to pick you up a new phone card so-"

"No, if they can trace my phone just with whatever he already has, a new phone card isn't going to do it. Listen, we should get radio band walkies or something. I don't know. I hate this. I'm going to cover my camera lenses with painter's tape and figure out what else I can do to muffle it. Christ, I really can't go anywhere without this thing, can I? I don't know what I'm doing. I need to— Brandon's calling. I gotta go. I love you."

"I love you, prettyboy. Keep me posted."

Griffin ended the call with Jun and answered Brandon.

"Hi Brandon."

"Be ready for pickup in ten minutes. We have work to do."

"Great. Great. See you soon."

18

The wastewater treatment plant loomed over the industrial zone, visible from a distance even through the dark sky of pouring rain. Four enormous, six story tall, silver, egg-shaped digesters were the defining feature of the complex, which Griffin had often seen in the distance when driving by, and  back then he had idly wondered about what the hell they were until he got into the business that would make him intimately familiar with them. Off to the side of the digester eggs was a shorter complex that dredged the water for incompatible solid waste products and detritus.

Brandon pulled the van into a small parking lot in front of a little office building adjacent to the plant. A tall, broad-shouldered thirtysomething woman wearing a lab coat and large yellow plastic gloves emerged from the office as Griffin and Brandon stepped out of the van, fully geared up in coveralls, respirators, gloves, boots, and blades.

"I'm Carolyn Lambert. Thank God you're here," she said to Griffin.

Griffin glanced to Brandon and smiled as he said "We get that a lot. What seems to be the problem?"

"Our best guess is that a fatberg primarily made of lard and tampons got soaked in improperly disposed of regeneratives."

Brandon replied, "Your best guess?"

"It's already grown too much to be sure. Please just come kill it."

"Lead the way," said Griffin.

The large solid waste removal chamber involved a mechanism that looked somewhat like a comb but on the scale of a wall of pitchforks dipping in and out of all the incoming water. When it functioned properly, the metal lattice plunged into the water merely filthy and emerged moments later covered in a repulsive slurry comprised mainly of "flushable" wipes, tampons, and assorted small weapons. This mess was then scraped off the latticework and onto an adjacent concrete incline, where they piled up and began a slow downhill journey to the byproduct extraction systems. When functioning improperly, it could be seen jammed up with innumerable varieties of oversized organic and inorganic materials, and most of the time this could be extracted with a bit of extra manual agitation by the workers. Things were not so easy during catastrophic regenerative-contaminated overflow events, as was happening in front of the Pearl Plumbing team at that moment.

Griffin knew that there was a metal lattice somewhere in there, but the teratomalith growing around it completely obscured that. There had apparently been small enough early growths as the storm hit that the first few layers of flesh were already piled up on the incline down to the byproduct extraction systems, cylindrical tubes of vaguely human-looking proteins that had been insubstantial enough to be dislodged by the machine operating as intended. As the rain picked up, the amount of organics and regeneratives in the water started creating new tissue on the lattice at an unsustainable rate. Where there should have been a metal lattice coming out covered in traces of inorganic material and depositing it safely upon the incline, there was now a wall of flesh wrapped around the lattice. It occurred to Griffin that it was not unlike the scaffolds he'd seen being used to grow cloned beef a few times at the Bear's Head factory.

What had grown and was still growing there had a web of muscle tissue holding everything else on the lattice together, with skin growing over it at irregular intervals. Griffin couldn't tell if he would've preferred all skin or no skin at all on the monstrosity, but half skin and half pulsing organs certainly seemed like the worst option, as it partially obscured and partially revealed a series of pulsing organs, *each one* appearing to have its own cystic core, with no clear origin point due to the array of different places growth could begin simultaneously on each lattice, where they would then grow together. There was a series of three separate lattices dipping into the flowing water at different spots, each one after the first catching a bit of what the ones before it missed. At least, that was the intention.

"Oh, fucking Christ," said Griffin, unsheathing his axe.

Carolyn yelled over the roar of the storm and the rushing water. "We need to clear this as fast as possible. If a TTL core gets into one of the digesters and starts growing, we are fucked beyond belief."

"Heard," said Brandon, who was wielding a glaive-like polearm and dragging a 55-gallon drum on a hand truck with a hose attached, atop all of which sat a large boombox-style radio. "Can you stop one of these at a time so we can let the others take some of the load?"

"Yes," said Carolyn.

"Go do that immediately. Growth's worst on the first one. Stop that one first, keep it in the top position. Block off the byproduct extraction area for now so that this stuff doesn't go anywhere once we cut it free. Got it?"

Carolyn said "On it," then ran off to the control room above.

Brandon took the boombox off the barrel, put it on the ground, turned it on, and turned it up. He wheeled the barrel over to the walkway beside the gate towards the extraction area at the bottom of the incline. Back at the top of the maintenance walkway, Brandon took a moment to stretch his legs and crick his back while waiting for the lattice to stop moving as a voice began to bellow forth from the radio.

*It's coming down hard out there today, folks! City recommends you get to high ground and stay inside on upper floors. Once you're there, don't forget to tune into the season premiere of The Contestant! tonight. We're staying high and dry here at WROT, but you know our true calling is to get down and dirty. No matter how bad it gets out there, we're good to go. No matter how hot it gets, we keep it cool. Every single day we're bringing you the best pre-war, pre-wipe music. We're all analog here in the bunker, so even if they drop the big one, we're gonna keep the records spinning all the way to the end. Now enjoy another half-hour of ad-free music.*

"Radioactive" by Imagine Dragons started playing.

Brandon and Griffin got in position next to the first lattice, which slowed as it exited the water and clunked to a stop over the incline. The men of Pearl plumbing were on the stairs to either side of the incline, able to brace themselves against the railing as they leaned over and held their blades aloft.

"It's just like pulling hair off of a brush," yelled Brandon.

"Oh, for fucking sure it is, man," yelled Griffin, as he swung his axe at the highest and closest point of connection between the flesh and the lattice. It was a small, tapered bit of flesh with a tendon-like point of attachment that snapped free and instantly loosened the twitching meat below it, which slackened down to a point and stacked up like a loose knee-high sock piling on the top of a shoe, indicating the next attachment point. On the other side, Brandon was putting the edge of the scythe against the metal and slowly sawing it back and forth as he worked it down the whole thing, not missing an inch as he went. Griffin hacked at the next attachment point and missed, the axe plunging through loose flesh and clanging off metal without severing anything important, and the entire teratomalith started writhing. Each swollen cystic core started showing more activity all at once as if whatever was growing within them was trying to escape.

Griffin swung at the apparent site of the attachment point again and missed again, the axe vanishing into bloody folds of collapsing skin and muscle and fat, as the erratic twitching of the cystic cores made the small target even harder to aim at. Griffin decided to pop a core and hopefully get out whatever was moving, thereby stabilizing the attachment point further up. He swung the axe at the highest core, which was shaking hardest but was large enough to hit easily. The axe sunk in near the bottom of the thing and a rush of fluid came out. When he drew the axe back to swing again, a mass of teeth and hair and eyes and pig ears began to poke out from the wound, so he drew his cleaver for precision work to open it up further, sticking the knife into the wound and cutting it wider.

The monstrous little homunculus came out, but not all the way, as it stopped mid-fall with a snap like a neck at the end of a hangman's noose. Griffin and Brandon paused at once to process the new development, which they saw was that the horrid clump of tissue covered in eyes and teeth was more body-shaped than such masses usually were, and it was hanging from the sac by an umbilical cord. Griffin and Brandon locked eyes.

Brandon said, "Take care of it."

"Fuck," said Griffin.

Griffin looked at the thing, which seemed to be looking at him, insofar as one of its grotesque eye growths was pointing right at him. He swung his knife and cut the thing in half. Blood poured from the half still attached to the cord until Griffin swung again and cut the cord and the whole mess fell. Blood poured from the flesh where Griffin had followed through with the cord cutting swing, and as the crimson liquid streamed away the top part of the mass grew paler and stiller, and after a moment of last-gasp frenzied thrashing the thing grew still enough for Griffin to swing on the next attachment point with his axe and sever it cleanly. A few more strikes followed to the dying tissue and soon the great mass of flesh separated from the lattice entirely and fell away as one, with the entire machine visibly snapping back up to its intended position as the hundreds of extra pounds of flesh no longer burdened it.

The wall of flesh on the incline slowly slid down to the collection area on a thick layer of blood and fat, where it came to rest against the metal door blocking the way to the next extraction zone. Looking down, they could see that the mass was still writhing from within the sacs.

Griffin asked, "Why isn't it dying?"

"Those aren't cystic cores. These are generated from tampon waste. Uterine tissue plus regeneratives can do horrible things."

"Oh. God."

"Yeah. That's why the umbilical cord. Now go kill everything in that while I go cut down the next one."

Griffin nodded, bent over, and threw up.

"You good, kid? Haven't seen you do that in a while."

"I'm good." He spat. "You know, it's just been a while since I've seen something new."

"Good. Take care of that. I'll cut the next lattice." He leaned back and yelled up to the window of the control room. "Carolyn! Next one!"

Griffin headed down the stairs and followed the trail of blood, stepping carefully, trying not to slip in the greasy liquid. He gingerly shuffled up to the mass, wherein each womb was kicking with monstrosities struggling to live. He knelt down to the first one nearest him, fully skin-covered, and excised the thing within with careful slices from his cleaver. He found yet another mass of human and pig eyes and teeth and hair and ears and found what he figured was probably the head and positioned the knife gingerly over the writhing thing before pushing down in one shove with his full bodyweight that made it quickly go limp as its body fell in half. He repeated this process with the next one, finding a body inside that was all too human in its development, except it was also too porcine in its development, and the fleshy infantile body had hooves and pig ears and yet eyes that were far too much like a human's for his liking, and he put the knife over its head and pushed down, and it ended, and he prepared for the next one.

And then he heard Brandon yelling to hurry up, there's too much to be so careful and precise, just start chopping it apart with the axe so we can get this done as fast as possible, and then he was swinging the axe into every pulsing nodule on the mass of flesh, and hair and teeth were flying up on every backswing, and these weren't cysts but they weren't alive and they weren't human and what was this and he kept swinging and his goggles were too covered in blood to see what he was doing so he tried to wipe them with his sleeve but there was too much blood on his sleeve and he just wiped it around and was still seeing everything blurred through smears of red.

Brandon yelled *INCOMING* and another wall of flesh started its slow slide down the incline, a little faster than the first from all the blood and fat the first on left behind on the surface, so Griffin stepped out of its path and waited for it to settle and then started swinging the axe again, killing each growth core one by one. Griffin swung the axe and hair and teeth and eyes went flying and umbilical cords severed and blood soaked every part of him and John Smith said he still owed Clearwater money but he didn't owe Clearwater money but those bastards were threatening Jun and Mr. President all for just a bit of money even though there wasn't even an apartment to pay for and all he wanted was to make a fucking living with some fucking dignity and be left alone to do his work and take care of the people he loved without some piece of shit landlord company treating him like an inhuman sack of shit just because he didn't pay them rent on a destroyed room and who did those motherfuckers think they were fucking with and

And Brandon yelled *INCOMING* and he turned and saw the next wall of flesh sliding down the chute, faster now that it had its predecessors trail of fat and blood to slide on rather than having to make its own, but instead of diving out of the way and preparing to handle it with any kind of methodical responsibility Griffin *ran towards* the fucking thing axe in hand like a berserker warrior of ages past and swung low and rising at a throbbing mass within it, and it went through like butter and a spray of blood and teeth shot upwards but the thing kept sliding and it knocked Griffin off his feet like a storm surge and he fell back and was getting pushed along on his side like he was getting dragged by a truck and turned in his last moment of clarity to see the first mass growing closer and then

*Boom* the second mass hit him from behind and knocked all the air from him at once and he tried to breathe in deep but the weight on his back was too much and it was piling up over and around him and warm and pulsing and he tried to breathe but nothing was coming and things started to go black when

Burning.

In every cell. Oxygen debt. Carbon dioxide buildup.

*Can't breathe.* **Can't breathe. CAN'T BREATHE. CAN'T—**

The weight on his back was lessening and his body's desperate measures spasmed his entire torso to maximize the influx of oxygen, his diaphragm pulling down and opening his lungs as hard as it could, drawing in everything.

Blood came in with the air and Griffin returned to choking and drowning within two seconds of regaining the ability to breathe, making deep guttural hacking and wheezing sounds as his body now attempted to expel foreign blood from his airway.

More burning. Burning harder. Burning. Left. Why burning left. Real burning. Hotter.

The teratomaliths crushing him on either side were liquefying. They were almost scalding hot as they poured around him and just barely missed getting sucked into his lungs, but that wasn't all of the pain.

It wasn't just heat.

Griffin rolled onto his hands and knees and coughed hard, pushing out as much liquid in his lungs as he could in every productively wet hack. Everything hurt. A rush of bloody slime poured over him from uphill and his left hand slipped out from under him, knocking him back down to his elbows.

He heard his heart pounding over all else and, distantly, the sound of frantic yelling muffled through the thick liquid slowly draining from his ears. He was hurt. He couldn't push himself up on his hands correctly. His right hand was working. His left side was downhill. He leaned right, leaned uphill, leaned against the onrush of liquefying flesh. He held this stable position for an endless second til a strong hand started yanking at the back of his collar and he was up on his feet.

He was up on his feet just long enough to get out of the rush of blood and over to the side where somebody else's hands pulled his contorted mask, still attached to his head but not blocking anything and now just full of gore, entirely away. He went to put his hands on his knees to cough up more effluvium, and somehow missed his left knee.

Sludge drained from his ears enough for him to hear Brandon's voice say, "Oh, no."

He wretched one last time, stood up, and held his hands in front of his face.

His left hand was dissolving. The flesh around the wrist was already gone and there was a gap where his radius and ulna were visible. The palm of his hand was sloughing away and the bones in the gap were bending under the weight of what remained as they softened.

The bones in Griffin's left arm bent and bent until his hand fell away softly, like a dead tree giving way under the weight of accumulated ashfall.

The stump sizzled for a moment and sealed over with the oddly smooth and shiny flesh of healed burns. Griffin stared at it for a moment, then let his eyes unfocus, where he saw the masses of teratomalith piles dissolving in the same way. Skin melted off of muscle and fat until they revealed pockets of hair and eyes and teeth and ears, and a wave of what looked like pain shot through the mass as sections of it in turn shuddered and went still, then sloughed away and melted entirely, filling the entire extraction gate with bloody foam.

Brandon stood in front of him, his left hand already covering the mouth area of his mask, his right hand holding a spray nozzle with a hose leading back to the 55 gallon drum.

Brandon lowered his hand and spoke. "I am so fucking sorry, kid."

Griffin didn't quite feel like he was really experiencing this. It was already just a bad memory, even as it happened. "It's fine. I can reattach it."

"Kid. Griff. It's gone."

Tears were pouring down Griffin's face and he was shaking, but his mind was empty and his voice was steady. "I always reattach it. I'm really good at it."

"I'm sorry, kid. I forgot you used to do that. This stuff is just supposed to melt abnormal growths and I forgot that includes reattachment points from within the past year. I'm so sorry."

"Jun will still think I'm pretty," said Griffin.

"I don't— I was just trying to keep you from getting crushed under the thing. I saved your life. I was just trying to save your life. The most important thing is we get to go home, remember?"

"When I met him my hand was off. He smiled at me even when my hand was off. He'll still love me. I'm tired."

"Griffin, we need to get you to a hospital."

"To do what? Put my hand back on? I'm still licensed to do that."

"Griffin, we need to get you to a hospital. Please."

"Did we clear the machinery? Is it clear?"

"Yeah. Yeah, we cleared the machinery."

"Am I fired?"

"What? No. No, kid, you're not fired, but you can't work like this. You need medical attention."

"What is that stuff?"

"What stuff?"

"The stuff in the barrel. The stuff that melted my hand off."

"Oh, it's, uh, I'm not sure of the chemical name, but the brand name is DeGrowth. They used to sell a consumer version called Tag Killer, I think."

"Oh. I tried to sell that when I was working at the call center."

"Okay. You still need medical attention."

"I'm going to call my boyfriend."

"Let's go back to the van. I'll take you to the hospital."

"My boyfriend sells medical supplies. I'm licensed for auto-surgery in extremis. He can get me a discount. I can do this. The new prosthetics attach with regeneratives at wound points. I can do this. Do not take me to a fucking hospital. They might just euthanize me or make me pay off my debt in a labor camp. Take me home. I'm calling Jun. I'm going to be fine. It's fine. Shut the fuck up about the hospital. It's fine. I can do this. Take me home. Jun will meet me."

"Okay, kid, fuck."

"Get an extra pair of the coveralls and bring it inside. I'm going to go clean off. Are there showers here?"

"I don't think so, no."

"Hold on, then."

Griffin turned and walked towards the exit. With his remaining hand, he unclipped his blade harnesses and dropped them. He stopped, pulled his rubber boots off, unzipped his coveralls, and stepped out of them, then fully tore off his t-shirt before pulling down and stepping out of his underpants and socks. He picked the blades back up and walked out the door and into the dark grey downpour. He walked out past the van and parking lot and into a side courtyard where no light reached him.

He stood in the rain, fully nude, as wind and water whipped the heat from him. He sobbed openly, clutching a nylon bundle of axe and cleaver in his hand. He pissed himself without realizing it, registering it only as a flicker of warmth that was immediately washed away in the rain. Greasy blood trickled off of his body, some of it his own, and he stood and screamed and sobbed and pissed until he was shaking violently from the cold and he felt a little more clean.

He stepped back inside, dripping wet and shivering.

Brandon, standing next to the barrel on the hand truck, handed him a fresh pair of folded coveralls and said, "Jesus Christ, Griffin."

Griffin took them, put them on, and slung his blade harnesses back around himself. He took a deep breath and said, "Take me home, Brandon. I've got to make a call on the way."

They loaded up the van and left.

The rain was coming down hard but the roads were still passable. Crews around the city were working to keep emergency drainage clear, and from the looks of things they were holding the line so far. Brandon drove, the radio off for once, as Griffin called Jun on speakerphone, too drained to hold up his arm. Brandon drove carefully and listened as Griffin spoke, his voice flat and monotone but for the sounds of shivering.

"Hi handsome," said Griffin.

"Hey there, prettyboy. What's up?"

"I lost my hand again. It's gone."

"What? How? Are you going to the hospital?"

"No. I'm not even bleeding. I don't want to explain the whole process yet but can you pick up one of those prosthetics that attaches with regeneratives right on the wound? And then also the regeneratives. And meet me at home. I'm going home. I can't work like this but I'm not going to the hospital. So meet me at home and I'll put the new hand on and then I can keep making money. I'll pay for everything. I'm making so much money this month."

"Jesus. Okay, honey. I'll get the stuff and head home right away."

"It's a little more than just the hand this time. It's like three quarters of my forearm left, I guess. I don't know if that makes a difference."

"Shouldn't make much of a difference. I love you so much. I'll see you soon."

"I love you, handsome. I'll see you soon."

Griffin hung up and Brandon drove in silence for a moment before saying, "That was Jun?"

"Yeah."

"You don't talk about him much."

"He's what makes it all worth it. He's what going home is for."

"You two really met while your hand was severed?"

"Yeah."

"You two have a really good energy. That was really good communication."

"Thanks. Yeah. I love him."

"I can tell."

They drove on together for a long while, slow and cautious through the heavy rain. Griffin eventually stopped shivering right around the time they finally arrived back at his apartment and Brandon stopped the van.

"Okay kid, go take care of yourself. Patch yourself up. Keep me posted. If you can't come back to work right away, that's fine. I can find a temp. I'm not gonna replace you. You do good work. I want you happy and healthy. Just keep me posted."

"Thanks, Brandon."

"You're a good kid, Griffin."

"I'm twenty-nine."

"You heard me."

Griffin got out of the van, barefoot, having not had the energy or hands to get his boots back on, and buzzed into the building. He was fully re-soaked between van and building. He trudged through the vestibule and lobby, leaving a trail of water behind him, and called the elevator up to the fourth floor. He staggered to his door, put his keys in the lock, opened it, and saw Jun sitting at the table, ramrod straight, a prosthetic arm and tub of regenerative coolant gel on the table in front of him, and behind Jun stood a man with a gun in his left hand, holding it to Jun's head.

# 19

"I'll pay you," said Griffin.

"I knew you would," said the man.

The man standing behind Jun could've been Griffin's brother. They were the same age, same height, same approximate build, similar skin tone. The difference was in the face. The man's face reflected an unusually low amount of hardship. This was the face of a man who smiled often, stayed out of the sun, kept up with his skincare routine, and had years of childhood orthodontia. The last one was obvious because of the wide, earnest grin he had on his face while holding the gun to Jun's head.

Griffin stood there barefoot, his soaked coveralls rapidly creating a puddle around him, and held up his stump for the man to see. "Can I sit? I've had a bad fucking day."

"Go ahead and sit down, Griffin."

"Please let Jun go."

"I'll let him go when you pay, you pathetic sack of shit. Christ, look at you. You look like a drowned rat. What fucking good have you ever done the world?"

"I do some good. Please just let him go."

Jun quietly said, "I love you, Griffin."

Before Griffin could respond, the man snapped, "You're the only fucking one."

Griffin narrowed his eyes at the man. "Are you John? John Smith?"

The man smiled wider. "Sure. The original. I fucked Pocahontas. You gonna pay?"

"I'll pay. I'll pay right now. Listen. I just lost a hand. I haven't logged into the tenant portal in nearly a year. I have safeguards on my account so that I have to manually authenticate any payment larger than my rent payment. I'm so soaking wet I can't type on a capacitive touchscreen. It is raining too hard to get to an ATM. Unless you have a way to make the payment go through just with a face scan on your part, I need to at least dry off enough to use my phone."

John pondered this, then saw the axe hanging from the side of Griffin's belt. "Give me the axe."

Griffin unsnapped the axe from the holder. "Man, fine. I'm not gonna kill you with an axe." He awkwardly pulled it up and out with one hand in little hops, then choked up near the top of the helve and gently tossed it aside onto the floor where it landed on the rug with a dull thunk. It was a terribly inelegant process that made him seem all the more pathetic and weak. "You kind of need two hands to use that thing right. Like I said, I've had a really fucking bad day."

John kicked it aside and stepped further back from the table into the room, towards the doors to the bedroom and bathroom, covering both of them with the gun. "You have permission to get up and get a towel. Griffin only. Jun, stay where you are. Griffin, hands up, face me the whole time, move slowly. Do not attempt anything stupid. To be legally clear, these are neutral instructions and are not conditional statements. I am not implying anything about what will happen if you do not follow them properly. Use your best judgment and act accordingly. Understand?"

"I understand," said Griffin, who raised his arms to keep his right hand and left stump visible, stood up, faced John, and began slowly crab-shuffling towards the bathroom. "Is this okay?"

"For now. Just get your fucking towel."

Bright white light flickered, illuminating the whole room and casting John's shadow over Griffin. The roaring crash of thunder followed almost instantly. Mr. President, already hiding in fear, dashed out from under the couch and sprinted into the bedroom, vanishing from sight. John's pistol swiveled to track the motion of the cat, and Griffin's pulse rose even higher, a drumming in his ears that he struggled to hear his own voice over as he said, "Leave him alone. I'm just getting the towel. Then I'll pay you."

"Sure. How much of what's dripping off of you is rain and how much of it is fear piss and tears? Hurry up." John crouched and picked up the axe in his right hand.

Griffin glanced over at Jun, who was still sitting at the table, hands visible and palms down, eyes closed and shivering.

*You're not taking anything from me.*

Griffin backed into the bathroom and realized he needed to step away from the door to grab a towel. He stepped halfway into the bathroom so his right arm was no longer visible, did something behind his back, put his arm back up, then looked at John. "I would have to step out of your line of sight from where you are now to grab a towel. You should step this way so you can still see me."

John stepped closer to the bathroom. "You're making this too easy. Takes the fun out of it."

"Do people usually try to be really tough to a guy with a gun threatening their loved ones?"

"I told you, I'm not threatening you. I'm just holding this, with no conditional implications. I'm not some lowlife crook. And, that said, yes, some people have a bit more spine. You just seem like a weak willed punching bag of a man. I was hoping I'd get to test that last part."

"Well, sorry to disappoint. Please keep pointing the gun at me instead of anywhere else while I grab this towel."

"Slowly."

"While I grab this towel slowly, yes, thank you," said Griffin, slowly grabbing a towel from the rack beside the shower. "Can I at least dry off a little faster? That usually takes some fast hand movements."

"Fine. God, you're pathetic."

Griffin threw the towel over his head and held it down with the stump while moving it vigorously around with his remaining hand, pressing hard into his hair and face, earnestly trying to dry off as best he could.

"Okay. I'm dry enough to type, I think."

Griffin shuffled back out of the bathroom with his hands up, facing John, who moved back in turn, and they continued their hostage shuffle all the way to Griffin sitting back at the table.

"Get your phone out," said John, who was now standing beside the table, gun in his left hand, axe in his right.

"It's in my left pocket. I need to use my right arm to get it out, okay?"

"Do it."

Griffin awkwardly rotated his right arm into his left pants pocket and produced his phone, which he put on the table in front of him. He started to shake hard again. His knee bounced up and down with jackhammer intensity.

"Well? Pick it up," said John.

"Hold on, I'm not used to using it one handed. I'm gonna prop it up against my left stump." He did, tilting the phone onto the patch of scarred flesh that used to be his wrist. "What do I type in? Faust Collections?"

"Yeah. Go to the Faust Collections website. Type in your-"

Griffin's attempt to type on the screen with one hand missing and the other shaking hard launched the phone across the table and onto the floor at John's feet. John casually tossed the axe behind him onto the couch and began to bend to pick it up as he said, "Jesus, you can't do anything right. How do you even hold down a job with—"

The cleaver entered John's head with surprising ease, burying deep.

In the moment that John had exposed the top of his head and the pistol had wavered away to point at nobody, Griffin had pulled the blade from his belt and swung with all the force his terrified body would allow. The handle protruded from the crown of John's head.

"Oh my God," said Jun.

John dropped the gun and stopped going for the phone. He stood up with blood trickling down his face, which half-contorted as his mouth slurred out, "What doing?" John's hands, wobbling and cupped as mittens, reached up and found the handle of the blade. His face dropped, somewhere between limp blankness and deep misery, and he murmured, "My momm."

Griffin grabbed the gun off the floor and pointed it at John, who started crying like a lost child upon seeing it, and said, "Sorry. Mm sorry. Throom." John turned and walked towards the bathroom with an uneven, lurching gait.

Griffin and Jun stood up and followed, glancing at each other to confirm that each moment of new horrors was, in fact, real, as the man who had appeared in their lives today solely to threaten them wandered into their bathroom to die. John seemed to have forgotten about them as soon as he looked away and, having made his way into the bathroom, stepped into the bath, where he sat down fully clothed and turned on the water by pawing at a knob with a limp hand.

"Duggy," said John, who then leaned his head against the wall of the bath, pushing the blade further into his skull, and died.

# 20

The next thing that happened was that Griffin turned off the water.

The next thing after that was that Griffin turned to Jun and asked if he was okay.

The next thing after that was that Jun said he didn't know.

As he and Jun held each other on the couch, unsure of what to do next, each waiting for the ability to speak and think to return to them, there was a part of Griffin that genuinely considered cutting off John's left hand and attaching it in place of his own. Part of him had, in fact, been hoping for an opportunity to cut off John's hand at the table. Maybe it was just that cutting off left hands was his go-to move, that it was the only thing he really knew how to do and he had to do something, but when he casually opened the cleaver's sheathe on the back of his belt, he had not been intending to kill the man in a way that induced a traumatic brain injury that rendered his last minute of life pitiably childlike. He had thought maybe there would be a moment where they would all be sat at the table and in the moment when his gun arm tracked from Griffin to Jun, he might cut it off in a single swift strike, dramatically saving his love and literally disarming their tormentor in a way that felt thematically appropriate and fulfilling.

Instead he had a dead man in the tub, who he had somehow managed to make himself feel very bad about killing, even though said man had been holding them at gunpoint. Griffin supposed that he didn't really feel bad about killing John Smith, insofar as he'd known John Smith. The problem was that killing John Smith, heartless debt collector, had inadvertently given brief life to John Smith, confused apologizing child, and that one that had existed so briefly seemed so much more worthy of life. By the first John Smith's apparent judgment of the relative value of the lives of Griffin Batt and Jun Saito-James, John Smith would likely have approved of the immediate death of the fragmentary childlike entity that briefly inhabited his body.

But from what Griffin could tell, that version of John could at least be sorry.

Griffin was sorry.

Jun was sobbing against his chest. Mr. President was still hiding. The two things Griffin loved most in the world were terrified. One traumatized by understanding. The other fortunately stupid enough that it would not be able to process the scale of the horror.

Griffin had, in fact, been intending to pay and to do it without incident until the moment John's gun had flinched towards Mr. President. In that moment, images had formed in his head of him cutting off John's hand. He had considered asking for permission to take the coveralls off while he was in the bathroom, then faking needing help with the belt due to his hand missing, and striking with the cleaver when he got close enough. He had imagined a moment of triumphant violence. He had imagined an opponent with enough remaining mental capacity to understand that he had been defeated by a man he had underestimated.

Griffin wanted to go home.

He didn't quite want to go home to his apartment with Jun and Mr. President, partially due to already being there, because though he knew that was the one place where he was most certain to receive adoring love and safety from those he loved in turn, it was now a besmirched place of fear. He wanted to go back to some old childhood idea of home, to an early memory of his mother rocking him in a chair. A time before he knew anything, when they had kept up the parental effort of shielding his little mind from the world. Before he started to grow and it became more and more obvious that he did not resemble his father. Before his father looked at him like a walking testament to betrayal.

And young Griffin would hear through walls at night. He would hear accusations, that the treatments hadn't worked, that his mother had just been cheating on his father, and she would beg him to believe her that she hadn't, and he would go quiet and things would slowly get a little worse every day until the next time he would hear something through the walls again.

His mother had died in an outbreak when he was fifteen, and this clarified things in the worst way. Griffin had felt, not incorrectly, that his father did not love him and had never been proud of him, and so he pushed himself hard in directions he did not want to go, trying to follow in his father's footsteps. University. Economics.

Present Griffin pondered that he may not have made a single decision for himself in his entire goddamned life. Everything he'd done had been to jump through hoops that were held in front of his face, and this had taken him as far as his first job, where he couldn't keep up, abused military-grade antinarcoleptics to try to keep up, and had a full on breakdown.

Now that he thought of it, though, there had been one single time where Griffin had made a decision for himself, fully on his own, instead of just stumbling through life and reacting to whatever coincidences were in front of him. His relationship with Jun was wonderful, but it was still, fundamentally, something he had wandered into through random coincidence and reaction to somebody else's advances.

The exception was Mr. President.

Shortly after he'd been fired from his finance job and found himself unemployed, living off his savings in his new horrid little first-floor apartment where he'd just installed the diffusion film on the windows, and he decided, all at once and all on his own, to get a cat. He set out on the bus to the shelter and came in asking a lot of questions and repeatedly apologizing for things he didn't need to, due to how unfamiliar it felt to do anything at all of his own volition. The workers led him into the back amidst the cages, where the room echoed with a chorus of meows and dozens of bright eyes regarded or ignored him with various degrees of curiosity. He looked from cage to cage. Plenty of kittens meowed at the sight of him, with a sense of novelty or acknowledgement or hunger, but one orange puffball toddled forward, older than the rest, and looked him dead in the eyes. Technically an adult already, said the rescue worker, but still in need of a home. It held the stare, then put its front paws up on the glass, stood up a little straighter, and meowed once with unusual clarity and confidence. It wasn't just meowing. It was saying hello to Griffin specifically.

In that moment, Griffin vowed: *I will protect you with my life.*

He took the puffball and named it Mr. President, which seemed fitting. He imagined wearing a black suit with an earpiece and diving in front of the cat to take a bullet. He had thought that that was unlikely. He imagined getting a new job and continuing to live instead of killing himself. He felt okay with his choice. His only choice.

Present Griffin decided to stay and deal with whatever came next. He had made a pledge to protect Mr. President with his life. If it came down to it, he would, but he wouldn't throw his life away just because Mr. President had a backup owner now. Mr. President loved Jun, and Jun loved Mr. President, but Mr. President was not Jun's cat. All the way back then, Griffin vowed that would protect Mr. President with his life, and, if necessary, with the lives of others.

Preferably the lives of others.

And what better way to protect your cat than to build a better world?

And what better way to build a better world than to burn the old one?

There on the couch, holding each other, Griffin whispered an endless stream of apologies into Jun's ear, sorry for doing that, sorry for bringing this into his life at all, sorry he didn't just pay, sorry he was such a fuckup, sorry to drag him into this, sorry for everything.

Jun pulled back and said, "I love you, Griffin."

Griffin waited, expecting the twist, and said, "But?"

"No buts. I love you completely. Thank you."

"...Thank me?"

"He was holding a gun to my head, Griffin. I don't care what you did. You saved me."

"I've ruined our fucking lives is what I did."

"Not if nobody ever finds out."

"How would they not find out, Jun?"

"If he just vanishes in the middle of a storm? People die every storm. There's always a few people who think they can drive across rushing water without a problem and get swept away in their cars. He'll be one of them."

Griffin paused. "Jun, even if we find his car, drag his body out, and somehow shove it into a river with him in it, no amount of water damage is going to cover up a huge cleaver hole in his skull."

"Then they won't find the body at all."

"What?"

Jun stood up and went over to the kitchen corner, where he dug under the sink for plastic gloves. "I'm going to put on gloves and go through his pockets. And clean. And. Whatever else I figure out I need to do in the process. For now, he's staying in the tub."

Griffin watched as Jun snapped latex gloves onto his hands, and he had never felt more loved. All the fear was gone from Jun's posture as he said, "When I got hurt the first night we were together, you patched me up and you went and took care of the thing that hurt me. You took care of me. You've never stopped taking care of me, and I'll never stop taking care of you. The thing you did that night, down in the basement, was the kindest and grossest thing anyone has ever done for me. And now you help people every day. I know the only reason you do that work is because you like the feeling of helping people. Of saving people. You're not a bad man, Griffin. You're not a murderer. You saw someone you love being threatened with a gun and you took care of it. Now we're going to take care of it together. We're going to take care of each other."

With that, Jun grabbed the prosthetic hand off the table, came back to where Griffin sat on the couch, and said, "Stand up." Griffin did. Then, once Griffin was upright, Jun kneeled down on one knee, presented the socket of the prosthetic to Griffin's stump, slid it into place, and looked up into Griffin's eyes.

"Griffin Batt, will you marry me?"

Griffin started weeping, said, "Oh my god, Jun, I—"

And passed out.

He awoke moments later to Jun's panicked voice repeating his name. It had been about fifteen seconds, but Griffin felt like his last period of contiguous consciousness had been a different lifetime. As his senses returned from blurred darkness, he made out Jun saying, "—I'm sorry, that was too much to put on you right now, that was impulsive, don't worry about it, you don't have to—"

"Yes."

Jun exhaled for a long time, inhaled deep and slow, and repeated, "Yes?"

"Yes, Jun Saito-James, I'll marry you."

"Oh, thank God. I was worried I had two dead bodies to deal with, for a second there."

"Fuck, I had hoped I dreamed that part when I blacked out."

"No, no, the horrible part is still real."

"The horrible parts always are. Before we deal with that shit, can we put this prosthetic on me for real now, first?"

"Of course, prettyboy."

"This is one of the ones that requires a fresh wound to bond to, isn't it?"

Jun studied the prosthetic hand. "Yeah."

"I'm going to need my knife."

"Oh."

"I can go get the knife if you don't want to, Jun."

"No, I've already got the gloves on. I was already going to go through his pockets. I can get the knife. You wait here. I'll clean it off. You going to need to sharpen it?"

"For this, yeah, I want it sharp as it can get."

"Okay. I'll get out your kit. You just wait at the table. Is there anything I'm forgetting?" Jun stood and looked around, scanning the room, whereupon he immediately noticed Mr. President sniffing at a the gun lying on the ground. "Oh, shit. What do we do with the gun?"

"Keep it for the next guy?"

"Is there going to be a next guy?"

"I don't know. I think I saw that guy at the old terrible apartment, right before everyone else moved out. He answered the door when I was looking for the two other guys upstairs, and then they moved out. Fuck, what did he do to them? Then I think he was watching me from outside the building. I know that he said he represents this collections company, but it's like he's been stalking me specifically for ages. Maybe I'm just paranoid."

"Nevermind. If there's going to be another guy, he won't be coming today. We have much more important things to deal with right now. If he has a phone, if there's any tracking information on it, if God forbid he was expected to report back to someone soon, we gotta take care of it. So just go sit at the table and we'll start getting through this."

Jun helped Griffin up from the couch to go sit at the kitchen table, then vanished into the bathroom. Griffin sat and listened to the muffled wet noise of a large cleaver being pulled from a dead man's head.

From the bathroom, Jun yelled, "You really lodged this in there, honey!"

"Sorry? I'll try and do it different next time."

"I'd appreciate that." A crunchy pop sound. "Oh God. Okay. I'm gonna clean this really good, honey."

As the noise of the bathroom sink joined the conversation, Griffin said, "Thank you, my love."

Soon Griffin sharpened his blade, tourniqueted his left arm, measured where the prosthetic needed to attach for his arms to be the same length, and cut his stump down even further to prepare for the prosthetic. The radius and ulna were thicker closer to the elbow, though, and he couldn't get through it in a single swift strike. Jun had been on standby to help push down hard on the back of the blade in case this happened, and he followed through unhesitatingly.

In matters of love, choose someone who will help you through anything, whether it's killing to protect you, aiding in home surgery, or navigating the Sisyphean onslaught that is weeknight dinners. The most beautiful acts of love are expressed when things get truly ugly.

Some of the other ways Griffin and Jun expressed their love for each other that night are as follows.

Once he'd completed the attachment with the regenerative coolant gel, Griffin held out his hand like he was examining a ring on his finger. There was, at least, visible metal at his left ring finger, as Jun had gone for the symbionic hand with clear synthskin both for the cyberpunk look— Griffin had mentioned wanting this if he ever needed a prosthetic— and for the ease of seeing what was wrong if maintenance became necessary. His nerves were still adapting to the neural map the prosthetic contained, so his fine dexterity had not returned, but he turned his hand this way and that and examined it from all angles as he declared that he couldn't wait to show it off to everybody.

To test it, he held Jun's hand and squeezed gently.

Then Jun, in a fresh new pair of gloves and full rain gear, went out to locate the dead man's car with the key fob he had taken from his pocket. He trudged through the rain, circling the block, trying the alarm button until something somewhere in the storm started howling. It was almost as dark as night under the storm clouds and rain, but the street lights hadn't yet activated, and the flashing red lights of the car alarm were a beacon in the dark. Jun examined the interior and the trunk and found an envelope stuffed thickly with cash in the center console, which he pocketed, figuring he needed it more for whatever came next than this car's owner did.

While Jun expressed his love for Griffin in this way, Griffin expressed his love for Jun by beginning to cut up the body. He wasn't sure quite what the final disposal method was going to be just yet, so he started by cutting the feet off, which was pretty easy with a fresh blade and new hand, then practiced using his new hand while blood drained out of the man, which would save a small amount of mess further up. He expressed his love for Jun by working the cleaver through the tendons at the back of the knee and wiggling just so until he navigated the blade through the cartilage around the kneecaps. He expressed his love for Jun by taking the hands off at the elbows, then the arms off at the shoulders, and the head off at the neck. He expressed his love for Jun by opening this man's abdomen and pulling organs out and into the same kind of heavy duty contractor bag that he used on teratomalith removal jobs when there was enough usable tissue to donate to BHAPAS. He figured cutting the ball and socket of the hip joint would be way more trouble than it was worth, so once the abdominal cavity was emptied into a bag, his blade made its way between the lower vertebrae, leaving him with a separated ribcage area and lumbo-pelvic-hip complex.

While Griffin expressed his love for Jun in this way, Jun took the car and drove it through the pouring rain. There was one spot known for being where a few people died just about every time it flooded, further down the hill from where Griffin's old apartment had been. Jun made his way through the rain-soaked streets in the borrowed car, making his way past what had once been Griffin's home and was now a half-finished construction site, towards the low bridge with thin steel guards over the drainage ditch which became a raging torrent when storms came. Every time, some number of hubristic fools would think that the laws of nature didn't apply to them, would bet their life on their car's ability to win a fight against a river, and lose. All Jun had to do was make it look like this guy made that bet. Half the time those people would try to escape the car when they realized what was happening, as if their ability to swim mattered in those conditions, and were swept away entirely, torn apart by the forces at play, and found fragmentarily or never again.

Jun was a little ways up the street and could see the water was well over the bridge surface already. The maximum historical height of the water was visible in lines of repaired asphalt and concrete, so he got the car up against the top line, and braked. He kept the car running, pointed it downhill, rolled the window down, tapped the accelerator gently, opened the door, stepped out, and simply let it roll. It made its way lazily downhill, not in a hurry, and lost speed as it hit the higher water that slowed it to a crawl.

His heart caught in his throat as it stopped entirely, and he thought he might be well and truly out of luck, but the water was rising fast enough that soon the car gently lifted off from where it sat and drifted towards the bridge where the current was an unstoppable force. Soon the car was up against the thin galvanized steel guardrail, bending it slowly, when finally the water reached the level of the open window, and poured in. Soon the guardrail gave way and the car went down the stream, gathering speed until it tumbled out of sight entirely and anything that had been in it certainly would have both died and been lost in a futile attempt to escape. Once the rain stopped, they would drag the system for debris and pull up the car and that would be that.

The contractor bags were tied tight, the air pressed out of the inner ones, then doubled up and compressed again, until a small mountain of black plastic grew from the tub. Griffin ran water over each bag, filled the tub til they floated in red water, drained it, filled it again, and washed them over and over this way until the water ran clear. Then he poured bleach over them all and filled the tub once more to let them soak in the solution. Each would have to be disposed of discretely. His arms ached. His left hand ached most of all, a phantom pain of the dull throb of long exertion, though the sensory feedback from the prosthetic was imprecise and distant.

The bathroom, besides the presence of the bags, was spotlessly clean. He needed rest.

Jun came home then, soaked to the bone, shivering, and found Griffin lying on the bed, over the covers, naked and clean and half-conscious. When Griffin heard the door open, he lifted his head, glanced at Jun, smiled weakly, murmured the word "fiancé," and dropped his head back down again. Jun stripped to nothing and crawled in to join him.

21

There were a few problems.

One, the rats. They always surfaced after a flood and went to town on whatever edible refuse they could find and would tear open bags to get at anything. He recalled the morning after Thanksgiving when he saw BHAPAS men in their tactical gear chasing giant rats carrying turkey carcasses through the street. Certainly most of those carcasses had been in plastic bags when they were disposed of— most people probably weren't handing their trash directly to the rats, though it would have been efficient— but they also likely weren't double-wrapped and bleached, so it wasn't clear whether the rats would drag them out and try to make a meal of them. The BHAPAS men were always on patrol for "alternative protein" these days, but he knew that, despite the broad spectrum of things that apparently fit that label, they were against harvesting human meat as a matter of policy. If they weren't against it for ethical reasons, it was at least a major concern in terms of PR and liability. People were willing to accept the true depths of mystery meat up to a point, but inadvertent cannibalism was sure to hurt sales.

Which meant any bags discarded carelessly into surface dumpsters were likely to get torn open and serve as a feast for rats, drawing attention.

Eventually, he settled on a plan so simple that the only way it could fail was if a cop was looking directly at him while he did it. He was going to drive to a block with several medium-sized apartment buildings that used standard curbside garbage pickup instead of having a service come collect from a harder to access dumpster. Then he would deposit the bags as part of the normal trash collection, shortly before pickup. He knew just the spot. There was one he passed that same morning after Thanksgiving last year, between home and his old place, where so many black contractor bags were stacked up for collection at once that the addition of one human body's worth of weight to it wouldn't draw any attention at all.

The problem was getting the bags there when neither he nor Jun owned a car. Jun rode his bike to work and Brandon just picked up Griffin in his van. So Griffin needed the van. And he needed the streets to be clear. And he needed the trash schedule for that building. And trash pickup was delayed due to the flooding. And he needed to get back to work as soon as possible because, despite recent incidents, he and Brandon were still in high demand to deal with ongoing teratomalith problems.

The next day Jun went back to work, because he had to, and Griffin informed Brandon that he had a new hand and was ready to get back out there, though he had another issue to bring up that he could only talk about in person.

Once Brandon had picked him up and the van was making its way through the rain, Griffin asked, "Do you trust me?"

"Of course I trust you. To try your best, at least, and to usually get it right, and to not be a dick. I'm not going to take investment advice from you, if that's where this is going."

"God, no. No. I, uh. What would you say if I needed help hiding a body?"

Brandon sat silent for a moment, thinking, and didn't take his eyes off the road. Eventually, his posture changed as he loaded up a first sentence and carefully dispensed it. "First, I'd ask how Jun's doing."

"Jun? Jun's fine, he's at work." Griffin's eyes lit up. "He asked me to marry him!"

Brandon exhaled. "No shit? That's great, kid, I'm happy to hear it. You say yes?"

"I said yes! I'm engaged now! He put this prosthetic on my stump like it was a ring."

"That's wonderful, Griffin. Then I'd tell you to shut the fuck up."

"What?"

"Less I know, the better, kid. Never confess to anything, never give details, never let anybody know anything who doesn't absolutely need to know it. Give people plausible deniability in court. Good news is I don't know shit, and I have no reason to suspect anything. Now, would you like to ask me a different question?"

"Okay, sure, let me try again. Do you know of any ways I could dispose of some contractor bags full of perishable organic material that's not suitable for BHAPAS recycling?"

"Sure. BHAPAS."

"What?"

"Not everything that goes through the mechanical separator and the enzyme bath is big fat rats, kid. Is it fresh? Elgin owes me a favor."

"I'm not sure if I— I was going to distribute it into the trash pile of a whole apartment building right before pickup."

"Terrible plan, kid. What if a cop looks at you? There's rules against dumping your trash into other peoples' trash."

"Are there not rules against disposing of—"

"Organic material for protein reclamation? There's regulations, mostly around freshness of source material. You have a deep freezer? You need to borrow a freezer?"

"That would help a lot, yeah. This is actually, uh. Thanks, Brandon. This is way more help than I was expecting. I had just wanted to use the van for my idea that you think sucks. Why are you being so cool about this?"

"Remember the second time we met?"

"You complimented my work and gave me your card."

"Before that. You assumed I was going to kill you, and begged me not to, and got really oddly specific with what you would do not to get killed. You got the kind of specific that let me know that you had thought I was probably somebody else entirely who wanted to kill you for, if I recall correctly, not showing him your mustard-covered asshole, or something. And then the first day I picked you up for us to work together, not too long after, you stepped into the van with extra mustard packets spilling out of your pockets."

"I really wish I hadn't made that so memorable."

"You just gave the clear impression that some maniac showing up to kill you wasn't entirely out of the realm of possibility, for some reason involving your asshole. Worried me. Then when you started working for me you actually seemed to get more relaxed and happy, despite the fucking work itself, so I figured whatever else was going on had gotten better. But maniacs tend to be a lot more persistent than normal people, popping up even when you think they've given up. So who knows."

"It wasn't actually—"

"And don't tell me if I'm right or wrong one way or another. You didn't do anything. You didn't do shit. You don't even want to kill things that aren't really alive, or are in a kind of monstrous half-life where their entire existence could be nothing but pure suffering. I see you trying to toughen up for this work and not always making it. So whatever's going on with you, and let me repeat, *nothing's going on with you,* I bet it wasn't your fault. You don't seem to like violence much. And yesterday you *lost your hand again.* So I don't think you'd premeditatedly do anything while you were missing a limb. But you've got a lot of practice swinging a cleaver into flesh. You get good at what you practice. Even if you don't always want to."

"Thanks, Brandon."

"No problem, kid. Now, for no particular reason, do you want to go back to your place and load up some stuff for me to put into a freezer until an opportunity presents itself, before we get to today's job? It's not an emergency rush this time, we just gotta clear some traps down in the stations, tagging along with BHAPAS. They'll be the ones carting out anything we dispose of."

"Uh, yeah. Thanks. Let's head back."

"Great." Brandon pulled a U-turn. "How's the prosthetic feel, by the way?"

"Better than I expected. My brain is still getting used to it. It feels like how your mouth feels right after going to the dentist when they really go wild in there, and you feel your mouth in such extreme detail that it doesn't feel like your mouth at all. Then I guess eventually I'll get used to it."

"When was the last time you went to the dentist, Griff?"

"Probably six years ago now? Shit, I should go to the dentist, shouldn't I?"

"Yeah, kid, you really fucking should."

"Wait, why, is my breath bad? Do they look bad?"

"Your breath is fine. You're just supposed to go to the dentist. Like you go to the doctor."

"I haven't gone to the doctor in years, either."

They hit a red light and Brandon looked over at Griffin, bewildered. "Your entire job was to cut off your hand and reattach it every day for years and you didn't go to the doctor?"

"Well, technically, I was going to the doctor every day."

"What the fuck are you talking about?"

"I was licensed to perform autosurgery in extremis, which is a medical licensure."

"Wait, yeah, you mentioned that yesterday. What does that mean? You had a license to sew your hand back on if you were going to die if you didn't? You need a license for that?"

"Well, you need a license to get paid for it."

"But *why did you get paid for it?*"

"Haven't we been over this?"

"No, kid, not in any way that actually gave me a good answer."

"Okay. Well, I looked into it a little more since you asked me. First of all, I was employed by Faust Medical Solutions, which owns both Faust Health Insurance and Faust Pharmaceuticals. We were all headquartered in the same complex, along with Faust Fertility."

"That monopoly is seriously a bigger problem than anyone talks about."

"Sure. So Faust Pharmaceuticals manufactures regenerative coolant gel."

"Of course."

"And I was basically serving as quality control."

"Did they really need you to cut your hand off to test each batch? I mean, pharmaceutical-grade manufacture doesn't usually have testers. I mean, they probably do, but it's supposed to be some guy in an on-site lab who checks it under a microscope or a spectrometer or whatever diagnostic doohickey they use for that. Not just a person trying it out. Tell me, is there anybody whose job it is to take pills at random from already-approved drug batches just to see if they get the same effect every time?"

"...No, I don't think there is, now that you mention it."

"Okay, so you were also licensed for conditional 'autosurgery in extremis' by the company that employed you, which was also giving you health insurance, which you definitely didn't use enough, but you were assigned one specific kind of injury, over and over, and you were fired when you did it slightly differently?"

"...Yes."

"And you said you were technically 'the doctor' every day, given the conditions of your license?"

"Yeah. Like I said, conditional medical license."

"So you were an insurance scam."

"What?"

"Griffin, you were an insurance scam run by the insurance company on itself. I think they figured out some way to make it so one specific type of wound would be appropriate to serve as the approved baseline test for quality control of the regenerative products so that that wouldn't instantly trigger all the usual problems of on-the-job injuries like worker's comp. Why they settled for cutting off your left hand in a single swift strike, I don't fucking know, but and then they also licensed you to serve as a doctor to yourself, and gave you the health insurance to do so. So they were getting paid out of the entire pool of insurance money every time you put your hand back on, but you were getting paid barely enough to live in that cave-like shithole where we first met. And they have a famously low official approval rate for the medical care they cover in the wild. And now that I'm putting it all together, I'm almost entirely sure that you and people doing the same thing as you were serving as almost all of the medical care they ever actually officially approved, which was to say anything outside of their own system.

"So, and I'm not writing anything down here, just spitballing, I'm pretty sure they almost never actually approved any medical care in the outside world and used their daily approval of 'autosurgery in extremis' to dramatically inflate the apparent rate of approval amid all their procedures. And even with that, their statistics were dogshit. So you were not just an insurance scam to get as much of the money going to them as possible while paying out pocket lint and bottlecaps to you specifically, even as you were serving as your own medical provider, but you were serving to fuck up the statistics to drive up their public palatability. Something like that. You were scammed into being a scam by the scammers to benefit the scammers scamming everybody else."

Griffin looked ahead into the pouring rain with a thousand-yard stare that went aimed well beyond the ten yards of visibility that the downpour allowed. They were quiet for a while, til Brandon pulled up in front of Griffin's apartment building again, ready to receive whatever suspicious cargo his young apprentice might have to deal with.

Griffin turned to Brandon and said, "You know, I know you said not to say things like this, but now that you've laid it all out for me, I feel like I might have to kill some more people."

"Kid, again, *shut the fuck up.* Now go get those bags of non-specific organic material."

# 22

The subways-turned-sewers were flowing as intended. Rivers of shit and meat and various indiscernible effluvia trickled merrily along beneath the streets of the ruined city, where Brandon and Griffin dragged up traps of recently-drowned giant rats for the benefits of their BHAPAS escorts, who happily harvested the protein for human nutritional benefit. At each station, they would bring down another one of the plastic bags containing the remains of 'John Smith' and toss them into the river while the BHAPAS crew were dealing with the cage of rat meat, shoveling it into the back of their garbage-truck-like vehicle, which used the same kind of compression mechanism to pack the organic material at maximum feasible density while squeezing out water.

Griffin briefly objected that this wasn't the plan that Brandon had proposed earlier that morning, to which Brandon reminded him that he hadn't seemed to want to contribute to mankind's casual ambient cannibalism any more than absolutely necessary, and that the sewers during a flood were about as perfect of a way to dispose of evidence as could be, so long as you hadn't written your name on any of the bags or body parts.

They'd never even made it to the point of getting the bags into Brandon's freezer, nevermind getting them to Elgin at Bear's Head for any kind of favor. Instead they would drag cages bursting with rats up onto the platforms at each station-slash-sewer-entrance, and the Bear's Head Alternative Protein Acquisition Squad would happily scamper back to their trucks with fresh plump rat meat, and Brandon would casually empty a gory plastic bag into the river of shit when nobody was looking, then toss the bag in after. Griffin asked if that was okay to do.

It was fine, said Brandon.

Who among us had never murdered anybody in a moment of desperate self-preservation, said Brandon?

I had thought that it was pretty rare, said Griffin. But also I meant why are you emptying the bags in and then tossing the bags separately rather than throwing the sealed bags in?

Then Brandon would give Griffin the look older people give to younger people who say foolish things while he threw a bag into the river at the same time as dropping the cage back in, and they would head back up to the van at the surface and resume their progress across the storm-dark city.

The glow of the dashboard lights was the only consistent light on their faces as everything in the outside world was distorted by raindrops, windshield wipers and motion. After a minute, Brandon started to talk.

"This town, completely sealed bags with body parts in them are sure to flag a murder. Plastic waste thrown into the water for no reason on top of human body parts probably ending up congealed into a teratomalith? Just another flood day. Now you're almost clear of it all. One more bag. How you feeling, kid? You good?"

"I'm good. I'm good. My heart rate is starting to go down for the first time in about twenty hours. This past day took a couple years off my life, probably."

"One bag left, kid. One bag of inconsequential, nonspecific organic material."

"Can I ask a question?"

"You better, because I'm sure not asking you for any details about anything anytime soon."

"Where did you get the DeGrowth? The shit that melted my hand off?"

"This is either gonna make you laugh or piss you off."

"What is?"

"Cold call from Faust Direct Sales."

"I *knew it*. That's basically the same shit I was selling when I was there."

"I know, you told me when you were in shock. Didn't think it would help to bring it up at the time."

"Who sold it to you?"

"I can't remember his name for the life of me. Absolutely the strangest accent I've ever heard, but such an oddly comforting voice. Just talking to him was like being wrapped up in a really confusing hug. I know the stuff's useful if it doesn't cause a horrible injury like it did, but honestly he got me on pure charisma and salesmanship."

"Schvantlfeim."

"Yeah, Schvantlfeim! You knew him when you worked there?"

"I got him the job, kind of. He started the day I quit and he got more sales in the morning I sat next to him than I did the entire time I was there. Which wasn't long, but still."

"How many sales did he get that morning?"

"I don't know, I only saw one. I didn't sell shit. I wasn't good at that job."

"You're pretty good at this one, if it's any consolation."

"Thanks, yeah. Just lost a fucking hand."

"Kid, that's more on me than it is on you. I was in a hurry cutting down those masses from the lattice, didn't give you enough warning. It was too loud from the sound of the water for you to hear me warning you. I fucked up and got you hurt, and then I poured DeGrowth on you to get you free. I knew it wasn't going to be pleasant but I was in such a panic trying to save your life that I didn't think about your hand."

Griffin started to raise his voice.

"No, Brandon, I was in a frenzy down there and I wasn't hearing you and it was on me. I— this guy had called and basically threatened me and Jun and my cat, and, like you said I shouldn't say anything about it and it's fine because nothing happened, but I'm just, I've spent my whole life just being a fucking punching bag for everything because it was the path of least resistance. I got my master's degree in economics because I didn't want to get yelled at, and I crashed out and got disowned, not that my dad liked me to begin with, and then spent years in a daze just cutting my hand off over and over, and this past year working with you is honestly the best I've ever felt. It's weird to say, because it means so much to me it's kind of hard to say, but you're the first employer I've ever had that actually treated me like a person instead of just some fucking broken machine.

"And then this guy threatened me and, I guess I'd spent enough time not getting constantly humiliated and threatened that I had lost my stomach for it. And when I was down there swinging that axe into that fucking monstrous mass, I stopped paying attention to my surroundings as much and I just got really, really fucking angry that no matter what I do, no matter that I'm actually contributing to society and helping, people will still come along and just try to make me feel less than human and scared and threatened just because they want money. I don't want much, Brandon. I'm not, like, trying to change the world or live in a huge mansion. I'm just some fucking guy, and I want to hang out with my cat and my fiancé and do my job and help people and not get harassed by heartless maniacs. But that's not even a fucking option. I would have to shut myself off from the world entirely to avoid it.

"I want to contribute. I really want to help. I don't know how. Cutting up teratomaliths is certainly helping, but it's, pun fucking unintentional but I realize I'm about to say it, so far downstream from the real problems. It's literally so far down-stream from the real problems. Like, I didn't know this job ex-isted a year ago, and now I realize we're absolutely essential to holding together the infrastructure of this city. I didn't know this job existed because this job definitely didn't used to exist, right? Teratomaliths are the opposite of naturally occurring. Like, great that they came up with these medical miracles to glue soldiers back together during the war, but we shouldn't need quite so much of it that it keeps ending up in the water enough to make this shit happen, right? Way back before I was born, we built the fucking world wrong. I was given this dogshit reality to navigate and I'm so fucking mad about it all the time and there's nothing I can do about it, really.

"And all of that hit me at once when I was down there, slamming an axe into things that shouldn't exist. I mean, a fucking blend of human uterine tissue and lard resulted in a web of uteruses containing monster pig babies. I know there is no way for them to have a viable life. I know that the only thing they can experience is pain. But one of them looked at me, for a second, moments after tumbling out of— and how fast do these fucking things GROW?— and I know this is some kind of mercy. I know. I fucking know, Brandon. You told me that the first day in the Bear's Head factory, that things make sounds and nerves respond even if there's no real soul or mind there. And I know it's definitely better for me to get in there with an axe and kill a monster and drag it out of the drain and get covered in blood and see things that were never supposed to exist than it is for me to give up and for the pipes to get backed up with growths full of teeth and eyes. That would be way worse for fully developed adult real humans to experience. I know. But it doesn't feel GOOD to slam an axe into the eye of an innocent thing that's looking at you."

Brandon sighed. "I know, kid. I know."

"And when I killed that guy—"

"Christ, kid, at least shut the fuck up to everyone else, okay? Like, I've tried to act like I didn't immediately know what you were asking, but there's only so much I can do if you keep talking like this. Okay, just tell me everything and don't tell anyone else shit if you need to talk about it that much."

"Sure, promise, right. Anyway, when I killed that guy, like, I didn't really mean to, but I didn't hesitate, either. He'd had a gun pointed at Jun's head and he wavered for a second and I just swung the cleaver like I would into any teratomalith and it went in easy, and... and after the knife hit his head he instantly reverted to this childlike state, and he got really sad and apologetic, and— I don't feel bad about killing him, Brandon. I don't. In the moment that he was threatening me and Jun and Mr. President, he was a monster and slamming a blade into his skull was the absolutely correct decision for how to keep the man I love safe and alive. But there was a moment there, the minute between me hitting him and when he really died, where he was this pathetic and childlike creature who kept apologizing and crying and, and he didn't really exist. And he could've been my stunt double to begin with, but once I actually put the knife in his head I felt like he actually looked like me.

"Me slamming that knife into his head made a pathetic creature that could only exist in a state of pathetic misery for one minute before dying, and these days my entire job is dealing with the fallout from people who built a world where the water is full of monstrous little creatures that exist for just a moment of pathetic suffering before they die. He died because of me and they die because of me, too. And I'm swinging a fucking axe and a cleaver and coming home covered in gore and yet I'm sure, I'm entirely sure that I'm right that I'm reducing the amount of suffering in the world. I guess if you kill everyone in the world you're also reducing the amount of suffering. I don't fucking know. I guess if you follow the same logic, you save a lot of time by killing yourself. You can't go to jail if you kill every cop. There's a lot of problems you can fix with enough killing, I'm realizing, though it immediately presents you with some new and interesting problems to deal with instead."

"That's an understatement, Griffin."

"Look, I'm a killer now, should I just lean into it?"

"What?"

"I mean, I love Jun and I love Mr. President and I don't want anything to hurt them ever. If I try to get away with all this, they're going to get dragged into it. I don't even want to make you have to lie on the stand. So just admit that I'm a murderer. Then I can try and make a difference. What's the fucking difference for me? I was never going to get to be happy. I got most of a year with Jun. He wants to marry me. That's more than I ever expected anyone to ever feel about me. There's no way the debt collection agencies aren't going to send more people and figure out what's going on, right? I mean, we sent a car out into the water and a man into the sewer part by part, but Jun and Mr. President can take care of each other now, right? Like, it's not like Jun depends on me for income. He was doing fine before I showed up, we're still living in the same apartment he was in the whole time, and if I give him permission to testify against me with no guilt then he'll probably get away scot free. I just want to make sure that he knows it's okay. I don't make his life that much better, do I? Mr. President will miss me and he'll never understand why I'm gone. I don't know. But if I keep going like this, my life will never add up to anything important and I've spent so much time ready to die. You can get a lot of important things done if you're ready to die."

In the ensuing moment of silence after that grim line, Brandon took a deep breath and started again. "You can get even more done if you're ready to live. You say you spent a lot of time ready to die and that you can get a lot done when you're ready to die, but for all that time you were ready to die, though it sounds more like you just wanted to die, you didn't get shit done at all and that's why you wanted to die. You cut your hand off every single day, and your life was hell, and you didn't much care if you lived or died, and look where it got you. You didn't get a damn thing done that you were proud of until you had enough to live for that you started fearing death. You don't want to die. You're just worried now that you might deserve to, since you made that choice for somebody else.

"But the choice you kept making for yourself day after day, even in the worst of it, was that you were going to keep on living. Even when all you had to do to opt out was to loosen a tourniquet. I'm sure you had no end of opportunities to hit the eject button and end it all, but you kept showing up to reality, day after day, even when reality was hell, because despite everything you actually had some hope it could get better. And you know what's wild? It did, for you, specifically, recently, and dramatically. You fell in love, you found somebody worth killing for, and now you want to throw that all away out of some misguided sense of protection or guilt or whatever the fuck it is? That's the easy way out. I know right now you feel like your world's ending, but here's the sad fucking truth, Griffin: world's ended.

"World ended a thousand times over. It ended, but then it kept going. It keeps ending and it keeps going. People keep hoping it's going to end in a way that wraps everything up with the neat finality of a cremation. I'm sure world war one seemed like the end of the world. World war two must have seemed like the end of the world. My dad said world war three seemed like the end of the world. And sure, we lost a lot of people each time, but also, each time, everybody who was left had to deal with the fact that they kept waking up and the sun kept rising and for everything we've lost, we're still fucking here. Survivor's guilt hits different when it's something you just barely survived and you saw somebody else die or killed them or whatever the fuck, but you were already a survivor to even be alive, Griffin. You just didn't know to feel guilty yet. At least not about that."

They drove in silence through the rain for a little while.

Brandon did not turn on the radio.

"Radioactive" by Imagine Dragons did not play.

Griffin eventually said, "Yeah. You're right. I just gotta toss this bag and put it all behind me. Pay the debt and they'll leave me alone."

"Yeah. You need to borrow some money? We're definitely getting paid plenty this month, I can advance you easy if it'll keep you from getting killed."

"No. I have enough money to cover it now. I really was going to pay. He just kept threatening."

"I know, kid. Now come on. This next station is the last stop for trap dragging, and furthest downstream, so there might be some real awful shit accumulated. Here we go. The Bear's Head guys are pulling over."

The organic-material-compression truck slowed in front of the hatch that led down the stairs to what had formerly been the last station before the train went under the river, where the water was frothing from a mix of whitewater velocity and regenerative heating froth, gathering foamy brown-pink clouds around the cage traps at the bottom of each chain. The traps were tethered to support columns all down the platform, and Brandon and Griffin made their way from upstream to downstream as they started dragging the traps.

The first came up as a solid cube of congealed rat material, all fur and tails and claws and teeth and eyes, really every feature you could find on the surface of a rat, assigned at unsettlingly varied intervals across the surface of the cube, as if that trap had caught the most material, held onto it early, and only grown more compressed as the storm kept pushing new things in. One of the BHAPAS crew yelled something through his helmet about it being an excellent specimen once they had visually inspected it and seen no proof of human flesh, which struck Griffin as a low bar for a specimen. Then the BHAPAS crew all turned to take it away, and the men of Pearl Plumbing discretely dumped out the final bag, which contained the loose slop that formerly inhabited John Smith's abdominal cavity. Brandon threw the final plastic bag into the filthy water, and it fell in it and was among it and became it and was gone.

The next trap contained a high density of congealed rat flesh but was marred by the obvious presence of two human hands melted to the sides. The BHAPAS crew groaned and marked it for disposal as they dragged it away. A similar thing happened with the next few traps. Each had plenty of perfectly good, recyclable rat flesh, marred by the presence of an obvious chunk of a human body adhered to it. Each time, Griffin's heart rate spiked, Brandon gave him a look of calm confidence to help Griffin attempt to feel the same, and the BHAPAS crew turned out to be remarkably nonchalant about it besides acting disappointed that the sample was set for disposal. When the lumbo-pelvic-hip area came up in the third cage, he was sure somebody would comment on it, but they were just so *used to it* that the idea of somebody in their vicinity having just fucked up an attempt at completely clandestine body disposal was nowhere near their minds.

When the final cage came up with the head in it, Griffin wasn't even surprised until it looked at him. They'd tossed the head first, simply wanting to be rid of it the most, as it felt the most human. Sure, every other part of 'John Smith' was still parts of a human body, but they didn't hold all of what had used to be his hopes and dreams and fears and those grey-blue eyes, just like Griffin's, that now stared back at him from atop a mass of rat flesh with a look that might have been accusatory or might have just been nothing but what Griffin was making himself perceive.

As they settled the cage on the platform, one of the BHAPAS crew said, "Oh, wow! This one looks just like me! I mean, marked for disposal, obviously, and please kill it when I'm done, but let me get a selfie first." The BHAPAS guy pulled off his helmet and mask and revealed a face that was almost identical to Griffin's. He took a knee in front of the disembodied, rat-adhered head, which was glancing around and gnawing mindlessly, held up his phone with the front-facing camera on, held up two fingers in a peace sign, smiled, and took a photo. "Perfect! I mean, gross, but what a coincidence, right? Wild. Should I post this? I shouldn't post this." He turned to Griffin as he stood up and pocketed his phone. "Anyway, you should kill it now."

In response, Griffin pulled off his full-face respirator. He nearly choked at the smell, but by the time he got his stomach fully under control, the BHAPAS guy was staring at him with a look of amazement. Griffin wasn't sure what he expected by this move, revealing himself to his doppelgänger, but he had felt oddly compelled to do it.

The BHAPAS guy said, "People ever tell you you just have one of those faces?"

Griffin stared back, slightly slack-jawed, and eventually said, "Sometimes."

The guy pulled his phone back out of his pocket and turned the camera back on. "I'm Danny. Group selfie?"

Griffin looked at Brandon, who looked like he was trying to figure out if he'd accidentally ingested any powerful hallucinogens and forgotten about it, then back at the guy, and said, "Yeah. Yeah, sure, fuck it."

So Griffin and Danny both knelt down, threw up a pair of peace signs, smiled, took a photo in front of the disembodied head of the man Griffin had recently killed, and shook hands. Then Griffin turned, chopped the head open with the cleaver until it stopped moving, and Danny yelled that it was clear for disposal. Griffin asked if he could get Danny's number so he could get a copy of the photo, and then they put the masks back on.

"So the ones with human remains are marked for disposal?" asked Griffin.

"Huh? Oh, no, we just cut around that. I think with sewer meat it's just a matter of contamination potential. If it has too many orifices on the surface then you have no idea how much sewage got inside. We're just looking for clean biomass. Orifices mean cavities, cavities mean sewage, sewage means overloaded filters and ruined batches."

Griffin nodded. "Oh. Got it. Horrible."

Griffin and Brandon walked back up to the surface with the BHAPAS team, and Griffin asked if he could just take a peek in their truck to see what it looked like at the end of a day of trap collections. Danny said sure, and let Griffin help him load up the horrific flesh cube into the back of the truck. The truck was full of their haul of biomass, and Danny commented that they'd got enough pieces that they could probably assemble a whole new guy out of the parts, Frankenstein style, and laughed. Then Danny hopped down and out, and Griffin followed. They shook hands, and the BHAPAS team got moving. Griffin got back in the van with Brandon and the men of Pearl Plumbing were in motion again.

As they drove the van through the rain, there was a long silence until Brandon said, "You do have one of those faces."

# 23

The rice cooker sang its little song just as Griffin got home. The sky was full dark and the rain had settled into a steady patter, calmed down from its earlier roars. Jun sat at the kitchen table, staring into space, his mind somewhere else until Griffin said, "Hey, love."

"Oh. Hi."

"You okay, handsome?"

"No. You?"

"Of course not. Is Mr. President okay?"

"I'm not sure how to tell. I haven't been home long. We'll see how he reacts when we crack a can open."

"Yeah. How was work?"

"Fine. Work was fine. Uh, how did your day go? Is everything taken care of?"

"Well, we disposed of all the body parts."

"Great. That's great, honey."

"Then they all turned up downstream reconstituted in bio-mass traps, and one of the BHAPAS guys took a selfie with the head, which was kind of reanimated, and the guy looked almost exactly like me, sort of in the way that the guy I was disposing of did, and then we all took a selfie with it before I killed it again."

Jun stared at Griffin for a long time. Then, "Are you fucking kidding me?"

"No."

"We're so fucked, honey."

"No, I don't think so. The guy who looks like me, the alive one, Danny, seemed completely unphased by it. I don't know what the BHAPAS guys find on normal days, now that I think about it. I didn't even get the impression they were going to alert the cops, necessarily. He said he wasn't going to post it because it was too gross, and that was the end of it."

"Seriously?"

"Seriously. And now I have eyewitnesses of me pulling it out of the water, finding it like that, and putting my knife in its head to kill it then and there. So there would be no reason for suspicion even if they did somehow match my knife to the wound."

"Okay. That's... that's so fucked, honey. Well, there's one piece of evidence I forgot to tell you about when I got home because I was just so drained and needed to pass out."

Jun pulled out the envelope and put it on the table, open towards Griffin, so he could see the density of money inside. "I took this from the car. Of all the things missing, I don't know that anybody alive is going to look for this specifically, but, uh, we have a little extra cash now, so groceries won't be an issue for a while, unless you have other ideas, but I don't know what to do with it. I mean, I have ideas. I'm not sure what I was thinking when I took it, except that I'd rather have more money."

"Yeah. Me too. We'll just put it towards small things for a while and I can use the balance to pay off the debt even easier. I can just say I paid it because he called me earlier. I don't know. That's besides the- listen. I know you said you're not mad at me for what I did and I don't need to say sorry. I'm still sorry. There's a lifetime of bullshit that led up to yesterday. You are the most important thing in the world to me and you're— you're not okay. I can tell. I saw it the moment I saw you. Why would you be? I asked if you were okay because I know asking is an expression of care in and of itself, I didn't ask to get an answer. I just want you to be okay."

"Griffin, don't—"

"I'm not saying that like I want to pressure you to be okay for me. By all means, lose your shit. Be not okay. If you need to cry more, I'll be here to hold you. If you need to... what do you need? Have you eaten? The rice cooker's ready. Is there anything else ready?"

"No. No, I... I would normally be cooking, I know, but when I got home all I could feel was how this place has been violated. And how... when that guy got here, I thought he was you. He looked so much like you. I knew you were coming home and I looked through the peephole and I thought maybe you'd just lost your key in the accident so I let him in and— and he— he. You know what he did. I don't know how long I sat there with him just breathing behind me. I don't know. It couldn't have been more than ten or fifteen minutes but it was an eternity. And now I'm— honestly I'm so hungry. And I need to piss so bad but I can't bring myself to go into the bathroom. I was being brave yesterday but at work I couldn't stop seeing his dead eyes, the way he looked lying there in the tub. And I just. I tried to stop thinking about it all so I realize I've now been sitting here in exactly the place he made me sit, holding still, not eating, not pissing, just getting increasingly uncomfortable in every way. I'm so hungry."

Griffin looked around the room. There was the pool of light from the kitchen, but beyond that the apartment fell into darkness. Jun hadn't even made it to the other areas of the one-bedroom apartment to turn the lights on. Griffin sat down and hugged Jun from the side. "I love you. If there's any ingredients I'm gonna cook for you."

Jun laughed a little, despite it all. "Cook? You?"

"I know all your darkest secrets, honey, including your most shameful secret of all: the curry is exactly the recipe on the back of the box."

Jun smiled, just a little, then turned to kiss Griffin softly on the forehead. He sighed and said, "I know this is silly, but will you come with me while I pee?"

"That's not silly at all. Come with me."

Griffin took Jun across the living room and around the corner to the bathroom, where he noticed that Jun was holding onto him tight and keeping his eyes closed as he navigated to the toilet, undid his pants, and sat down. Jun hugged Griffin around the waist, keeping his face pointed away from the tub, and Griffin ran his fingers through Jun's hair to comfort him as he cried softly while urinating. Griffin realized that, despite what he'd managed to convince himself was normal, Griffin was a man dramatically more encased in emotional scar tissue than the average person. Even with Griffin and the others in his former line of work as outliers, the average person still had experience with less than one amputations. The average person may have been ground down a great deal by the ambient agonies of the world, but they hadn't been acclimated to the extremes of pain. Jun had been strong for Griffin the day before, but he hadn't been conditioned to the horrors like Griffin had, and he needed to be protected. The trickle of urine slowed to silence after a minute of Jun tenderly clinging to Griffin's torso, and Griffin bent down to kiss the tears from his cheeks and softly ask, "You done?"

"Yeah. Yeah. I'm sorry."

"Why are *you* saying sorry?"

Jun grinned a little through the tears. "Good point."

"Come with me. Lie down on the couch. I'll play some old movie and cook you dinner. We got ingredients?"

"Yeah. Thank you, my love."

Griffin helped Jun stand, pulled his pants back up, and as he did so he felt how little energy was left in his fiancé, who was leaning on him for balance. Like he had done in his cozy cottage memory of dancing to "Sweet Agnes" by Masayoshi Takanaka, Griffin bent lower, let Jun fall over his shoulder, and fireman-carried his exhausted lover to the couch, where Griffin laid him back down as gently as possible. He turned on the tv to the public domain movie channel, then knelt down to look under furniture while making gentle psst psst psst sounds until a furry orange sphere gingerly extricated itself from beneath the couch. Griffin beckoned the cat over and into his arms, whispered *take care of him while I cook,* then set Mr. President down upon Jun's chest, kissed each of them on the head, and headed to the kitchen while some ancient movie played on the tv.

Griffin hadn't really cooked for most of a year, and hadn't been good at cooking to begin with, but in that first night of relieving shelter in this apartment, Jun had said that the recipe that tasted better than anything Griffin had ever cooked was exactly the recipe that was on the back of the box of Japanese curry mix. Griffin rummaged through the cupboard for the box, found it, read the recipe, and turned around to put it down on the table before he used it, where he was greeted with an envelope thick with cash that had to be brushed aside before he could continue. He tried to put the cash out of his head. All that mattered was cooking for the man he loved.

The recipe on the box turned out to be so simple it was funny. Cloned beef, carrots, potatoes, and onions, then add the curry mix and serve with rice. Almost entirely comprised of the kinds of hearty root vegetables that made up most of their humble pantry. Griffin brought water to a boil and got to chopping up the vegetables in ways that seemed similar in scale to what Jun made every week, albeit with knife skills that had developed through a brutally non-culinary tradition. Griffin decided to define the resulting oddly shaped hunks of carrot and potato and onion as "rustic" and not worry too much about the aesthetics of the individual components of something that would end up being engulfed in thick brown sauce as their delivery mechanism. Soon his fork easily entered each potato and carrot and the onions softened away to a suggestion, and he popped open the long-delayed rice cooker to finally serve dinner.

He first opened a can of Mr. President's wet food to distract the beast from Jun's incoming meal, and the immediate reaction of the creature was to jump off Jun's chest with piston force, jolting Jun back into the present tense with indifferent percussion. Jun began to sit up on the couch as Griffin brought over the bowl of their traditional weekly curry and put it on the coffee table in front of his love. Jun took the steaming bowl, and as he waited for it to come down to an edible temperature, asked, "Have you been following this movie at all?"

"No. What's going on?"

"Some maniac runs a candy factory and, in search of some heir to take over his empire, I guess, he puts a bunch of children through this insane gauntlet. It's not as explicit about it as anything these days would be, but I'm pretty sure he keeps killing the children who fail his tests in some psychopathic filtering process to find one child who will be pure enough to deserve his empire. It's... oddly brutal, but they frame it like it's a heartwarming comedy. There's orange little people who sing after every execution. It's so fucking weird it's distracting me, so that's good."

Jun took a steaming spoonful of the curry, from which an interestingly trapezoidal chunk of potato stood tall. He raised it to Griffin in a silent cheers, blew on it, and put it in his mouth. He started to chew, then started to laugh, then started to cry, then combined all three. "Oh, honey," he said, tears streaming down his face, his words distorted around the food, "I don't know how you fucked this up this bad. This is... you have to try this."

"It's exactly the recipe on the back of the box!"

"I don't know if it is, honey. Try it." Jun held up another spoonful of creatively geometric potato prism and extended it to Griffin, who bent down to eat it. It occurred to Griffin at that moment that he should probably taste things before serving them. Well, the flavor itself was fine— it's hard to fuck up a pre-mixed block of spiced roux, flavorwise— but the inside of the potato, which had been cut far too large, was raw. Hot, but raw. Not to mention that the spice block clearly hadn't been given the time to fully dissolve, and as he got an overthick blob of hyper-concentrated spice, he too started to laugh.

"Oh, fuck. I'm so sorry, my love. This is the worst thing I've done all week. Will you help me dispose of the evidence?"

Jun laughed and cried to the point that he started coughing, then had to gasp his breath back as he intentionally gathered his composure. "Oh, God, I needed that. No, no, I think we can bring this one back to life." He took the bowl, stood, and kissed Griffin on the cheek. "Come on." They went over to the pot that contained the remainder of the ostensible curry, where Jun scraped his bowl back in. "I guess maybe it's not exactly the recipe on the box." He checked the level of water in the electric kettle, which stood at just two cups, and clicked it on. "That boils water faster than the stove, so I usually boil all the water in there while I sauté the onions first. I cut them thin so they just sort of vanish into the texture of the sauce at the end. Did you add the onions last?"

Griffin shrugged and stammered, "I, fuckin, yeah, I, I, I just wanted to—"

"Honey, don't worry. I've been cooking this since I was a teenager and I haven't thought about it this much in a while. Do you want to know the way I do it?"

"I do, yeah. I love your curry. It feels like home."

"Then I want you to know how to make it the way that feels like home. This batch isn't gonna quite get there, but it just needs more time and tenderness to get good. I mean that literally." The kettle clicked, and Jun poured the water in, turned the stove on low, and stirred it up again. "So you sauté the onions on low til they're tender. Usually I cut the onions first, put them in on low, and let them get up to speed while I cut up the carrots and potatoes and beef. I do the beef first so I can brown it in the pan while there's just the onions and oil in there. I try to get everything to pretty uniform cube-ish shapes, though I go a little smaller on carrots because they're a lot sturdier. After the beef is browned— I also just remembered that I usually dry brine the meat very first thing, usually even the day before, but I forgot to do that this week because... because. Then I toss in the potatoes and carrots, deglaze the pan with the first splash of boiled water from the kettle, and once that's clear, I dump in the rest of the water and get it all up to a simmer before I put in the curry roux. And I also cut up the roux so it dissolves faster and more evenly. But right now, I'm just gonna let this get up to a gentle simmer, stir it up every once in a while, and then we just wait for it to soften everything and reduce."

"Reduce?"

"Honey, you should watch me do this more often. Reducing is when the water steams off so it concentrates all the flavor and literally reduces in volume. See, right now, since I added more water and stirred it up, it looks like the chocolate river did."

"Chocolate river?"

"Right, you weren't watching that part. In the movie on TV where those little orange guys are singing right now, there's an earlier scene where a fat child falls into a river of chocolate and gets sucked back up an extraction tube into the fudge room."

Griffin looked at the TV. "What the fuck?"

"And that chocolate river is similar to the current thickness of this curry. But the curry should be thicker than that."

Griffin looked at the pot of thinned-out curry swirling and was reminded of the rushing river of sewage he'd pulled John Smith's head from.

"Sorry, all the workers in this nightmare factory look the same, and a child was sucked out of a river of chocolate back up a tube into the depths of the facility?"

"To the fudge room."

Griffin looked at the thick envelope of cash on the table. "Jun, I have an idea of what to do with the money."

"What?"

While the pot on the stove quietly bubbled, Griffin explained some suspicions he'd been having. He showed Jun the photo of himself with Danny Wilson and the head of 'John Smith,' talked about the revelations about the purpose of his old work that Brandon had helped him realize, and then went into the other reasons he had been theorizing about regarding the demand for ritualized work that always resulted in large samples of biomass-and-DNA-laden regenerative gels at the end of the day. Griffin dove into a few other things on top of that. The talk went on for a long time, and their hunger was forgotten as these unspoken nightmares came to the surface. The carrots and potatoes were beyond soft, the cubes of beef falling-apart tender, and the roux fully integrated and flavor saturated everything within it.

When Griffin finished talking, Jun sat for a minute, just staring into space, still sitting in the same spot where he'd recently had a gun to his head, the same spot he'd been stuck in when Griffin first came home, but the dead-eyed dread had been replaced with fury. He stood, his eyes wide under a furrowed brow, and whispered, "Make them pay."

"I will, my love. But first, I have to call Clara."

# 24

Schvantlfeim sat at a wide, solid desk in his own office, a monolithic thing that seemed proportional to his stunningly broad shoulders. His horseshoe-bald head had been trimmed to a level of neatness that indicated that his baldness was a choice, that he was doing it on purpose, and that he was proud of it. His greying temples marked the transition zone down to his beard, where the splendor of his hair reached its true potential. His mustache was thick and walrusy without going too far over the lip line, and the beard itself had the deep uniform lustre of a black bear's fur. He wore small round golden glasses with wire arms slightly too narrow for his head, which only served to emphasize his hugeness. His wrists seemed as wide around as loaves of bread, which Griffin noticed as he shook the man's hand and in turn was nearly lifted straight up off the ground on the upswing.

"Griffin, my boy! My good man! You do not know how much your call has changed my life. When last I saw you, I was still bemoaning life as dog killer, living in storage unit, unsure what to do. You and your call led me to this life, this wonderful life of sales! Is so easy! I make so much money thanks to you and your call. I understand you have built respectable life of physical work. This, I respect. I am not as young as I once was, and grow tired more easily from such work. I see your shoulders as well have grown to a more respectable width. You have given me the gift of sales work, and I see you have found the joy of using your body when it is still young and powerful. You are good man, Griffin, good man. Tell me what I can do for you today."

"Hello, Schvantlfeim," said Griffin.

Clara stood off to the side, her tight curls thrown forward over her shoulder, wearing a wide smile on her face to complement her pantsuit. Griffin realized he too was smiling wide, solely from the energy Schvantlfeim brought to the room, and considered that this level of infectious joy was likely the cause of his apparent success as a salesman and progress within the company, even if it was absolutely baffling that a giant man who talked about killing dogs with such nostalgia was somehow so charming and apparently harmless.

"He's genuinely always like this," said Clara. "He credits you as part of his success whenever the subject comes up."

"I'm honored," said Griffin. "But I do want to get to why I'm here."

"Please do," said Schvantlfeim.

"So you know my job now involves dredging weird growths out of the sewer and cutting them up. Extremely gross stuff. Sometimes I find stuff in the growths. Usually nothing good, usually just trash. But during the storm the other day, I was dragging these biomass traps down in the sewers when I found a sealed plastic bag of cash sticking out of one of them. Absolutely grossest way to get a sudden windfall. Now, don't worry, I'm not trying to launder this or anything, I'll tell the IRS I got it, but it's pretty difficult to spend cash in this volume unless you want to get into drug dealing. I don't. But I know you're already selling pharmaceutical grade stuff in bulk, and I want to reinvest this into the business. I'm just wondering if there's any way that you two can, as friends of mine, help me put this cash towards a large volume of DeGrowth and an additional several tubs of regenerative coolant gel. We're already in a pretty good place in terms of positioning ourselves as the premiere teratomalith removal specialists in the city, but thanks to that we're going through DeGrowth at a stunning rate. And also I need the regen gel for personal use."

Clara said, "Personal use?"

Griffin held up his metallic left arm, at which both Clara and Schvantlfeim gasped slightly. Griffin said, "I don't want to get into the details, but this needs regular maintenance to sustain the flesh interface, and the DeGrowth can be hazardous in that regard. Don't ask me how I know. Easiest way to keep it solid is with a fresh dunk in the gel."

"Griffin, good man, I will help you with this challenge of currency. I, Schvantlfeim, am now what is called rolling in it, due to being good at sales, and for coming up with idea of selling bulk to business instead of low volume to consumer. Give of me the currency and I will log the order in our system."

"Thanks, Schvantlfeim."

Clara said, "How much do you need, exactly?"

"I'd say one barrel of DeGrowth and then, uh, as many tubs of regen gel as that amount of cash will cover. And can you ship it to yourself, Schvantlfeim? I'll come pick it up in the work van and get it to storage, but I don't think I'll be able to receive these at my apartment."

Clara and Griffin locked eyes while Schvantlfeim typed in the order information. Clara squinted at him and cocked her head a little. "Personal use, huh?"

"Personal use," said Griffin.

They hashed out the details of the transaction, all shook hands, and then he turned to leave. At the door, he turned to Clara and said, "Hey, can I actually talk to you on the way out?"

"Sure, Griff. What's up? I'll walk with you." They stepped out into the main floor of the call center, which had its usual cacophonous blend of sales chatter and weeping.

"This is actually pretty hard for me to talk about, Clara. I've been thinking about it a lot, and I haven't really told anybody about it."

"I'm listening, Griff." They passed a man smashing his headset into his console with animalistic fury.

"It's about something that happened the other day, during the worst of the storms. The worst flood day."

"What happened?"

"It's about what happened right around when I lost my hand. Promise you won't tell anyone?"

"What are you about to say, Griffin?"

"I ended up in a water treatment plant in the large debris filtration area where a teratomalith had formed on the filters. It was grown mostly from a mass of tampons and coagulated lard, so it was formed of uterine tissue and pig flesh. I ended up basically doing like fifty axe abortions on pigs coming from human wombs and I'm worried if I ever tell that story it's going to seem weirdly misogynistic in its symbolism."

"Jesus fucking Christ, Griffin."

"Is it bad?"

"Mainly it's just obscenely gross and I don't think anybody's going to want to hear that story. I don't think anybody can fault you for doing your job dealing with whatever ends up in the sewage systems. More importantly, why in the world are you asking me?"

"I just wanted a woman's opinion."

"Wait, am I your best female friend?"

Griffin's mouth opened and no words came out.

Clara sighed. "That's really the problem you should be worried about, Griffin. I mean, I like hanging out with you when I do, but I'm your former boss from a job you had for like a week, and mainly we just see each other at karaoke every week or two."

"I don't know many people. I don't know how to know people."

"I could've sworn you were good friends with Poppy."

"That was probably Chandler you were thinking of."

"Oh, yeah. You guys look almost exactly alike. It throws me off."

"I know. I have one of those faces."

"It's a good face. Hey, Griff, we should hang out more. We could grab a drink sometime, or how about Bell and I come over for dinner at your guys' place sometime soon?"

"You know, I'd love that, but I've been working too much to play host anytime soon. How about dinner at your place?"

"Sure. Bell makes an amazing cricken tinga."

"Can't wait."

When the apartment building that had once housed Griffin Batt, Wesley Sweat, and two Mohammeds suddenly burst with teratomaliths all throughout its plumbing mid-way through its renovation, nobody at Clearwater Property Management suspected vandalism. It had happened before in the building, and the idea of somebody sneaking into the sewers nearby to pump regenerative coolant gel back up through the pipes did not, for a second, cross anybody's mind as an option of what the cause might have been. That would be an insane waste of expensive medical supplies, not to mention expertise in navigating the sewers. A more reasonable use of money, by far, was to call up Pearl Plumbing, the premiere teratomalith removal specialists in the city, to come and see what could be done to salvage the place.

Unfortunately, the good men of Pearl Plumbing, who the Clearwater representative only consciously processed as Young White Guy and Middle Aged Black Guy, said that it was irreparable without completely gutting the building to the bones and starting all over again. The pipes were packed with pulsing flesh from top to bottom, and after swinging an axe into the second floor bathtub to open up a cystic core containing a wad of misshapen hands, which killed the entire thing, there was nothing more they could do but call in BHAPAS to help with extraction. The Young White Guy seemed to smile way too wide when delivering this news, which the representative took as the usual smirk that these types would give when they didn't even actually have to do any work and still knew they were going to get paid. These fucking goons didn't even do anything to help and still demanded to get paid.

What fucking parasites, thought the representative from the property management and real estate investing company.

When the offices of Clearwater Property Management burst with teratomaliths, tearing open every pipe and causing the entire place to flood with bloody chunks of cancerous flesh floating in sewage, well, that sure was a hell of a freak accident. When Pearl Plumbing and BHAPAS showed up to clear it out, it seemed pretty clear to the representatives of the property management and real estate investing company that Pearl Plumbing and BHAPAS were some kind of brother-owned businesses giving each other referrals and kickbacks, especially when, at one point, the young white guy from Pearl Plumbing started taking things from the back of the BHAPAS truck and nobody stopped him.

On a rainless night soon after that, certain of a few things he hadn't been before, Griffin Batt ventured into the sewers alone through one of the abandoned station entrances, his pack fully loaded, his batteries charged, his map in hand. He was sure he would be coming back out of the tunnels, his pack much lighter than when he went in. He had work to do.

## 25

"**T**HANK GOD YOU'RE HERE!"

Brandon and Griffin rolled up to the front of Faust Medical Solutions headquarters in the van, clearly labeled with the company name on the side, so the pale man in the grey suit knew exactly which vehicle to run towards, through the pouring rain, while screaming and waving his arms. The men of Pearl Plumbing were already masked up, having been told the details such as *"It's so bad"* and *"Oh my God it's so bad"* and *"get here as fast as you can"* that let them know to show up as prepared as possible. The pale man waved them around to the side entrance, where they unloaded their weapons and barrels of DeGrowth as another suited man opened the door for them to the Fertility section of the facility.

The pale man in the dark grey suit, which had probably been medium grey before he ran into the rain, squeaked forward through the brightly lit, sterile hallways of the facility. Griffin and Brandon followed behind him, axe and cleaver on Griffin's belt, glaive and machete over Brandon's back, Brandon pushing a hand truck with a barrel of DeGrowth and Griffin pushing a wheelbarrow loaded with shovels and contractor bags. Griffin wore a backpack, stuffed to capacity, which yet moved with pillowy lightness high on his spine.

The pale man babbled as he walked. "Something must have gone wrong with the bioreactor. We usually put the used regenerative coolant gel through a full digestion cycle to process all latent reactions as harmlessly as possible before we break it down. We follow *proper* disposal procedures around here, so I'm not sure what happened."

Griffin nodded. "If it's as bad as you say, we're probably going to need to call in backup for extraction of the material. We personally don't have the kind of carrying capacity to do a full removal at this scale, but we have partners who do. We'll make the call when we see the specimen so we can let them know how many trucks we'll need."

The pale man turned, nearly slipping on the water coming off of himself onto the linoleum, as he said, "Can't you liquefy and pump it with the DeGrowth?"

Brandon shook his head. "DeGrowth is good for loosening stubborn attachment points and really solid chunks, but it's still too thick to pump. With the amount of surface area you said this covers, we'll need the DeGrowth to get whatever residue is left loosening off the floor and walls, once we cut and carry the majority of the bulk of it."

"Okay. Whatever you say. You're the professionals. Here we are. Brace yourselves." The pale man approached a pair of double doors and threw them open, revealing a vision of hell.

It wasn't quite the hell Griffin had expected. The bioreactor had probably once looked like a smaller version of the digesters at the water treatment plant, but now it looked like the remains of a water balloon frozen in time at the moment it popped, half-peeled away, the break point like the weak spot in the skin where a cyst decides to burst open when you squeeze it hard without first cutting a designated escape route. The burst had clearly been that same kind of unpredictable high-pressure pop, as an arc of flesh started growing up on a portion of the ceiling in a kind of splatter pattern that continued on to the wall and all the way down, before flooding the entire floor. The ground was covered in a mountain of flesh where undifferentiated and partially-digested human organic matter had been reactivated into uncontrolled growth, looking as if a colossal mound of melting candle wax were made out of cancer. The entire thing twitched and throbbed under the fluorescent light, which, fittingly for the tone, was flickering, as several of the initial jets of the high pressure burst appeared to have knocked out some of the overhead light panels. Near the bioreactor, the flesh was at twice Griffin's height, and where it had piled up like snow against the door they stood in front of, it was up to his waist.

The men of Pearl Plumbing regarded this for a moment, then Griffin turned to the pale man and said, "Yeah, let me make that call."

The pale man nodded. Griffin took out his phone, tapped a recent text conversation, made a call to the person it was with, and waited for a moment. He spoke. "Yeah, Danny? It's Griffin with Pearl Plumbing. We're at the headquarters of Faust Medical Solutions. Yeah. Teratomalith. There's a big one. The motherlode. Noncontaminated, clean origin environment as far as I can tell. Yeah. Side entrance, got a guy who will meet you there." Griffin looked at the pale man as he said this, and nodded his head towards the door, and the pale man ran back the way he'd come, where he immediately slipped and fell on his ass before getting up and continuing to run again. Griffin stifled a laugh and continued on the phone. "Yeah. Yeah. Bring fucking everybody. Get the trucks. See you soon."

Brandon propped the door open with his barrel of DeGrowth and put his little radio on it. He unsheathed the glaive, turned on the radio, and proceeded to stretch his legs and limber up while the voice crackled through the speaker, the facility around them distorting the signal, with the static fuzz on the voice adding nicely to the nightmarish atmosphere of the scene.

*—other news, the hostage situation with* The Contestant! *is entering its eighteenth hour, as The Contestant has held the rest of the cast of* Get Bit The Most By Venomous Bugs For A House *at gunpoint as he claims that he has been the same guy for every season and they just keep telling people his name is different and nobody notices for some reason and they won't let him go home. But we're not a news station, we're WROT. Keepin' it as splashy and trashy as floodwaters, we here at WROT don't need to hold you hostage to keep you hooked on our line, but don't be a sinker!*

*Deaths from people trying to cross rushing water in their cars are surging, so if you're thinking of trying to see if your car can float, don't! Stay safe, stay dry, and stay tuned in to the best pre-war, pre-wipe music from the good old days. Our bunker's stocked with enough beans that I can make sure the vinyl plays all through the final days. What have we WROT? How about another half hour of ad-free music? Yeah, you got it. Only here on WROT.*

"Radioactive" by Imagine Dragons started playing.

Halfway across town, Danny Wilson of the Bear's Head Alternative Protein Acquisition Squad relayed the news to his team. They geared up. At rest, on standby, the team was always ready to go at a moment's notice— they had their waterproof pants tucked into their high boots as a matter of course. It was just a matter of getting the protective tops on, strapping on the signature vest emblazoned with BHAPAS in huge letters across the back, and popping on the filter masks and helmets. His gear was still gross from the other day, but his backup gear was missing and the replacements hadn't come yet. The wonders of corporate bureaucracy and its many efficiencies never ceased to amaze him. No matter. The places they went were always filthy enough to begin with that people hardly ever noticed the smell, and who were they to complain if they did notice it? What, did they prefer the giant rats? Fuck 'em. From what Griffin said, this was going to be the kind of job where nobody would give him a second look if he walked in already filthy and reeking.

Still, after this one he would be throwing his gear in the station washing machine immediately. It was getting to be a bit much.

Danny Wilson drew the full-face mask and respirator down over his blue-grey eyes and handsome face and joined his team in the deployment van. There was work to do. There was protein to harvest.

The men of Pearl Plumbing were doing their fucking jobs.

The BHAPAS team hadn't shown up to aid in disposal yet, but that was fine. They were excising cubes of flesh from the mass with the practiced efficiency they'd honed on their best days. The irregular growths sometimes came out in clean cubes, and sometimes burst halfway with hidden blood vessels. The hard part was piling up the flesh in reasonable spots for extraction once they'd cut it free. Brandon was cutting through the closest exposed layer in a grid pattern, horizontal then vertical to the depth of the blade of the glaive, so then a subsequent cut at the back would free a cube of flesh for Griffin to add into the contractor bag currently occupying the wheelbarrow, which he would wheel off to a side hallway and plop against the wall in low piles, trying to keep walkways clear.

Danny Wilson had forgotten about the side entrance where the pale man was waiting to let them in when he had been re-laying the information to his team, which is what led to a group of foul-smelling men in black tactical gear barging through the front doors of the Faust Medical Solutions complex, brandishing machetes and screaming, ***"WHERE'S THE FUCKING PRO-TEIN?"***

The initial hubbub in the main lobby was quickly defused, but it wasn't made much more productive. The BHAPAS team smelled like sewage and decomp, which they seemed to have grown oblivious to, but it was obvious to every worker they passed, who had to stifle gags. The BHAPAS crew were told that the teratomalith crisis was in another part of the building, which the receptionist gestured towards as she said it, and they started running into the bowels of the complex before she could give clear instructions or recommend they pull the material receiving truck around to the side entrance which was much closer to the problem. Soon there were men in BHAPAS gear storming the halls blindly, making wrong turns, until eventually one found the crisis and the rest swarmed to him like ants that had located a fallen pastry. They still hadn't found the side entrance they were supposed to use, though, so when they located Brandon and Griffin and the stacks of contractor bags, they ran back through the facility they way they'd came.

Unfortunately, by the time they did this, the man in the truck had been instructed to pull around to the side entrance for receiving organic material, so a group of BHAPAS men arrived in the lobby with contractor bags in each hand to find that the truck was not there waiting for them. When told it had moved, they did not stop to think that maybe they should ask to move it back out front for the first unloading and then move it to the side entrance for the subsequent work. No, instead they immediately turned around and started running back into the facility again, but there was enough accumulated rainwater on the floor for them that in the process of this reversal of momentum, one slipped and fell into the bag another was holding, dragging that man down with it and tearing the bag open, resulting in a chain reaction of men falling onto and tearing bags that contained cubes of flesh and general gore slop.

This triggered a resultant "vomit wave" throughout the facility that truly plunged things into chaos for anyone who was walking through the corridors.

The radio was playing "Disco Inferno" by The Trammps at around the time all this happened, and Griffin had been thinking about how he'd read some post somewhere that that title roughly translated to *"I learn through suffering"* if you read it as a Latin phrase. But amidst the storm and the facility above and around them, the radio fuzzed out long enough for Griffin and Brandon to make out the screams in the distance, which caused them to look at each other in alarm.

Griffin said, "I'm going to go check that out. See if the BHA-PAS team needs any help."

Brandon just gave a thumbs-up and kept cutting into the mass of flesh. They were deep into it now.

Griffin had learned that, as long as you weren't dripping enough blood for it to be a major concern to the custodial staff, or if there was already a much more concerning amount and source of blood somewhere else, people would stay out of your way if you happened to be strolling through a building holding an axe and soaked with blood, your face fully obscured under a respirator, protective glasses and a cap pulled low. He wasn't sure about the precise psychological explanation for it, but something about the look of a man in blood-spattered coveralls wielding a large axe made people just get out of the way and try not to draw any attention.

Especially, as he was seeing right now, if those people were running screaming down the hallways, pausing only to vomit as they did. In that case, people would just keep on running and screaming.

Soon Griffin found himself at one of the entrances to the lobby, looking upon a mess of men in tactical gear who were all soaked head-to-toe in blood and gore, screaming and slipping as they struggled to stand up amidst the enormous mess of rainwater and bodily fluids on the floor.

*God, this is going even better than I hoped*, thought Griffin.

He stepped over a BHAPAS goon who was retching into his helmet, and then Griffin vanished down familiar corridors from a previous life.

# 26

Griffin walked the way he had many times before. He left a trail of bloody footprints through the windowless corridors and made his way past the supply station, where of all people was Dave, the attendant, who was still here, and seemed to be taking better care of himself. He'd gotten a haircut, his shirt fit better, and his skin was smooth, which was all remarkably apparent even when he responded to Griffin's habitual "Hey Dave" with a terrified scream and another contribution to the vomit wave.

Griffin found himself standing in front of the door he'd gone through hundreds of times before, the door that led to the small windowless room where he had, for reasons that were now clearly absolutely insane, subjected himself to daily amputations without anesthetic for three years. But there had been one thought that stuck with him from his final day, one thing that he hadn't stopped wanting from this job, one goal he was yet to achieve.

*Maybe I could be on the other side of the mirror one day.*

Griffin stepped through the door into the wedge-shaped room. On his right sat the same metal table he'd grown so familiar with, where there sat a handsome young man with blue-grey eyes who had a carbon steel Serbian cleaver in his raised right hand, now staring up at the bloody axe-wielding man in front of him in terror. He looked incredibly familiar, and Griffin knew he had never seen him before.

Through the respirator, Griffin growled, "This isn't your job anymore. Get the fuck out. Now. Or I'll cut it off for you." Then he held the door open and gestured towards it with the axe. The young man wordlessly put the knife down and ran out the door. As he did, Griffin closed the door behind him, and in one unhesitating motion whirled around and smashed the axe through the glass. It went straight through, shattering the rest of the pane, and in a few swipes of the axe he had cleared away enough of it to see an old man, frozen in place with fear, his pants around his ankles, his small erect penis in his left hand, peeking out from a tuft of white pubic hair. His face was a mask of horror, stuck in a silent open-mouthed rictus, not just from the obvious threat of the blood-soaked axe-wielding man now stepping through the window into the same room as him, but in the shocked shame of somebody caught masturbating to something they really shouldn't be.

That shock came through bright and clear from his blue-grey eyes.

Griffin looked around and realized there were two other windows in the room. The wedge shape of his workspace had been to accommodate other rooms and access hallways in a radial shape around this single panopticon masturbation chamber. These were clearly also two-way mirrors, and beyond them sat handsome young men with a resemblance to Griffin, and the hideous old man before him, and each was holding a cleaver in his right hand but looking at the mirror in curiosity, having heard the commotion beyond.

"Don't you fucking move," said Griffin, before smashing the axe through one mirror, then the other, and yelling, "GO HOME. YOU'RE FIRED."

The men in the rooms beyond got the message and evacuated promptly. Now he was alone with the hideous old man, who was shaking in fear. Beside him sat a small cooler, similar to the one Griffin used to store his hand in during his lunch breaks. It was packed with concerningly well-filled sperm sample canisters.

Griffin laid the flat of the axe blade on the man's shoulder. "You know, when I got here today, I thought I would find some kind of high tech facility growing clones or something. I used to think I just had one of those faces. Then I started wondering why there were so many of those faces. All this high tech medical shit. I thought you were implanting clone embryos as part of the fertility treatments. Growing them fast with the regeneratives, somehow, maybe. But it's just this, isn't it? It's just an old man jacking off into a cup all day?"

The old man croaked out, "Who are you?"

Griffin pulled his respirator and sunglasses off.

The old man's face dropped as his eyes widened in recognition. "Oh. Griffin."

"Why? Why all this shit, you fucking maniac?"

"To repopulate our ruined world. To be a new Genghis Khan. To cement the dynasty of Faust."

"What is this fucking nightmare? How did you make everyone so okay with this? This isn't a job, this is just ritualized self-mutilation. What the fuck is wrong with you? Why are you doing this?"

The old man looked him dead in the eye and said, "This is the only way I can cum."

Griffin couldn't think of anything else to say.

He loosened his grip on the axe as he pondered the disgusting, pathetic man sitting in front of him, who at that moment decided to lunge and use both arms and his full body weight to press the handle of the axe away from him, which Griffin allowed, as he used his prosthetic left hand to unzip his coveralls, grab the pistol from inside, and fire it into the old man's genitals.

Roderick Faust's penis and testicles ceased to exist in that moment, and he screamed a high piercing wail that reflected his level of pain and horror at this new development, as well as its effect on his worldview and priorities. He cried something that was probably, "Why, my son?" before Griffin fired another bullet through his left kneecap, causing the screams to become completely nonverbal, painting the room with even more blood. Another round through his right kneecap caused a level of shrieking and weeping Griffin hadn't really prepared for.

Once all the fight was out of the old man and he was experiencing an amount of pain beyond what most humans will ever approach, Griffin grabbed his withered left hand, drew it out onto the table beside him, knocking over the cooler, and he chopped off Roderick Faust's left hand in a single swift strike. The old man went silent at this, the scream so complete it had drawn all the air that was left in his lungs and his eyes bulged from his head.

Griffin cut off the old man's other hand, then slapped him. The old man's eyes were wide and searching as he grew paler, blood flowing freely from him, and Griffin grabbed his head with both hands and stared him directly in the eyes as he calmly said, "Fuck you. You deserve this. You ruined the world. You deserve this. You're going to die soon and I'm going to keep telling you how glad I am that you're in pain right now until you're dead, because you deserve this. Everything you ever worked for led to this moment of your illegitimate son killing you. You deserve this. You're a fucking piece of shit. You deserve this. My only regret is that I can't keep you alive longer to make you feel this forever. You deserve this. I wish I had the time to fucking peel you. You deserve this. You deserve this. You deserve this. You deserve this. You deserve this. You deserve this. You deserve this."

The light went out of Roderick Faust's eyes, and Griffin smashed the axe through his head. He kept hacking away at the body for a long time, swinging until he was gasping for breath and his arms ached, and when he came to he was standing in front of a thick red puddle with a few remaining discernible bits of what had once been a person.

He pushed the remains into a pile, then stepped back into his old room and grabbed the day's tub of fresh regenerative coolant gel, which he poured directly over the slop that had once been Roderick Faust, causing it to bubble and froth and coagulate into a grotesque pulsating mass. The mass had a few blue-grey eyes over its surface, presumably where pieces of the old eyes had ended up, and they all swiveled to look at Griffin.

"Hi again," said Griffin, and he slammed the axe down once more.

To the workers in the lobby at Faust Medical Solutions, it was downright comical to see yet another BHAPAS goon come stumbling out of the depths of the facility, soaked in blood, carrying yet another contractor bag, apologizing profusely for having gotten lost in there, saying he was just gonna go around outside to the other entrance anyway. Coming in so late after all the others, apologizing and lost, was the cherry on top of the slapstick gore pile that they had just finished shepherding out of the lobby. At least this one's bag hadn't ripped. The masked BHAPAS goon went out the front door with his bag, and nobody thought twice about that compared to the huge mess that preceded him.

"Took you long enough," said Brandon as Griffin returned, freshly soaked in rain for some reason.

"Yeah, well, the BHAPAS guys royally fucked up out there. I don't know if they told you quite how bad, but they royally fucked it and spilled a bunch of gore right in the lobby. Hey, I'm gonna borrow the hand truck and use the DeGrowth to get some of the residue they spilled, alright? I'll be back in a minute."

"Fuckin' amateurs. Yeah, go handle it. I'll keep cutting."

"You're the best, Brandon."

"No problem."

Griffin completed the remainder of the day with utmost professionalism. The BHAPAS crew, once wrangled, managed to load the segments of the teratomalith into their extraction trucks with something resembling competence, and it was prime high-protein biomass suitable for refinement. People would be well fed. Brandon said that, except for the hiccup the BHAPAS guys caused, it was Griffin's finest work yet, and that one of these days he would have to teach him something about how to actually do plumbing so he could take over the business one of these days. Griffin thanked him, but said that he wasn't sure he wanted to grow old in this line of work.

# 27

Jun Saito-James came home to find his fiancé dancing with the cat in the living room. Griffin held Mr. President in his arms, the confused feline tucked against his chest with the prosthetic arm as he grooved out to "Ready to Fly" by Masayoshi Takanaka, one of Jun's dad's old favorite records. The storm that had been raging all day had tired itself out and the lowering August sun was peeking beneath the remaining clouds to scatter orange light all around their humble apartment. The music was up too loud for Griffin to hear the door, but as he completed a twirl he spotted Jun and his eyes lit up.

Griffin shouted "My love!" over the music as he went to turn it down, and as he bent over to lower the volume on the speaker, Mr. President squirmed out of his arms.

Jun smiled as he set down his work bag. "Hey, prettyboy. What's gotten into you? Did it— did you do it?"

Griffin came up, took Jun's head in both of his strong hands, and kissed him hard. Jun came out of the kiss with a dazed little smile, and repeated the question. "Did you do it? What happened?"

Griffin answered, "Hi honey. Yes. I'll get into the details later. I don't want to ruin the moment with the details. It turns out there wasn't a clone lab. Even besides that, I had the most wonderful and illuminating day, because I had the most awful and grueling day."

"Please say that in a way that makes sense."

"I love you so much. You mean the world to me. You mean everything to me. I love you completely. Your daily little rituals of love and care and tender mercies have made me feel like a complete person, deserving of love, for the first time in my life. My job is horrible. It's fine, I'm good at it, it helps people, it makes money, but it's a bummer. I'm tired of hurting things. I'm tired of this city. I want to get out of this place and go somewhere better with you."

"Much as I want to get out of this specific place," said Jun as he gestured to the apartment around them, "I'm not sure how much better things are anywhere else, Griff."

"Not to the middle of nowhere. Not to the central steppe or anything, but maybe just on the other side of the mountains where the storms don't pass as often or hit as hard. They've got farms there, raising cows again for dairy. Warehouse management probably has some application in farm supplies. Or hell, maybe there's a way to make it as a ceramicist out there. And I could be a farrier. I used to want to be a farrier and I think I still do."

"Well if you, you know, did what you intended to, and that's not what you want to talk about, then what happened at work today?"

"Well, you remember what my job is?"

"Of course."

"Well, my job happened. And I did it really well. So much that Brandon complimented me on it and said I could really make a career of it. The moment he said that, I realized that if I'm still doing this in five years I will be the most miserable man on Earth. I liked it at first because it wasn't just cutting my hand off, but there's so much more out there. I love you so much and I want to see more of the world with you. I'm tired of sewers."

Jun's face visibly shifted through a range of worries, then cleared and softened as he said, "Okay."

"Okay?"

Jun smiled. "Yeah, okay. I mean, we can't just run away. We need to figure out how we're going to do this, but yes. Fuck it, yes, let's find a way out of this godforsaken town."

Griffin kissed him hard again.

Mr. President chirped at some passing bird, and the two of them looked over at the fat orange furball illuminated on the windowsill.

Jun said, "What do you want, buddy?" and Mr. President hopped down from his perch, jogged over to Jun, and stretched against his leg to ask for uppies, which Jun wordlessly granted him.

The two men stood in the soft orange glow of the August evening, their beloved cat held between them, as Griffin tried to think of what to say next. How to explain what madness he'd found instead of the clone lab he'd expected. How he'd killed again in what had been an utterly unforced moment of ecstatic bloodlust. How he wasn't sure if he was going to get away with it this time. All of these concerns coursed their way through Griffin's body and, somehow, gently dissipated into the air. He could get there in a minute. He didn't want to ruin the moment with the details. And as he knew that, and as he looked at the man he cherished entirely and the cat he protected with his life, he suddenly knew something else, too.

"There is one thing I want to talk about," said Griffin.

Jun, who had been cradling Mr. President while regarding the sunset, said, "What's that, prettyboy?"

"I want to get another cat so Mr. President can have a friend."

# Acknowledgements

Thanks to the guy who cold called me and aggressively tried to sell me skin tag remover over the phone a few years ago. You gave me more than you will ever know.

# About the Author

Hugh Neill is an American male writer. He is the human shambles behind the work. He once had an angry hornet get trapped in his shirt while he was riding a roller coaster. He has never written a math textbook. The math textbook Hugh Neill is a fully separate guy.

**Also By Hugh Neill**
*As Though Before A Vengeful God*